THE JOURNAL

THE JOURNAL

Linda Lee Keenan

Dedication

*To all who assisted in saving individuals
and families from the grip of the Nazis
during the Second World War . . .
you positively impacted our dignity
as well as our legacy.*

"The highest tribute to the dead is not grief but gratitude."

Thornton Wilder

Acknowledgements

I wish to thank my parents, Beverly and David Conway. They are my constant cheerleaders, as well as my brain trust. Throughout the writing of this book, they encouraged me and offered constructive thoughts and ideas that helped to shape the storyline.

A debt of gratitude goes to all my Swedish and Irish relatives - to those who still walk among us, and to those who went before. They are an innately compassionate, intelligent and intuitive group. I take my cues from them.

Thank you to my sister, Diane Conway. She piqued my interest in Central Park and it became part of the story with a dedicated chapter.

A big thank you goes to Karen Bruno Roos for her encouragement and undying enthusiasm. And for finding unexpected treasures that relate directly to this book as I wrote.

Last and not least, I want to thank my history professor, Dr. Eric Roman, for sharing his vast knowledge. He was one of the great teachers and writers of our time.

Introduction

War leaves scars - emotional, physical and spiritual. It is an ongoing human tragedy, for reasons that defy logic. Nevertheless, wars are a fact of life that hasten death and leave life unbearable for many.

The First World War took the youngest and the best of an entire generation. It was said to be "the war to end all wars" and yet only twenty-one years later the Second World War broke out in Europe.

Europe offered few safe havens for some who did not conform to Nazi ideology. The Nazis kidnapped, raped and murdered thousands upon thousands of innocents. They ransacked, pillaged and burned the homes and businesses of civilians. Those of the Jewish faith were most at risk, but others who did not accept Hitler as supreme leader were also at peril.

Many heroes saved people from the Nazi terrorists in the 1940s. One of those heroes was Raoul Wallenberg, a Swedish diplomat. His work has been the subject of books and movies over the past many years.

Wallenberg managed to save thousands from the Nazis by providing protective passports.

While the writing of this book was inspired by Raoul Wallenberg and others like him, it is not based on the life of any person. The characters are fictitious, as are their acts and deeds.

The story within is wrapped around actual history. Research of dates and places is historically accurate with a few exceptions.

After war. After all. Love does not die.

Table of Contents

Chapter One

THE SIGNAL

There was that smell again, impossible to ignore, a sweet and pungent tobacco aroma. Julia had come to recognize this as the signal that she should go to her desk and continue writing about the life of her Great Uncle, Per Lundgren. He was a member of the Swedish Royal family, a diplomat during World War II and most of all, a humanitarian.

Uncle Per came to know the plight of the Jews even before the Second World War broke out in Europe. The suffering, especially that of the helpless children at the hands of the Nazis enraged him. He was compelled to help, to save as many as he could.

His story resonated with Per's great-niece, Julia. It went right to her core. During her years at Columbia University studying European History, she researched her heritage. She was struck when she read about Great Uncle Per. She was aware of her royal heritage but had never put much thought into it, that is, until now.

It was becoming clear why she was repelled but intrigued by the Second World War, why she *had* to tell of the work of her great-uncle. He seemed to be speaking to her—asking her to tell what he could no longer tell.

Long ago, Julia had accepted her clairvoyant ability, it was easier than fighting it. And so, she took out the fat journal she'd begun writing in, re-read the most recent chapter and continued to write.

The tobacco aroma would dissipate as she wrote.

Chapter Two

THE DESIGN

Julia Hamilton was a successful Interior Designer who enjoyed living and working in Manhattan's Upper East Side. Her penthouse apartment at 74th and 5th Avenue overlooked a wooded area of Central Park. On a clear winter's day, Julia could watch from her balcony window as people skated on Belvedere Lake. It relaxed her and made her feel happy.

She lived alone. The solitude suited her. She worked at home, often for long stretches. When she worked on a design project, it took over her mind completely. Sometimes she'd work twenty-four hours nonstop, after which she would fall into an exhausted sleep.

Julia learned years earlier to keep her project notes on her bedside table. No matter how many hours later she awoke, she would immediately recall the dreams she had and hurry to write them as best she could. Her dreams usually solved the issues she was dealing with in her current design project. It never ceased to amaze her how helpful the dreams were.

Julia feverishly worked on a design for Mrs. Ellis Pulaski Wellington. She wanted to impress the Grand Dame of 5th Avenue.

An issue arose regarding the indoor fountain that Mrs. Wellington wanted in the plan. Her co-op apartment did not allow indoor fountains or pools.

There seemed to be no answer to this dilemma. Julia worked on numerous other details of the design all day and into the night before she drifted off to sleep with the problem of the fountain on her mind.

When she woke the next morning, she grabbed her notes and began writing about the dream she had.

At first, the dream made no sense, but she kept writing anyway. She drew pictures to illustrate information that explained what she was being told by an elderly gentleman dressed in a tweed suit and top hat. He said his name was Martin and that, indeed, there *was* a way to legally install Mrs. Wellington's indoor fountain.

In her dream, Martin went on to explain that there had been an indoor fountain in that very building's lobby and that it had been abandoned in the 1960s. The fountain was connected to a waterway running under the building. Before vanishing from her dream, Martin said that this was a little-known fact but it was easily verified.

Julia re-read what she had written. She was astounded. She had so many questions, the first one being, could this be true? If it *was* true, maybe Mrs. Wellington's fountain could be installed, her apartment was right next to the building's lobby.

Her next step was to find the apartment's property records at the City Clerk's office. As she hastily dressed, she made mental notes of the documentation she hoped to collect at City Hall.

She donned what she referred to as her work uniform—always at the ready for quick exits. The sleek, tapered black slacks and cream-colored cashmere sweater was perfect for dressing up or going casual. This day, she added her turquoise necklace, a gift from her boyfriend, Tom. He had bought the fabulous necklace on one of his business trips to the southwest. As he presented the gift to her, he reminded her that the American Indians had owned Manhattan first, so he thought it was appropriate to add to her collection of jewelry.

Julia thought the turquoise would bring her good luck. After all, she was investigating Manhattan property records.

On any other day, she would enjoy the long cab ride south to the Civic Center. The driver navigated along 5th Avenue to Broadway at Madison Square, past Union Square, through Greenwich Village and Little Italy, across Canal Street to the Chambers Street entrance of City Hall.

As she gazed out of the window of the cab, she was not aware of anything other than her thoughts. She wondered who this Martin fellow was and if he had been a real person who lived in Manhattan. Judging from his suit, he might have lived in the early 1900s, around the time the subway system was built. It was also a mystery why Martin would see fit to help her—*if* what he told her turned out to be true.

Julia was beginning to feel a bit foolish. Was she on a wild goose chase?

City Clerk Sally Hughes was lovingly referred to as "Old Sally." She greeted Julia with a big grin. Old Sally was barely tall enough to see over the counter. She laughed along with everyone when a man at the counter asked her if her Mommy was home. Old Sally had a great disposition and she'd been a joy to all her coworkers for more than fifty years. If Sally did not know something about a property record, no one did. And she had an elephant-sized memory. Why, she had facts in her memory bank of events that occurred long before the age of computers!

Sally asked Julia, "And how may I help you this fine day, young lady?"

Julia replied somewhat hesitantly, "Oh, I just need to know if there is an underground waterway in Manhattan." She expected to be laughed out of City Hall.

Sally seemed surprised by the question. "Why, of course, there are several underground waterways in Manhattan, although few people are aware of that fact. How did you come to find out?"

Julia quickly replied, "I heard a rumor there was once an indoor fountain connected to an underground river on 5th Avenue. If this is true, I can apply for a permit for my 5th Avenue client to install a fountain as part of my interior design.

"We've never been formally introduced. I'm Julia Hamilton of Hamilton Interiors. I'm an Interior Designer. I've been working in Manhattan for about fifteen years. Maybe you've seen me here before?"

Julia realized she was rambling. She was so excited to find that what Martin had told her was true.

Sally said, "Why yes, I remember seeing you here before, Miss Julia, I remember your beautiful hair and your fancy jewelry!"

Julia's hand went to her turquoise necklace. Perhaps it *did* bring her luck!

"That waterway would be called Minetta Creek or Minetta Brook. There's actually a plaque on the outside of a building on 5th Avenue that tells of the brook. I'll get you the Viele Map. It shows the underground waterways. That will give you all the information you need."

"Wonderful!" Julia replied. She was already rehearsing in her head what she would say to Mrs. Wellington. She laughed at herself as she mused that Mrs. Wellington was going to think that Julia could walk on water. Now *that* was funny.

Julia thanked Sally for her help, paid for the map copy and fairly ran to the elevator to get to the street and hail a cab.

As soon as she arrived home, she laid the map out on her oak desk. As she examined the details, she marveled at how much water ran beneath the streets of Manhattan. It boggled her mind to think how difficult it must have been for the subway system to be engineered around the waterways.

She also searched online for the plaque that Sally had said was on a building on 5th Avenue. She found an image of it. It read:

A brook winds its erratic way beneath this site
The Indians called it Manette or Devil's Water.
To the Dutch settlers it was
Bestevaer's Killetje or Grandfather's Little Creek.
For the past two centuries familiar to this
Neighborhood as Minetta Brook.

Julia dialed Mrs. Wellington's private number. Mrs. Wellington recognized Julia's number and answered. "Julia, I did not expect to hear from you for another three weeks. I hope there is not a problem with my design, dear."

"Oh, no, Mrs. Wellington. I'm calling because I am very excited to tell you good news! Today I confirmed there is an abandoned fountain in the lobby of your apartment building and that it was once connected to an underground waterway. That means you can have the fountain in your solarium!"

"Why, Julia! I cannot begin to tell you how happy this makes me! How *ever* did you find this out? Oh, never mind about that, when can you show me your design plans? You know I want this design one hundred percent complete and perfect before my annual ball for people who survived the war."

"I know how important the ball is to you and your family, Mrs. Wellington. Don't worry, I'll finish the plans tonight and call the contractor tomorrow after we meet. Do you have time to meet me tomorrow, Mrs. Wellington?"

"Yes! I will cancel my morning meetings and see you here at nine AM sharp. I will not be able to wait a moment longer!"

"I will be there with your design plans promptly at nine tomorrow morning, Mrs. Wellington. We have plenty of time to complete your design before spring arrives. I am looking forward to meeting with you. Goodbye, Mrs. Wellington."

Julia's next call was to her friend, Seth Schmidt, a well-known architect. She had met him when she was commissioned to design the interior of the downtown office where he worked. They'd formed an instant bond. She admired his intellect and they shared a similar sense of humor.

Seth was out of the office, so she left a detailed message telling him she needed him to help her with a residential design that included an indoor fountain.

It would be an easy task for him. He was accustomed to much bigger projects, like the Grand Central Station renovation in the 1970s.

Julia ended the message by asking if he could meet her at the coffee shop two blocks east of his office, hopefully at four o'clock, and to please text her as soon as he got the message.

Seth knew the place. They'd often met there to catch up over a cup of their favorite French roast. Julia was quite sure Seth would make time to meet her if he could.

She went back to work on her design and ten minutes later, Seth texted to say he would love to meet her at their coffee shop, and he'd be there at four sharp.

Chapter Three

THE PRESENTATION

The sound of a rooster startled Julia awake. It was the alarm tone set on her cell phone. She kept it under her pillow when she had to get to a morning meeting.

She squinted at her phone and confirmed that it was seven-thirty AM. She had plenty of time to cab over to Mrs. Wellington's with her final design plans.

When Julia and Seth had met, he'd offered his architectural expertise about the fountain. He was greatly enthused that a bit of history was being reclaimed by connecting to Minetta Brook.

As Julia suspected, it was a simple task for Seth. He even offered to call the contractor to instruct him on the best way to plumb the fountain.

Julia had wanted to spend more time talking with Seth, but her morning design deadline loomed large in her orderly brain.

So with an apology to Seth for rushing off, she promised to call him to meet up again after Mrs. Wellington's design was on its way to completion.

Julia finished dressing in front of her mirror wall. The wall was her own design with variable lighting dependent on whether she was dressing for day or evening.

With a self-satisfied grin, she grabbed her leather briefcase that she'd carefully packed with her drawings and headed for the elevator.

As was his habit with all the residents, the doorman, Javier, greeted Julia with a smile and a bow when the elevator opened into the lobby.

Javier was not talkative with most people; he did not want to intrude. However, he always had a compliment for his favorite resident.

"You're looking radiant today, Miss Julia! May I hail a cab for you?"

"Thank you, Javier. And you are looking quite dapper!"

Julia knew Javier had lost virtually all his family during World War II. He had told her he was only three years old in 1940 when the Nazi soldiers stormed into his family home in France.

From the enclosed eaves in the attic, tiny Javier watched through a knot hole as his parents and his three older brothers were pushed down the stairs by the bad men who Javier later came to know were Nazis.

He recalled it all: the scuffling and breaking of glass and especially the shrieks and screams of his family and the yelling and laughing of the merciless captors.

Those fifteen minutes of horror had stayed with him for all the years since. He was now seventy-eight years old.

Two days later, Javier was miraculously discovered and rescued by a kind, blonde-haired young man. He never knew who the man was but he thanked him every night in his prayers.

A year later, Javier was living with his adoptive family in rural New York State. He was relatively happy on their farm. He had three older sisters, one baby brother, two cats and lots of dogs to play with.

He did not know what had happened to his family in France. He consoled himself with the idea that they would have somehow escaped across the border into Switzerland, a neutral and safe country.

He imagined that they lived on a farm much like the one where he lived with his adoptive family. He referred to this new home as his vacation home and prayed every night that his parents would find out where he was and take him back to his real life. Javier believed in miracles.

Julia recalled that when she began writing about her Great Uncle Per, she discussed the war with Javier. He'd been intrigued with what she was writing and she was happy to share each segment with him as she finished it.

She was aware that sharing with Javier might somehow help both of them, though she was not sure how.

"Yes, I do need a cab, thank you, Javier. Have a wonderful day. And oh, I almost forgot to tell you that I have another piece of my journal for you to read. I'll see you when I get back, okay?"

She saw the joy on his face but could not hear his reply because she spotted a cab at the curb, sprinted to it and jumped in saying, "5th at Washington Square North, please!"

At eight fifty-five, Julia pressed the intercom button for Mrs. Wellington's apartment and was immediately buzzed in. The inside apartment door was open for her and she went directly to the solarium where she knew Mrs. Wellington would be.

When Mrs. Wellington saw Julia, she said, "It's nice to see you, dear. Let's get started right away, shall we? I'm so excited to see your finished design!"

Julia was accustomed to her client's abrupt manner and did not mind in the least.

"Of course, Mrs. Wellington, I hope you will be pleased with the final plan."

With that, she spread out her drawings on the writing desk that had been cleared for her.

Julia held her breath as she waited for Mrs. Wellington to say something, anything, about the detailed drawings she was looking at.

Finally, she looked up at Julia with an expression that Julia could not interpret.

With tears in her eyes, Mrs. Wellington said, "Thank you, Julia. This is going to be so much more than I dared to hope for. Your drawings are masterful. They illustrate just what the end product will look like!"

"I'm so happy you like the plan, Mrs. Wellington. Is there anything you'd like me to add or change before the contractor comes on board?"

"Oh, no, you've thought of *everything*, Julia! I can see that my solarium will look just like my shop before it was demolished during

Kristallnacht. Now that we can add the lighted fountain, it will be perfection!

"Pardon my manners. I did not even offer you anything to drink. Would you like a cup of coffee or tea?"

"No thank you. If you don't have any questions, I will go back to my office and make some calls so your work can begin. Do you mind if the workers arrive as early as tomorrow morning?"

"I do not mind at all. The sooner the better. I'll move my workspace to the den so that the solarium can be transformed."

"All right then, Mrs. Wellington, I will see myself out and I will let you know exactly when the work will begin. The contractor will have to secure a permit for the fountain, but there is plenty of other work that can be done before they begin the fountain."

Julia breezed out, saying, "Please call me with any questions that you have on the design. Have a wonderful day!"

At the curbside, Julia waited for a cab. She reflected on the conversation she had with Mrs. Wellington at their very first meeting three weeks before.

Mrs. Wellington said that she was Jewish and lived in Germany in 1938 when Kristallnacht, The Night of Broken Glass, destroyed Jewish homes and businesses throughout the German Reich.

Her family was originally from Poland. Her parents named her Netti and her family name was Pulaski, which she used as her middle name after she married Ellis Wellstein.

Upon immigrating to the States in 1939, the Wellstein name was changed to Wellington to avoid being discriminated against. Wellington sounded British; the Brits were far more welcome in America than were the Germans during the war years.

Before Kristallnacht, the Nazis harassed German Jews, but they had not become violent, until on the night of November 9, 1938, the Jewish family stores in Mrs. Wellington's neighborhood were destroyed by the Nazis.

The Wellington's shop merchandise was all burned that terrible night. The priceless antiques could never be replaced—not the porcelain sculptures from China, or the sets of Limoges dishes, or the wood carvings from Bavaria.

Their livelihood, as well as their home was gone with their shop. Worse than that, most of the Jewish men in their community were corralled by the Nazis and taken to prison camps to be exterminated as part of Hitler's final solution.

Mrs. Wellington had painted a mental picture for Julia so that she could create a design to replicate her beloved shop, right in her 5th Avenue apartment. To be authentic, the design would need to include an indoor fountain.

That's when Julia knew she had a major design challenge on her hands. She had wondered how she would be able to solve this dilemma.

Thanks to the gentleman named Martin in her dream, the problem was solved.

Chapter Four

THE JOURNAL

There was some staging to be done before Julia would continue writing about Great Uncle Per.

She sat at her oak desk with a world map spread out; she needed a physical frame of reference. A gooseneck lamp lit the pages of her journal.

Her cognitive skills worked best with what she called her "other worldly abilities" after the sun set and the room took on mysterious moving shadows. Julia realized that the shadows were a manifestation of her intuition, like a silent black and white film playing right in front of her.

Julia began to write as the jazz music CD she'd chosen started to play. The dulcet tones of Vera Lynn both soothed and saddened Julia; so very many lovers were separated during wartime. Julia knew the bittersweet taste of love and loss, and she would discover that her Great Uncle Per Lundgren knew that same sting.

The heartache of others was what drove him to risk his life to save people from the depths of hell in Europe in the early 1940s.

The music faded into the background. The lamp flickered once and Julia heard the familiar voice of her Uncle Per as clearly as if he was sitting with her.

He asked her to write his story exactly as he dictated it. He knew Julia was more than capable. They shared the same clairvoyant abilities. In this case, he would be the sender and she would be the receiver.

She wrote in the first person - that of Per Lundgren:

In 1940, I was twenty-seven years old and a member of a Swedish diplomatic agency.

I was an expert mediator and therefore often asked to intervene when political tempers flared, particularly in Europe, but also in Canada and the United States.

It was a time of great fear and uncertainty. Hitler had already attacked and occupied Czechoslovakia, Norway and Poland. A political posture of appeasement by the major military powers allowed Hitler's advances to go unchecked.

Initially, Sweden declared itself to be neutral. Their economy was in large part dependent on exporting iron ore and ball bearings to Germany.

Between 1936 and 1939, Sweden's defense budget was increased nearly one thousand percent, and the primary cigarette company had been nationalized to raise government funds for defense as well as for government pensions.

Suffice it to say that Sweden was prepared to defend itself if necessary.

I was asked to arrange diplomatic talks in Berlin between Sweden and Germany in the spring of 1940.

Talks were going fairly well after the first week. My objectives were to keep Sweden out of war with Germany and to negotiate within Sweden's policy of neutrality.

The sticking point was that Germany wanted to maintain trade relations and use the Swedish railroad system to access occupied Norway for its strategic military position and resources.

In the end, Sweden agreed to the German demands. It was the lesser of two evils—to get along economically with the Germans or risk being attacked by them.

What that meant to Sweden was that they were no longer considered neutral, but non-belligerent. Sweden did not openly help Germany in the military sense, but did not block access across Sweden to Norway. I had accomplished only the objective of staying out of war with Germany.

After three long weeks of talks in Berlin ended, I decided that I needed a break from work. I had heard there was a jazz club downtown called the Blue Tango—it sounded interesting.

I went alone to the club after dining with my associates at the inn where we were staying. We were scheduled to travel back to Stockholm on an early flight the next day.

I intended to have a drink and enjoy the music for only an hour or so; it was already late by the time I headed to the club.

The Blue Tango was a very popular club, especially with the military. It was crowded, smoky and noisy.

As I stood in the entry looking for a place to sit, I thought, "I can't hear myself think in here. This was a bad idea."

The crowd pushed me toward the only seat that was available - directly in front of the empty stage, which was at the same level as that one seat. I sat at the tiny round table right in front.

A waitress asked what I'd like to drink and I ordered a stein of Berliner Pilsner Boch Beer.

When she returned with my beer, she leaned close and said, "The gentleman at the next table has paid for your drink and sends his regards."

I looked to my right and I recognized the uniformed man as Hans Hermann. He nodded as he caught my eye. He had been involved with the German diplomatic team that I'd been in talks with over the previous weeks.

I nodded in return and toasted him with my beer stein. I wondered why he would be so agreeable after being the most argumentative one at the talks from beginning to end.

My thought was interrupted when a singer stepped onto the stage. She stood barely two feet from where I sat.

She had lush chestnut-colored hair that fell in soft curls over her bare shoulders. The flowing sky-blue material of her strapless gown accentuated every curve of her petite figure.

She began to sing "Dream a Little Dream of Me." Her deep brown eyes drilled into me. It seemed she sang only to me.

Before I knew it, her song ended and she spoke into the microphone, "I'm Raya Simone and I thank you for joining me here tonight. Before I leave you, I would like to sing one more song called 'We'll Meet Again.' I hope you like it."

Raya still sang directly to me and my heart felt as if it was in my throat! For me, time stood still and flew by all at once. If I could have stayed in that time and place indefinitely, I would have done so.

Suddenly, I heard clapping and cat whistles from the crowd and I became aware that Raya was no longer singing. She had walked into the audience and was talking to Hans, the man who had sent me a drink.

The patrons were leaving, the lights were turned up and Hans came to my table with Raya at his side.

I stood. Hans shook my hand and said, "Per Lundgren, please allow me to introduce you to my sister, Raya Simone.

"Raya, this is Per Lundgren, he is the Swedish diplomat that I told you about."

Raya offered me her delicate hand. I was struck by her strength and by the electrical current that shot straight through me.

She spoke first, which is fortunate because I was quite speechless.

"Per, I've been anxious to meet you. My brother has related to me how instrumental you have been in assisting Germany in the talks. You are quite an accomplished negotiator."

I could not decide how to respond. One might assume she was pro-Hitler and I was in Berlin to protect Sweden from Hitler.

I simply said, "I enjoyed your singing very much, Raya.

"It was so nice to meet you and I'm afraid that I must take my leave as I will travel back to Stockholm early tomorrow morning.

"I will say good evening to you both."

With great reluctance, I let go of Raya's hand and headed for the door.

I took a step and turned back to see who grabbed my right arm. It was Hans.

He was smiling but his eyes were very intense, and he had not taken his hand from my arm.

Hans leaned in and spoke into my ear. He said, "Raya and I would like you to join us at the after-hours club with some of our friends. I'm certain you will find this meeting to benefit both of us."

Without waiting for my answer, he added, "There is a car at the back door right now waiting to drive you to the place. We will be there by the time you arrive. You will need a password in order to be given access; it's 'zodiac.' Speak to no one until you see us again."

He left me standing alone. There was no reason for me to trust Hans Hermann, and I didn't know who his friends were.

I could not think of a scenario that could benefit me. This was far too mysterious and dangerous for my taste.

Add to that the fact that I had no idea where I would be taken. If this was a scheme to abduct me, it was likely to be quite effective. I would simply get into a car in an alley and disappear into the night.

That was my logical mind at work—the left side of my brain.

I chose to focus on using my right brain. Those ideas did not occur in the same way; they weren't really thoughts, but did add a certainty to the creative thought process.

My decision to ignore what both sides of my brain warned me not to do, would alter my life in unimaginable ways.

On high alert, I slipped out the back door of the Blue Tango Club and saw the door of a limousine being held open by a man in Nazi uniform.

He motioned for me to get in.

My mouth was dry and my heart was pounding. I knew that what I was doing was foolhardy, but there was no turning back now.

I got into the back seat of the limousine, the door slammed shut and seconds later the car screeched out of the alley toward my destiny.

The lamp on the desk flickered and got brighter. Julia sat in stunned silence. Uncle Per had left the building, so to speak. Apparently, he had finished telling his story for the night.

She touched the world map on the green "X" where Manhattan was, to confirm that she was completely in her apartment—body and mind. A second before, she was sure she was in Berlin.

The music CD had looped and was replaying, "We'll Meet Again." It was haunting, and it was confirmation that she had been writing for nearly an hour.

She shut off the music, folded up the map and turned off the desk lamp.

Aloud, Julia said, "I will read what Uncle Per dictated when I wake up tomorrow."

She walked to the bedroom, dropped onto her bed, fully clothed and fell fast asleep.

Chapter Five

MONDAY

Monday was always Julia's busiest day of the week. She would go about completing the previous week's projects, toss that list and begin a new "To Do" list for the week.

On this Monday, the very first item to be completed was to read what she had written the night before. Only bits and pieces had come to her conscious mind as she listened to Uncle Per and wrote what he told her.

She was anxious to get to the reading, but not before she had two cups of rich, dark coffee to clear the cobwebs from her brain.

With her third cup in hand, she sat in the comfy chaise that was warm from the morning sun shining in and began to read.

She read it through once, then again, all the while thinking that what Uncle Per would reveal to her in upcoming sessions was likely to be shocking, based on what he'd already related to her.

Julia had been told that he died during the war but she didn't know the details.

When she read that he got into the limousine to be taken to a secret meeting, Julia thought, *"Oh, no! What did you get yourself into, Uncle Per?*

She put her journal on the coffee table. For the time being, she had as much intrigue as she could digest. Besides, it was Monday and time for her to get crackin'!

Both her business line and her cell phone began to ring at the same time. The caller ID on the business line read "Seth Schmidt."

Her cell's caller ID read "PII," which was Pierson International Investigations.

She knew that Seth would leave a message. She answered her cell; Pierson was the company her boyfriend Tom worked for.

Julia settled back into the chaise and answered, "Good morning, Tom. How are you today?"

He answered as if he had all the time in the world and that she was the only person on his mind, "Hello, my love. It's wonderful to hear your voice. I'm well and how are you doing, Julia?"

She decided to stick with a logical answer. Tom was not given to what he would consider flights of fancy or wild imaginings. He could never understand her penchant for writing from a channeled conversation with her dead uncle.

"Well, the design for my 5th Avenue client is going forward with the fountain in her solarium. Mrs. Wellington is very happy and in fact so am I. What do you think of that?"

Without waiting for his reply, she continued, "You may remember my friend, Seth, the architect."

Instantly, Tom felt a pang of jealousy when Julia mentioned Seth. He knew they were good friends and suspected that Seth had designs on her. He'd only met Seth once, at "their coffee shop." He didn't care for the way Seth looked so adoringly at Julia. She seemed to be oblivious of that look and ultimately Tom determined not to mention what he thought to be true.

Tom maintained his composure when he said, "Yes, my love. I do remember meeting Seth with you last winter at that coffee shop."

"Oh, right, I completely forgot about that. Anyway, Seth was able to design the indoor fountain so that it connected to an abandoned fountain in the lobby. And get *this*—the original fountain was connected to an underground brook. I have the map from City Hall showing numerous waterways under Manhattan! Isn't that amazing, Tom?"

Of course, Julia neglected to tell him how she came to know about the waterways. After all, dreams could not possibly impact his reality as they did hers. Anyway, he didn't ask and she didn't tell.

"Oui, mon chou, that is wonderful news and will be good for your business. I am very happy for you.

"Julia, I'm afraid that I am scheduled for a video conference in ten minutes, so I must say goodbye for now. I just wanted to hear your smiling voice, and to tell you that I will be going to my company's conference in Paris tomorrow for three weeks. However, after that, I will be all yours for an entire weekend before I head back to our offices in Toronto."

She was about to say how much she missed him when he was interrupted by another call.

He simply said, "Goodbye, my love."

Their call was disconnected. She was thrilled that they would have an entire weekend together, but not so happy that it was three weeks away. She decided she would ask a friend to join her to go to the new Egyptian exhibit at the Metropolitan Museum of Art.

I need to socialize more, she thought.

Her business line started to chirp again. The bird ringtone made her grin.

She answered, "Good morning, Seth. I'm sorry I missed your call a few minutes ago. I have not checked yet; did you leave me a message?"

"Hi yourself, Julia. No, I didn't leave a message."

There was a long silence. When he spoke again, he seemed uncertain.

"Julia, if I asked you to go on a date with me, would you accept?"

She was not sure she heard him correctly. He was aware she was involved with Tom.

"Maybe you know about the Egyptian exhibit at the Met. It's opening tonight and I'm going. Will you join me?"

He sensed her hesitation and added, "Some people that I work with will be there. How about if you meet us there, say at seven?"

Wow! Seth seemed to be reading her mind about needing to socialize more, about going to the Egyptian exhibit and about the fact that she couldn't accept a formal date.

She responded immediately, "I would love to meet you at the museum tonight, Seth. I was just thinking that I would ask a friend to go with me. I'll see you at seven. And Seth, thanks for asking."

"You're welcome, Julia. It will be fun and I look forward to seeing you. And Julia, thanks for accepting. See you later." Click.

Julia looked at the phone in her hand.

Suddenly she sprang into action. She had many things to accomplish before the clock chimed seven.

The next item on her list was to confirm that the contractor for Mrs. Wellington's job had applied for the required building permits.

She left him a message and was busy for the remainder of the day.

Julia glanced at the clock every so often and was amazed at how fast time slipped away.

Finally, at five o'clock, she quit working so she'd have plenty of time to dress to go out to the museum. She sighed happily…the thought of going to an opening at the Met was thrilling.

She didn't hear her cell phone ring. She didn't know it was Tom calling, so she didn't know what he had to tell her.

Tom did not leave a message. Julia would not like to hear that they would not have their weekend together, and that he would not be in New York for at least two months. He didn't like it either, but he had landed the biggest case of his career and couldn't take a break from work in the foreseeable future.

Seth waited at the museum's main entrance for Julia. He watched as she got out of the cab. She was wearing a red ankle-length coat over a close-fitting black body suit and red open-toed heels.

She seemed not to notice that heads turned as she passed by. Seth mused that Julia had turned his head from the moment he met her.

She caught sight of him and waved. He returned the wave and walked toward her.

He kissed her lightly on the cheek and said, "My God, Julia, you look positively amazing! Here's your ticket. We were fortunate to get tickets for this important exhibition on the opening night. The press is out in numbers!"

"Yes, I noticed the news trucks, and the traffic was barely moving on the way here. This is so exciting, Seth. How did you manage to get tickets?"

He playfully nudged her shoulder. "Oh, just one of the perks of being the best architect in Manhattan.

"Actually, my company has a sponsoring membership at the Met, which gets any of our staff access to opening nights such as this one."

Julia was reminded why they were friends. They were comfortable together and had a lot in common.

They both enjoyed the exhibit immensely. They met up with a couple of Seth's coworkers and they each shared what they knew about the artworks.

Mack and Sheila were part of the group and they'd both been to Egypt twice; their enthusiasm was contagious.

The four hours to closing passed by almost in the blink of an eye; none of them wanted the night to end. Seth suggested they go to the corner coffee shop and they all agreed.

They sat side by side at the coffee bar and each ordered their coffee of choice. Julia ordered French roast decaf latte. Seth followed suit.

Mack pointed to a television on the wall, "Look! We're on the news!"

All eyes went to the large screen television. At first, Julia was excited to see that the exhibit got so much publicity and that they were part of it.

Seth and Julia saw themselves on the screen at the same time. They appeared to be immersed in each other as they walked around the museum.

Julia panicked. She thought they looked like a couple rather than just friends—right there on the eleven o'clock news!

She realized that sometime in the last few hours, she may have slipped into that undefined relationship space between friendly associates and something more.

If she was watching herself on the news, maybe Tom was too.

She thought, *Tom will not like seeing me with Seth.*

Seth saw her panicked look. "Well, folks, morning comes early, we should be going."

He leaned toward Julia. "Let's find you a cab."

She did not want to chance being seen again in the news footage with Seth.

She managed a smile and said, "Thank you for a wonderful evening, Seth. I'm so glad that you asked me to join in.

"It looks as if I can easily get a cab right out front, so stay with your friends, and we'll talk soon."

She left him with a friendly pat on the shoulder. She said goodbye to the other members of the group.

They all chimed in with "Good night, Julia! Let's get together again soon!"

The moment she stepped out of the coffee shop, a cab stopped in front of her. She hopped in and said, "74th and 5th Avenue, please."

Her evening out with Seth and the others had been fun and extremely interesting. She loved history and had learned so many things she didn't know about Egypt.

She mentally reviewed some of what she saw—art exhibits depicting magic and ancient Egypt, women's role in society and the afterlife beliefs of the culture.

Everyone in her group was especially taken in by the sculptures and replicas of the monuments. The tombs on display combined the features of architecture, culture, religion and mythology.

Ancient Egyptians thought of death as a rebirth. To assure an afterlife, they preserved their dead through the process of mummification.

A museum guide explained that the canopic jars were made of clay or stone. The jars were used to store the internal organs that were removed during mummification. They were closed with stoppers made in the image of one of four protective spirits—a human to protect the liver, a baboon to protect the lungs, a jackal to protect the stomach and a falcon to protect the intestines. These deities were also referred to as the Four Sons of Horus.

Julia interrupted the guide and asked, "What about the heart?"

The guide smiled and said, "Isn't it just like a woman to ask about the heart. Well, the heart was weighed against a feather to test if the heart was pure and truthful enough to go into the afterlife. It was deemed to be the most essential organ of the body and therefore left in the body to be transported into the afterlife; that is, *if* it did not outweigh the feather. If the heart was heavy with wrongdoing, it was given to a beast to devour and thus the body would suffer complete and final death. If the heart did not outweigh the feather, that body passed into eternal afterlife in paradise. This is all written in the 'Book of the Dead.'

"The brain was thought to be simply an organ to dispense with mucus and so it was discarded."

She thanked the guide for his informative answer.

Julia cringed when Seth took great pride in informing her that the brain was sucked out through the nose.

With a wide grin, he said, "That is my contribution to tonight's learning!"

That was Seth; he was a comical, intellectual genius. His comments made everyone laugh.

Seth added, "Actually, I know something about these burial masks over here on the left".

Pointing out the colorful masks, he added, "Funerary masks were used extensively throughout Egyptian history. The most elaborate were made for royalty out of gold, believed to be the skin of gods. They also added precious gemstones as ornamentation.

"The mask of Tutankhamen conveys his actual facial features, although most masks were in the image of a god.

"The masks were made of wood, poured plaster or cartonnage, which is layers of linen mixed with plaster."

Seth stopped and looked quite pleased with himself as he turned to Julia.

"How do you know so much about burial masks, Seth?"

With a big grin, he replied by tapping his index finger on his head.

The cab traveled along 5th Avenue toward home. Julia smiled as she recalled seeing the statue of Anubis, the god of mummification, standing tall as he sailed on a barge through the narrows into the Hudson River, past Lady Liberty. That was in early 2010 and the press was out in numbers then too.

January 2010 was when she received the news that Jed, her beautiful brave husband, had been killed in Iran. He was a member of a special ops company contracted to assist U.S. troops in combat.

The story as she got it from his company spokesman, was that the group that Jed was with returned to their camp after a mission and drove over a land mine that had been set by dissidents just outside their camp.

Jed was in the lead Humvee that was demolished and all three men were killed. The two vehicles that followed were severely damaged but no one else was killed.

It still seemed like a bad dream to Julia. She was the only family that Jed had and so there was no one to grieve with, no one who truly understood her loss.

She became a recluse and went out only when she needed groceries. She spent long hours looking at pictures and videos of their short and glorious marriage.

Some of her most precious memories were captured in photos of their three-day honeymoon at Niagara Falls. Julia could still feel as if Jed's arms were around her when they rode on 'The Maid of the Mist.' That's when he told her that she was the woman of his dreams. They were very happy.

When she felt water from the great Horseshoe Falls on her face, she realized it was her own tears and she was plunked back into the present.

She worked very little and lived on Jed's life insurance policy that paid her enough to last for two years, then it was time to get back into life.

She pulled herself up by the bootstraps and began reconnecting with business contacts in 2012. Hamilton Interiors began to take on new business and she breathed life into herself.

That was when she met Tom Pierson. They were introduced at an art gallery in SoHo; they'd both been invited by acquaintances of the artist. They never found out who they had in common and they didn't really care. They just figured their meeting was kismet.

Tom told her that John Lennon and Yoko Ono also met at an art gallery. Those two considered their meeting to be "instant karma" according to news sources.

Tom swept her off her feet with his charming personality. He was self-assured but not egocentric.

He asked for her number and said he would call to set up a dinner date. He called that same night and they agreed to have dinner in a quaint little restaurant he knew in Greenwich Village the following evening.

That was the night when Tom said that he'd fallen madly in love with her, and if she didn't feel the same, that he would throw himself off the Brooklyn Bridge!

Julia laughed and said, "No, don't jump, Tom! I would have to save you and I don't know how to swim!

"Besides, I have also fallen in love with *you*."

She thought of Tom and wondered again if he'd seen the eleven o'clock news that showed her out with Seth at the Met, looking a bit too cozy.

The cab stopped. She was relieved to see that she'd arrived at her apartment building. She was suddenly very tired.

The foyer light came on automatically as she unlocked the front door. She went directly to her bedroom, turned down the bed and changed into her nightgown.

Her evening clothes got plopped unceremoniously on a chair.

She set the alarm on her cell phone to be awakened at seven and noticed that Tom had called while she was out, but he had not left a message. She thought it was odd and assumed he was busy and that he would call her in the morning.

Chapter Six

A SECRET MEETING

A few nights later, as Julia sat at her desk eating her favorite chicken and vegetable takeout, she had the urge to play some music. She chose a special edition CD of "Songs that Won the War." This collection was especially romantic and idealistic. It included songs such as: *Accentuate the Positive, Sleigh Ride in July, Manhattan Serenade and Buy, Buy, Buy Bonds.*

She was enjoying a steaming cup of Yogi brand ginger tea when she heard *There'll Be a Hot Time in the Town of Berlin.*

It was her cue that it was time to connect with Uncle Per again.

She thought about the secret meeting Uncle Per was going to, when they last communicated.

With her desk set up to write, she had only to wait for a minute before she began to hear his voice.

Good evening, Julia. I see you were expecting me and you are prepared to hear about my secret meeting.

Well then, let us begin, shall we?

The limousine headed west on the Unter den Linden and through the Brandenburg Gate.

Just as we entered the Tiergarten, the driver veered sharply left into the driveway of a private estate. He cut the engine and turned the headlights off.

I asked what was wrong; he did not reply. He seemed only interested in what was or was not reflected in the rearview mirror.

Once satisfied that we were not being followed, he spun the limo around and drove straight back through the Brandenburg Gate toward the city center.

I thought, "What the hell is going on here? Now I understand why Hans said that he and Raya would be at the meeting before I arrived."

Two sudden left turns and we were parked behind the Reichstag building.

Then the driver said two words to me, "Get out!"

It was obvious that I had no choice but to skedaddle out of the limo, and I did exactly that.

Once again, the limo screeched away. I was left standing alone.

Aloud, I said, "Where is this blasted meeting?"

In the darkness, I pivoted ninety degrees to my left and stopped. I looked at the basement level of the Reichstag building.

Upon closer examination, I could see the lit outline of a door. Cautiously, I walked toward it.

There were three steps down to the door and before approaching, I checked all around for followers. There were none.

I thought this had to be where I was to meet Hans and Raya. The limo driver must have known where to drop me.

I knocked lightly on the heavy oak door and got no response.

I waited for a full two minutes and then I summoned every ounce of courage I could muster and rapped sharply on the door. Immediately I heard a deep male voice shout, "What do you want?"

I was startled out of my wits and had no idea what to say!

After what seemed an eternity, I remembered that Hans had told me that I would need a code word to be admitted to the meeting. With my lips almost on the door, I blurted, "Zodiac!"

Nothing happened. I stood looking at the closed door.

I wondered what my next move was.

Finally, the door opened and a burly man grunted, "Enter."

I tried to appear confident as I scanned the room for the only two people I would know.

Hans spotted me and strode across the room to where I stood.

I must admit that I was greatly relieved to see him.

He shook my hand and said, "Per, I'm glad you decided to join us. Come, I will introduce you to everyone."

Then he stopped me and said, "First, I need to tell you what this is all about. You will then tell me if you wish to stay. Look around the room, Per. Do you recognize anyone else?"

There were a few other men gathered in a group, talking in hushed tones. And of course, Raya was there. She was speaking to a handsome young man who was casually dressed.

In fact, I did recognize many of the faces. It took me a moment to register that they were Germans who had been at the talks I had been at during the previous weeks.

I said, "Hans, I do not understand what you have gotten me involved in. I hope you have a good reason for bringing me here."

By this time, I was irate and in no mood for political game-playing.

"Come over here where we can talk privately, Per. I assure you, there is good cause for you to have been invited to our meeting.

"All of the people in this room are committed to stopping the Nazis from capturing and slaughtering people.

"I discussed your joining us with each member of our group. We took a vote and it was unanimous that you would benefit our efforts with your particular skill set in the diplomatic community. Shall I continue, Per?"

Saving people from the Nazis was definitely my first priority. I said, "Yes, please continue."

"All right, this team's mission is to divert people from death camps or concentration camps, and to provide them with safe passage to new homes, ideally with their families intact.

"As you would expect, we will encounter all manner of dangerous situations in the pursuit of moving people away from the grip of the Nazis.

"We are also fully aware that it will not be possible to save everyone, thus we will establish protocols to follow to give us the most beneficial outcome for as many families as possible.

"We have been assembling this group for just a few weeks and we hope that you will agree to round out the team.

"As you can see, we are in the Reichstag building, therefore, we must take care to meet only occasionally and to align ourselves with the most trustworthy individuals."

At that point I interrupted him. I said, "Hans, I appreciate your confidence in me, truly I do, but I fail to see how I might be of any help here. After all, in just a few hours I will be back in Stockholm. These people are all Germans and can blend into Hitler's affairs, while I cannot."

"That's the beauty of your joining us, Per. In Sweden, you have direct access to German communications as they use your lines. Isn't that right?"

I was beginning to see the method to this madness. Normally I did not think in terms of espionage. I was trained to deal with aboveboard politics, not underground operations.

"Yes, Germany has access to our communication lines for telephone and telegraph, plus they have use of our railroads to access Norway.

"Hans, say no more. I am convinced that I can help save lives as a member of this team. Count me in."

Hans clapped me on the back and loudly announced so that everyone in the room could hear, "Listen here, Per Lundgren is joining our effort!"

Suddenly, everyone stopped talking and looked at me. You could hear a pin drop in that room.

One man began to clap and everyone followed his lead. I felt self-conscious being the object of their applause.

Hans held up his hand for quiet and said, "Let us begin our meeting. Please take a seat and you can each introduce yourself to Per."

Everyone found a seat at the large oval table. I sat next to Hans and across from Raya. I cautioned myself to keep my mind on the important business at hand. I told myself that I didn't know how she fit into this ever-growing puzzle and it was best to stand down. Still, I could not help but wonder what role a female might play in this treacherous situation.

It was apparent that Hans was the man in charge. He called the meeting to order.

"As you all know, we have a limited window of time in this room. We've a great deal to accomplish. Raya, would you please state your team position so Per can begin to get a handle on our operation?"

Raya stood. I noticed she'd changed from her evening gown and was now wearing a black cape over loose-fitting black slacks. Even so, I was still distracted by her presence.

She was every bit as self-assured in this setting as she was on stage at the Blue Tango.

She said, "I intend to use my singing talent to divert the attention of the Nazis while our team accomplishes their missions.

"Over the past three years, I have gained notoriety throughout Europe and particularly here in Germany. Since Berlin is our headquarters, my performances at the Blue Tango are the perfect cover for us."

Raya sat and the man next to her stood. He was the huge hulk of a man whose voice I had heard at the door say, "What do you want?" His voice was intimidating and certainly matched his physique.

"I am Henrique Duff, the doorkeeper here and security guard at the Blue Tango. My position with the SS is Communications Officer in charge of Intelligence."

He sat.

I was stunned. The level of infiltration into the SS was astounding. And I had not heard from the others who sat at the table yet.

Next, a rather small man wearing round frameless glasses stood to speak. He looked anything but menacing.

"My name is Will Bates and I am the strategist for our team. My field is mathematics and I calculate the variables and come up with the odds of success for each of our missions."

His humor surprised me when he added, "I work closely with these two monkeys in the departments of mechanical engineering and cryptology."

He motioned to the two men who sat to his right.

Everyone laughed, but only for a moment.

Then the one Polish-born member of the team introduced himself—he was the cryptologist.

He bowed as he stood and said, "My name is Karl Klein. I am one of the few Polish Cavalrymen who survived the German massacre last September.

"Before that fateful day I had been working on reconstructing the Nazis' most prized coding machine, the Enigma. Our crew managed to figure out all but the settings to unravel the Nazi codes. That's when we teamed up with the Brits and they set up an entire unit to break the Enigma. As a result of that work, I have a direct connection to British Intelligence."

He turned to me and said, "You may wonder, Mr. Lundgren, how it is that I came to be part of this team."

I nodded. Karl answered my unspoken question.

"Well, on the day that my brothers-in-arms were killed, I quickly changed out of my cavalry uniform into casual attire. I assumed because of my youthful appearance, fair coloring and blue eyes that the Nazis would likely herd me into a group of young people that were being sent to Germany to be integrated into their culture. I was correct in my assumption. I was picked up by the Nazis within a matter of hours and taken to a holding facility before being transferred to a youth hostel here in Berlin. I was placed in Hitler's Youth Corps and given a German name. I kept my mouth shut, learned all that I could and moved up into the SS unit that I am in today, using my skills as a cryptologist.

"I'm sure you've heard of Aryan-looking youth being Germanized, Mr. Lundgren?"

The full meaning of Germanization was not lost on me. I had to take a deep breath before speaking. I said, "The Nazis kidnapped many of our beautiful young Swedish girls and either married them off to soldiers or used them as baby-making machines.

"They were force-impregnated by purebred Germans and the healthy girls churned out a baby every year. By the time a girl had given birth two or three times, she was no longer healthy mentally or physically. The babies were taken from their birth mothers and sold to whoever paid the highest price, which of course, added to the misery of the poor young girls.

"As you might imagine, the girls became very depressed and thus were no longer of use to the Germans. Most were sent to death camps and met immediate extermination.

"I understand that currently some of our girls have been kept and used as servants in the homes of officers of the SS.

"The Swedish government has made numerous attempts to rescue the girls, however, their location is unknown. Add to that, the fact that the Nazis do not admit to the kidnappings.

"We've considered taking drastic measures such as kidnapping children of high-level officers within Hitler's military and offering trades for our girls."

I noted the raised eyebrows all around and quickly added, "Of course, that is not our first choice for obvious reasons. Tonight, I have reason to hope that our girls will be rescued along with as many other people as this team can manage to save."

The next and last member to introduce himself was tall and lanky. He looked goofy wearing a checkered shirt with a bolo tie. He didn't seem to fit in any group, much less in this prestigious team. My thought was, "Here's a square peg in a round hole if I ever saw one." I soon learned how wrong I was.

As he stood up and up to his 6'5" height, he said, "I am Wilhelm Weber and I too am a member of the SS. I have the distinction of being both a mechanical engineer and a behavioral psychiatrist.

"As a doctor, I specialize in the field of the paranormal and the occult. The Nazis base much of their military strategy on the unseen influences of the occult. So, with this expertise, we can often stay ahead of whatever maneuvers they plan.

"Because I am a mechanical engineer working in the SS, I am privy to what's going on, technologically speaking, within the German military."

Abruptly, Wilhelm sat.

Everyone had spoken, and Hans looked at me for my reaction.

He said, "Well, Per Lundgren, are you ready to work with us against the Nazis?"

I cleared my throat, pushed back my chair and stood on very shaky legs. At that moment, I felt humble. Emotions knocked around my brain like a pinball machine.

I felt a blast of anger at what the Nazi devils had done and were continuing to do to anyone not their own. That anger threatened to debilitate me. Yet there was an outlet for my anger—to join a team that could offer defense against unimaginable atrocities and hope for those who believed that all hope was lost.

This venerable group was committed to unleashing their considerable power on the Nazis who would never see it coming— right from inside their ranks.

I cleared my throat again to give myself extra time to collect my thoughts.

"First, I commend each of you for having the courage to take a stand against the Nazis. We have all been deeply affected by what has happened to our world since Hitler came to power seven years ago. He has chipped away at humanity in the name of being Germany's savior.

"Second, I am honored and humbled to be considered to join with you. I accept and I promise that I will do everything in my power to support our goals. Thank you."

I sat and Hans got up and walked around the table as he spoke to the group.

"And so, my friends, now we see that our team is complete with the addition of our Swedish diplomat.

"Our time is up for tonight. As usual, we will pass the word about our next meeting via Mr. Duff at the Blue Tango. At that meeting we will discuss strategies for our first mission.

"Until then, we will all be thinking about exactly how we will blend our special talents.

"I bid you good evening."

At that point, Hans, Henrique, Will, Karl and Wilhelm stopped to shake my hand and to say good night.

Raya stayed back and waited until everyone was gone. She walked toward me and with that beautiful smile on her lips, she said, "May I give you a ride to your hotel, Per?"

Until then, I had not given a thought as to how I would get back to my hotel.

I said, "I would appreciate that, Raya."

"All right, shall we go?" She shut off the lights and we walked out into the night. The door slammed behind us. I assumed it locked automatically.

I looked around the parking lot for her car - there were no cars to be seen.

I said, "Where is your car?"

Raya grinned, linked her arm with mine and said, "Come along, you'll see."

It was indeed a night of surprises.

Around the side of the building was a Harley-Davidson. She got on it and said, "Hop on!"

I had never been on a motorcycle and I cannot say that I was anxious to "hop on" as Raya suggested. However, I also was not anxious to walk to my hotel either, so hop on I did.

I must admit that Raya was an excellent driver and I almost felt secure with my arms around her waist, riding on the back of that cycle.

She slowed as we neared my hotel and I saw that she was driving around the dark side to avoid prying eyes. I was not well-known in Berlin, but Raya certainly was.

The bike came to a stop and she motioned for me to get off, which I gladly did.

Before I could thank her, she waved and drove on down the alleyway. This was not the first time that I was left standing alone in the dark on that night.

My hopes were dashed. I thought I would have some time to get to know Raya.

I went around to the main entrance of the hotel and walked up one flight to my room.

I checked my watch. It was two-thirty AM. My flight would depart in seven hours.

Rather than try to sleep, I decided to finish up some paperwork from the diplomatic talks. I was grateful to have something other than the night's events to fill my mind.

Julia dropped her pen and sat back in her chair; she was in a daze. Suddenly, she realized that the writing was complete for the night.

She felt as exhausted as Uncle Per must have felt that night all those years ago in Berlin.

Until then, her journal writing was conducted without her conscious mind being present. Every other time she'd written what Uncle Per dictated, she had not comprehended until the next day after resting.

That night, there was a change. She was acutely aware, on all levels, of what her uncle was saying *while* he was telling his story.

Did that mean she was in both places at once—in Manhattan in 2015 *and* Berlin in 1940?

She was spent. With crossed arms on her desk, she put her head down and slept.

Chapter Seven

LEAVING BERLIN

Julia woke with a start and realized there was a small pillow under her head. It was one she displayed on the antique rocker next to her desk.

She thought, *I must have reached for the pillow sometime during the past six hours. That is the only possible way it could have moved from the chair—right?*

She was glad for the comfort of the pillow although her neck was stiff from sleeping on her desk.

The rocker moved slightly; she smiled. The chair rocked on occasion when it was occupied by the spirit of her Aunt Margaret. The rocker, now Julia's, had sat next to Aunt Margaret's desk as she wrote stories of far-off exotic lands. When Julia was young, her aunt read those stories to her and it sparked her imagination and curiosity.

She told Julia writing is a noble profession and it could expand your mind and take you anywhere you wanted to go.

She spoke aloud to the rocker, "Right, Aunt Margaret, and writing can take you to places you didn't even know you wanted to go—such as back to Berlin in 1940!"

Uncle Per chuckled, "So Julia, my cousin Margaret visits you. I'm glad you have her penchant for writing.

"Now then, since I'm here, would you mind continuing our communication? I would like to tell you about leaving Berlin."

"Of course, Uncle Per. I will be back as soon as the Keurig brews me a cup of coffee. Don't you wish you could have one too?"

"Ah, Julia, you are a funny one, aren't you? I will share your enjoyment of that first cup of morning coffee without need of a cup."

Satisfied with her little joke, she hustled to the kitchen. As she waited for the coffee, she thought how natural it was to speak to the spirit of her uncle.

She heard him chuckle again. Of course, he could be wherever he wanted to be.

A sip of the rich, dark brew perked her up considerably. He began to speak before she picked up her pen. She thought it might be a good idea to have a recorder for these sessions, but then again, she knew the energy didn't work that way—she was the medium, a recorder could not do the job. Julia quickly scribbled the first lines of what she had just heard.

I finished my paperwork and still had three hours before my flight was scheduled to take off. I allowed myself to think of Raya.

Until then, I had never mixed business with pleasure. I argued with myself that it wasn't business that brought Raya into my life. Meeting her was a chance encounter after my business was completed when I went to the Blue Tango Club.

Raya affected me as no woman had before. Sure, there was physical attraction, she was a beautiful woman, but this was much more. I thought I saw my future in her eyes. I had no idea if it was simply wishful thinking on my part, or if it was possible that it was mutual. I had to know, even if Raya felt nothing for me, I had to find out.

At once, I realized that I had to move quickly if I was to find Raya and still have time to make my flight.

I packed with speed and was about to leave my hotel room when, thankfully, I glanced in a mirror. Although I had showered and changed into travel clothes, I'd forgotten to shave.

That would never do. I tossed my suitcase onto the bed, located my toiletries and rushed to the bathroom to shave.

One should never rush such things. I managed to cut my neck in two places and had to wait until the bleeding stopped before putting my shirt back on.

Finally, I got to the lobby only to find no concierge to hail a cab for me. Rather than wait, I decided to walk the four blocks to the Blue Tango Club.

I didn't know where Raya lived. She had told me only that she had a small flat near the club.

Nevertheless, I sallied forth. I hoped I was not chasing windmills. As I neared the club, I began to search the windows of apartments. I was sure I would find the clue that would lead me to Raya.

I passed by the Blue Tango. I knew there were apartments around the next corner at the back of the club and headed there.

I stopped near the front door when I heard her voice— she was singing at that early hour!

Well, I could not believe my good fortune. I jiggled the door handle of the club and found it locked. It was just as well not to scare the wits out of Raya.

I waited until she stopped singing. I rapped sharply on the wooden door and after a moment she peered out of the small square window and saw me.

She opened the door and invited me in. There was no one else in the club.

We both spoke at once, "What are you doing here?"

Then we laughed.

"I know what I'm doing here, so please, you go first, Per."

"Raya, I wanted to see you, to ask you, I have to know, if you will please tell me…"

She stopped my stuttering by gently taking the suitcase from my hand and setting it down. Then she put her arms around my neck and kissed me so completely that I no longer knew where I was, nor did I care.

She took her lips from mine. "Does that answer your question, dear Per?"

She saw I was at a loss for words—me, the man who always had the right words no matter what the situation.

"Come, let's sit and talk at the bar. I've perked coffee. Would you like some, Per?"

I replied with a nod as she led me to the end of the bar near the kitchen. I sat on a stool and waited. A minute later, she emerged from the kitchen with two mugs of steaming coffee.

"I assume Swedes take their coffee dark and sweet?"

"Yes, thank you Raya. I really need this. I didn't get any sleep last night."

She smiled and gazed into her cup as if it might tell her what to say next. When she looked up at me, there were tears in her eyes.

I put my cup on the bar and stood at her side.

"What is wrong, Raya? Why are you crying?"

She turned on the stool, faced me directly and was silent for a moment.

"Per, I fell in love with you the moment I met you and I was afraid you did not feel the same. Knowing that you do, is a great relief to me, and so you see, these are tears of joy."

"I understand completely. I set out to see you before leaving to go home this morning and I had no idea if I could find you. I never dreamed that I would find you here. As you know, I was so happy to find you that I could not speak."

We giggled like school children.

I glanced at my watch and saw I was nearly out of time. I could not miss the only flight to Stockholm that day.

"Raya, you know that we will have to be very careful to let no one know of our relationship, primarily to keep you safe. But I promise you that we will find ways to safely spend time together. Perhaps I will arrange a singing engagement for you in Stockholm."

"I'm not worried, Per. Hans knows how I feel about you. He noticed the way we looked at each other last night and asked me what was going on. Hans is my brother and a friend to you. He is in favor of our relationship and he will be helpful to us."

I grinned. "And in addition to being my friend, Hans is much more observant than I!"

With a sigh, I said, "I'm sorry that I must be going now, Raya."

She hopped from the bar stool and fairly fell into my arms, then kissed me again until my mind was numb. I groaned as I let her go. I said, "I wish this was hello instead of goodbye, Raya. I hate to leave you."

She smiled and tilted her head. I could see love in her eyes.

"That kiss was only until we meet again, dearest Per. Now hurry away before I refuse to let you go!"

The plane trip was uneventful, unlike my time in Berlin. Leaving Berlin was more difficult than I could have imagined.

I thought, this just proves that you never know how life can be altered at any time, by any person...with no advance notice.

The communications from Uncle Per had taken on a more personal tone. He no longer simply expected her to write what he spoke; it often became a two-way conversation.

He surprised her. "Now then, Julia, what do you think of me falling in love with Raya?"

"Uncle Per, I'm happy for the two of you, you seem perfectly matched. What happened, did you marry her?"

"Whoa there, Missy, you will find out in due time. Allow my story to unfold. Meanwhile, don't you have a life to attend to in Manhattan?

"I'll be back soon. Enjoy your day, Julia."

Chapter Eight

CENTRAL PARK

The voice recorder in the front hallway blinked insistently. Julia took note of the two messages.

She pressed "Play" and heard Tom's voice. He sounded somewhat hurried, or was his tone clipped?

The knot in her stomach indicated that it might not be a pleasant conversation. Tom had likely seen her on the news with Seth. Tom's call would wait for the moment.

The second message was from Seth. She perked up when she heard his cheery voice.

"Call when you can, Julia. And, I had a great time with you at the Met. No rush to return my call. However, I think you will want to hear what I have to tell you. Talk later." Click.

Seth picked up on the first ring. "Hey Julia, that was a quick response; I just called you. How are you today?"

"I'm fine, Seth and how are you? You sound very happy."

"I *am* very happy, Julia, and you will be too when I tell you the latest!"

"Well then, please keep me in suspense no longer…what's up?"

"Okay, as you know, the opening at the Met that we attended garnered a great deal of publicity."

Julia's stomach did a little flip as she thought of Tom again.

Seth continued, "Thor Bjorn called me after seeing us on the tube. You know, he's one of the biggest real estate developers in Manhattan. I met him when I was involved with the Grand Central renovation project."

Julia jumped up from her chair. "Wait! *Thee* Thor Bjorn called you? That's amazing! What did he want?"

"It sure *is* amazing! He told me he's heading up a festival celebrating the original architects of Central Park and he invited me and anyone else I would like to invite. Would you like to go, Julia?"

She could hardly wait to say, "Yes, I would love to go! I have wanted to meet Mr. Bjorn in person ever since I moved to Manhattan. When is the festival?"

"That's just it; Thor apologized for the late notice. It's this Friday evening. Do you have plans?"

"I have a dinner meeting but I can reschedule it and be free for the festival."

"Great! We will be rubbing elbows with some very influential movers and shakers in our respective professions. Shall I pick you up or would you rather meet me at the park?"

After a moment's consideration, she said, "My apartment is right next to the park, so come here. She gave him her address and said, "I can see the park from here; it will be a short walk. I will tell the doorman to expect you, his name is Javier."

"Very good, I'll come by at seven on Friday evening. Be sure to dress in warm clothes. The festivities will be outside and it's forecast to be thirty degrees. We'll walk to the Bethesda Fountain; that's where Thor will address those who will be present for the opening ceremony."

"I will see you at seven, Seth. Thank you for the invitation. Goodbye."

"Goodbye, Julia. I'm glad you can join me."

Tom was not available when Julia returned his call. She kept her tone light when she left a voicemail, "Hi Tom, I received your message. I should be free all day. I'll wait to hear from you."

Just as she hung up the phone, the intercom summoned her.

Before she could speak, she heard Tom say, "Julia, buzz me in."

"Okay, Tom, I'll see you in a minute."

She opened her apartment door and Tom brushed past her without a greeting.

"Hi Tom. You seem upset."

"Damn straight I'm upset, Julia! I've called you several times in the past few days. You're never at home and you did not have your cell phone on.

"*Then* I hear from one of *our* friends that you've been seeing that architect guy, Stu or whatever the hell his name is!"

"Tom, Tom…can I please explain?"

"No! There is nothing to explain. It's perfectly clear to me what is going on!

"I'm here for two reasons: first, to tell you that you and I are no longer dating. And second, to take the personal items I have in the bedroom."

He headed for the bedroom and Julia followed.

She reached for his arm and he pulled away.

"Please, Tom, you don't understand. Seth and I are only friends. He invited me to the opening of the Egyptian exhibit at the Met and I joined him and a couple of his business associates there. Seth and I are not dating."

"Actually, this is what I want *you* to understand, Julia. You are free to see anyone you wish."

He tossed a few items into the small bag he'd brought with him and left as hastily as he'd arrived.

Julia stared out of the window overlooking the park. She was shocked, hurt and angry that Tom was being so unreasonable.

She wondered if there was some other reason for him to break up with her. She knew him well enough to know if there was another reason, he wouldn't tell her.

Tom walked toward the lot where his rental car was parked. His palms were sweating. Breaking up with Julia had been gut-wrenching, but it had to be done, for her sake.

He thought how fortunate it was that her friend, Seth, yes, he knew his name, came onto the scene and could be used as an excuse to end his relationship with her.

The client who contracted his investigative services insisted that Tom have no distractions whatsoever while he went undercover on assignment in Canada.

Having Julia on his mind would be a distraction and possibly put her in harm's way.

Yes, breaking up with her had to be done. He'd be in deep cover for the next year, or maybe two.

His rental car would serve as his office until he reached the border. Then the car would be exchanged for another rental car and he would disappear until the job was complete.

He hoped that Julia would not try to contact him or any of his friends. She would only be upset to find that he was unreachable.

Even *he* did not know exactly where he would be.

By the time Friday arrived, Julia was beginning to get over the shock of Tom breaking up with her and she was looking forward to the festival at Central Park.

Seth arrived promptly at seven and Javier called Julia to let her know that she had a gentleman caller.

She could hear the pleasure in Javier's voice. She grinned.

"Thank you. I'll be down in a jiffy."

With hat, gloves, scarf and coat, she headed to the elevator.

The lobby was empty but for Seth and Javier; they were engaged in an animated conversation.

They both turned and smiled as Julia walked toward them.

"Hello, Seth. I see you've met Javier."

"Ah, Julia, it's so nice to see you. Yes, Javier and I have been talking about the monuments in Central Park."

To that, Javier added, "Your friend is most interesting. He knows a great deal about all sorts of architecture. I would love to hear all about the festival when you two return."

"Absolutely, we'll gladly share the details with you, Javier. Have a nice evening.

"Oh, I have a chapter or two for you to read. I'll catch up with you sometime this weekend."

Seth gave her a quizzical look but simply said, "It was nice to meet you, Javier. I hope we meet again."

"I do too, young man. You two have a pleasant time and stay warm."

Curiosity got the better of Seth. As he held the door for Julia, he said, "What's this about chapters? Are you writing a book?"

She laughed, "Well, not exactly. I've become interested in a historical connection between my Swedish uncle and World War II. I'm doing some research and taking notes. Javier's family was taken by the Nazis during the war; he was only three years old. He hid in an attic space and was rescued a couple of days later. He's very interested in the history of World War II so I share my research with him.

Javier is very special to me; it's as if he's an older brother. We look out for each other."

"I can tell that he's very fond of you, Julia. He lights up when he talks about you.

"If you wouldn't mind, I would like to read what you've written sometime."

Julia quickly said, "Sure, I will let you know when I finish the current section of my research."

She was pretty sure Seth was not prepared to know that her research was channeled from Uncle Per. Maybe she would let him read what she'd written sometime later—that was a *big* maybe.

Central Park was sparkling with white lights that had been draped in every tree, or so it seemed.

The sky was clear, with twinkling white lights of its own, accented by the March full moon.

"Are you warm enough, Julia?"

"Yes, thank you Seth. We're almost at the Bethesda Fountain. I can see a crowd gathered. What time is Mr. Bjorn expected to arrive?"

"He should be here at seven-thirty. Wow, doesn't the park look fabulous? Let's find our way to the terrace where we'll hear Mr. Bjorn better and it might be a little warmer with so many people around."

"Okay, sounds good, Seth. There's a little bistro right there. I'll buy you a hot chocolate with marshmallows on top."

He laughed and said, "You are a temptress. I love hot chocolate; however, I'll take mine without the marshmallows. I hate to hear them scream as they are boiled in chocolate! But I'm buying. Save our place and I'll be right back."

She giggled and watched him as he walked to the bistro. He stopped two or three times along the way to shake hands with people he apparently knew.

It seemed to Julia that everyone liked Seth. She realized how much she liked him too. Everything was easy with him.

Television camera crews were in place at the fountain. The crowd grew restless when Thor Bjorn, aka the Mayor of Manhattan Development, had not arrived by seven forty-five.

Suddenly, people began pointing at a light approaching in the sky.

Seth said, "Thor loves to make a grand entrance; that would be his chopper."

Everyone watched as the helicopter landed.

Seth had always been intrigued with helicopters. He recognized this one as a Eurocopter. It could fly in all sorts of weather conditions.

The chopper shut down its engines, the door opened and Thor appeared clad in a tuxedo and top hat, which he tapped with the end of a cane. The crowd roared with laughter. He was quite a showman, obviously in his element—front and center.

Thor was handed a microphone. "Welcome one and all! Thank you for coming to this wonderful festival in honor of the master architects who gifted our park with bridges, arches, fountains, buildings and pavilions that we are fortunate to be the caretakers of in our time!"

He waited for the applause to end.

"Tonight, we have the privilege of being led through the park by those who know the park well…the Cultural Guide Group of Central Park.

"They're here waiting to take groups of thirty people to some of the architectural features of this great park.

"We have ten guides who will form your groups. So let us begin. I will go with the first guide, along with the television crew.

"Please—enjoy your tour and we will host a reception at ten PM at the Delacorte Theater."

Confusion ensued for the next few minutes.

A man who looked like he could be a Secret Service agent tapped Seth on the shoulder and spoke into his ear, "Mr. Bjorn asks that you and your guest join his tour group, Mr. Schmidt. Will you follow me please?" It didn't sound like a request.

Seth said, "Of course, we would be delighted to join Mr. Bjorn."

Seth whispered, "Okay, Miss Julia, you are about to meet the Great and Powerful Thor…we're invited to join him."

Mocking the 'secret service' man, he said to Julia, "Will you follow me please?"

She laughed. "Absolutely, let's go, Seth."

Julia was glad she'd chosen to wear her wool hat and scarf; the wind added a chill to the night air.

Thor saw Seth immediately and broke off his television interview to greet him. He grabbed Seth's hand and shook it. He said, "Well, well, Seth, I'm so glad you could make it!"

He glanced over Seth's shoulder and said, "And who is this beauty you have with you?"

Seth moved over and Julia stepped forward and offered Thor her hand.

"This is Julia Hamilton, one of Manhattan's premier interior designers. Julia, this is Thor Bjorn."

"It's a pleasure to meet you, Mr. Bjorn."

Thor's eyes bored into hers. "Well, Julia, I would like to hear all about your work sometime.

"Now then, let's get on with our tour, shall we?"

He finally let go of her hand, only to put his arm around her shoulders and lead her next to him.

"You don't mind if I keep your friend with me, do you, Seth? You can jump into the back of the cart with my assistant here."

It was the man who had advised Seth that Thor wanted them to join him.

Seth did as Thor suggested with a pasted smile on his face.

Thor said, "Julia, you sit right up front with me. Do you mind the television cameras? Just imagine that they're not there."

Julia had a déjà vu moment as she recalled being on TV the night of the Met…also with Seth.

Thor interrupted her thought when he leaned over and spoke so as not to be heard by the TV microphones. "You make me look good, Julia. You're very beautiful."

She smiled.

He then motioned to the driver and the guide that they were ready to begin their tour.

Their guide was a student on a fellowship at Columbia. He knew everything about the park; it had been the subject of his master's thesis.

He said, "Just call me 'Guide'—that way you won't have to remember my name."

The cart jolted forward and traveled along an eastern pathway, northward to the top end of the park.

It was a windy night. Julia pulled her scarf tighter around her neck and covered her face as best she could.

Guide began, "Our tour starts with the Huddlestone Arch, one of the many arches. The wonder of this design by Calvert Vaux is that it contains absolutely no binding material. It's held together by gravity and the pressure of the roadway above. It's made with uncut boulders."

Our cart stopped for a moment while Thor commented to the interviewer about the arch.

Guide continued, "Next, we find the Untermyer Fountain, which is cast in bronze and modeled after a sculpture in Berlin. It was donated by the family of American lawyer and civic leader, Samuel Untermyer and it remains a mystery how he came to have this fabulous fountain of 'Three Dancing Maidens' in his possession.

"We will now cross over to the west side to see The Ladies Pavilion, designed by Jacob Wrey Mould. It's a charming example of Victorian architecture. It was built in the late 19th century, originally intended to be a cover for passengers awaiting the trolley."

The tour stopped again and Thor got out so the cameras could get his picture standing in the pavilion.

He returned to the cart laughing and joking. He looked at Julia and said, "I hope you are enjoying the tour, Julia."

"It's wonderful, Mr. Bjorn. I am really enjoying it."

The guide directed the driver to the middle of the park to the mini-castle, aka Belvedere Castle.

"This castle was designed by Calvert Vaux and Frederick Law Olmstead who combined forces with Mould. It has many whimsical features as you will see when we slow down here.

"It has become the home of the New York Meteorological Observatory and is an official weather station.

"The castle has shown up in many movies over the years, such as 'Hannah and Her Sisters' and 'Stepmom' just to name a couple. It was even a location in the videogame 'Alone in the Dark.'"

The cart traveled along east and south until it came to another bridge.

"Here we are at the Vine Arch Bridge, also known as the Gapstow Bridge. It strongly resembles Ponte di San Francesco in Italy, also a segmental arch bridge. It's been rebuilt entirely from schist—that's our local bedrock and designed by Howard and Caudwell. Schist was chosen due to its hardness and it is also used to anchor Manhattan's skyscrapers. However, the original architectural designer was Mould. He had this bridge built of wood with cast iron rails. As you might imagine, the wood deteriorated over time and so it was replaced by the schist.

"The bridge is at the northeast corner of a pond named 'The Pond.' We will travel to The Pond's southern point, which is also the southeastern corner of the park."

The guide stopped the cart and shut off the electric motor. It was surprisingly quiet there, even though both 5th Avenue and Central Park South were nearby.

For a moment, no one spoke.

"Again, we find a design of visionary architects Olmstead and Vaux." The guide grinned. "Some refer to those two as the magicians of Central Park, and I tend to agree.

"Birdwatchers gather here to partake of the two hundred and forty migratory bird species. I'm not a birder, however, I have been at this spot on a clear day at sunset and the bird sightings are amazing.

"This is the last stop on our tour this evening. I hope you enjoyed it, I know I did."

During their televised tour, Thor had been in conversation with his interviewer and Seth seemed to be intrigued with his seatmate.

Julia was left to simply enjoy the sights and sounds of Central Park at night.

When Guide announced the tour's end, the camera crew shut down and thanked Thor for his time.

Seth was anxious to reconnect with Julia. He went to her side of the cart and helped her out.

"That was fascinating, Seth. I realize how little I know about this park. I intend to spend a lot more time investigating every square inch of it!"

"It sure was, and getting acquainted with Thor's assistant was equally fascinating. He told me that he travels the world with Thor and meets many interesting people.

"Julia, we're invited to the Delacourte Theater with Thor's group. It's quite a walk from here and it's an open-air theater. What do you think about saying goodnight to Thor and then we can head to a coffee shop?"

"That sounds good to me, Seth. I'm chilled to the bone."

He grabbed her hand and they made their way through the crowd that surrounded Thor.

"Whoa…it looks as if you two are headed away! I don't blame you. If I could go with you, I would. But duty calls."

Thor reached into his pocket and produced a card. He handed it to Julia and said, "I'm very glad that Seth brought you along tonight. Here's my card. I want you to call me first thing on Monday morning so we can discuss you coming to work for *me*. I need a talented interior designer."

She took the card, "Of course, Mr. Bjorn. I will call you on Monday. It was nice to meet you."

Seth shook Thor's hand and said, "Thank you for inviting us tonight. It was a great event, very good for Central Park. Goodnight, Thor."

The crowd pressed in closer to Thor and he shouted, "Goodnight to you both!"

Chapter Nine

CHANGES

Julia sat alone in the darkness of her living room. She was not the least bit tired, although it was well past her usual bedtime.

Her head was swimming with details of meeting Thor Bjorn, Tom breaking up with her and what had happened in the adventures of Uncle Per.

Any one of those events was enough to overwhelm her sensitivities; but all three together was too much.

She decided to try to declutter her brain by writing. First, she tackled the issue of whether to accept a position as an interior designer with Thor Bjorn.

She grabbed a yellow pad and drew a line down the center. She labeled the columns "Pro" and "Con" and titled the page, "Work for Thor Bjorn?"

Over the next hour she employed her logic and intuition to add points to both columns. Each point was assigned a number between 1 and 3, which denoted a level of importance, 3 being the most important.

When she tallied the points in the columns, she wasn't surprised to find that the points in the "Pro" column outnumbered the points in the "Con" column by a large margin.

Clearly, it would be a good move to work for such a mogul. It would include travel and she'd meet many important people.

That would also divert her mind from the issue of Tom breaking up with her.

She determined that a big life change was her best course of action. She would accept his offer, assuming his terms were fair.

Her thoughts went to the last session with Uncle Per.

"Good evening, Julia."

She laughed, now accustomed to his unexpected visits.

"Good evening to you, Uncle Per. Are you going to tell me about you and Raya?"

Once again, she was surrounded by sweet and pungent cigarette smoke.

"Does the smoke bother you, dear? I cannot seem to break the habit. I still smoke the Swedish brand, you know, before they were contaminated with chemicals."

"No, it's fine. I find the scent pleasant."

"Excellent, smoking relaxes me and keeps me focused. Now then, where were we? Ah, yes…you were wondering about Raya and me. I will satisfy your curiosity, my little chickadee!"

Julia smiled as he continued his story.

I thought of nothing other than Raya during my trip back to Stockholm. The moment I arrived back at my office, I put my plan into action.

I called my assistant, Inga, into my office and asked if she was still in charge of the Summer Celebration in Stockholm.

She said, "Yes, I am, Mr. Lundgren. Everything is in order. It's only two weeks from now. Why do you ask?"

"Could you possibly add a singer to the list of entertainers, Inga?"

She gasped. "Mr. Lundgren, you know what I always say… everything works out perfectly as long as you stay calm. Just yesterday, the performer who was to open our celebration called to say that his wife had taken ill, and he is not able to honor his commitment to sing.

"I told him not to worry about us, and to take care of his wife. I must admit that I had to take a few deep breaths to stay calm. And now you are asking me if I have room for a singer! Well, that's kismet. Wouldn't you agree?"

"Indeed, Inga. It certainly is kismet!"

My thought was that Inga had no idea just how appropriate the term kismet was as it regarded Raya.

"When I was in Berlin I met Miss Raya Simone. She is a singer at the Blue Tango Club. Maybe you have heard of her?"

"Oh yes, Mr. Lundgren! I have heard of her and she has quite a following. I hope she is available to come to Stockholm!"

"I hope so too, Inga. I will call her today and if she says yes, I will ask you to make the arrangements for her. Thank you very much. I will let you know as soon as I reach Raya, that is, Miss Simone."

Judging from the grin on Inga's face, I surmised that she gathered what Raya meant to me.

"That will be all for now, Inga."

I picked up the telephone and dialed the switchboard. I told the operator who I wanted to call and that I wanted to be advised when the party was reached.

While I waited, I looked at the calendar—two full weeks before I would see Raya—if she could arrange to come.

Thankfully, I did not have long to wait. The operator called back within minutes.

I heard a click, and then a pause before her voice sang into my ear. My heart skipped a beat.

"Raya, it's so good to hear your voice. How are you?"

"I'm well and I'm so glad you called, Per. I was just thinking about you."

"You were?" My heart skipped another beat.

"Raya, I was just talking to my assistant about you. I've arranged a singing engagement for you...right here in Stockholm. It's for our annual Summer Celebration and it's in two weeks. Do you think you can be here?"

"Per, your call has come at the perfect time! The Blue Tango is being renovated to accommodate the upstairs rooms, which will be used as a hotel for German officers. The plan is to close the club for a month beginning next week. Yes, I would love to come to Stockholm!"

"That's wonderful, Raya. My assistant, Inga, will make the arrangements for you and I will call again very soon."

"Yes, I look forward to hearing from you again.   Goodbye for now, Per."

"Goodbye, Raya."

I put the phone back on the hook and took out a lined pad. I wanted to write an itinerary for Raya's visit.

It was fortuitous that the Blue Tango would be closed for a month. That would leave Raya free to stay with me longer.

To the list, I added a particular place I wanted to show her—the palace where I was raised, and especially the pond in the back.   I spent my summer days there fishing, swimming and just daydreaming.

I also wanted Raya to spend time with me at my family's country home. It was a log cabin, simple and lovely, surrounded by pine trees on a small private lake.

I decided to ask Inga to have the cabin prepared for us to stay for the week after Raya's performance.

When I gave the list to Inga, I asked her to let me know when she finished the arrangements and to use my personal account for the expenses.

She did not look up from her steno pad, but she paused just for an instant when I said I was paying for everything.

That told her anything she may have wondered about.

Raya arrived on the morning of her performance. I met her myself, without a driver. I was not about to share her with anyone unless or until I had to.

The airport was a small private one so I drove onto the tarmac and parked next to her plane just as it came to a stop.

She stepped onto the plane's stairway and waved. How radiant she looked!

I hopped out of the car and held the passenger door open for her.

A steward delivered her luggage and I stowed it in the trunk and got back into the car. I leaned over and kissed her.

"I'm happy to see you, Raya. How was your flight?"

"It was wonderful; thank you, Per. I am looking forward to spending time with you. Where are we going first?"

"I thought you would be hungry after your travels, so we will check you into your hotel and then have brunch in the hotel's grille.

"After that, we will go to the stage where you will sing tonight, introduce you to the band and you can have a practice session.

"And then, I will drop you back at your hotel so you can rest and prepare for your performance.

"How does all of that sound to you?"

"It all sounds just perfect, Per. Let's get started!"

At that, I shifted my 1927 Volvo into first gear. It lurched forward and stalled. I tried again, it lurched forward and stalled.

I apologized, saying I usually had a driver and I was out of practice.

We laughed. We were happy.

Inga had made sure that every detail of Raya's visit fell into place flawlessly.

Our eight days together were blissful and ended far too quickly. The time we spent at the country cabin was the best time of my life, and Raya said the same.

We arrived at the airport early for her return flight.

As we sat in the car, Raya said, "I nearly forgot to give you something. It's a message from Hans."

She handed me a sealed envelope.

I opened it quickly and read it.

"Well then, we don't have to wonder when we will be together again. Hans has set a meeting for our team in the renovated rooms at the Blue Tango for three weeks from now."

"Oh, that is bittersweet news, Per. I will be looking forward to seeing you, but this meeting will determine our first mission, which will lead us all into harm's way. I know these missions are what we signed on for, but that was before I met you. I don't know what I'd do if I lost you, Per."

"My thoughts exactly, Raya, but I refuse to imagine my life without you. Please, let's focus on the present, and we will do what we must.

"There is your plane. I will say goodbye here."

We kissed, and she said, "Until I see you again, Per, remember that I love you."

"And I love you, Raya."
Then she was gone.

The next weeks dragged on, but I kept my mind busy with my work during the day, and every night I planned and imagined my life with Raya.
Finally, it was time to return to Berlin.

"Julia, that will be all for tonight. I bid you good night."

"Wait…you're leaving me hanging yet again?"

He laughed. "To my way of thinking, I'm not leaving you hanging at all. I *did* say I was planning my life with Raya, did I not? The rest is history as they say. Clever, eh?"

"All right, Uncle Per, I'll be satisfied with that, but only for now. Good night, Uncle Per."

"Good night, Julia."

Chapter Ten

Thor Inc.

It was a short trip from Julia's apartment across Central Park on the 79th Street Traverse Road to Thor's office.

Everyone in Manhattan was familiar with the most impressive skyscraper on Central Park West with its huge silver letters that spelled T H O R.

Thor Inc. was headquartered on the 38th floor of the building, just below the penthouse, which was, of course, used exclusively by Thor Bjorn.

Mr. Bjorn had not waited for Julia to contact him. His assistant called her on Sunday to set up a meeting for Monday at noon.

Julia arrived promptly at noon and was immediately escorted through three locked doors to the library level of Thor's offices.

The guard apologized for asking if he could perform a security check on Julia's coat and purse.

She handed them over and said, "You certainly *are* security-conscious here."

The guard thoroughly checked her belongings, handed them back to her and replied, "Yes, ma'am. Please have a seat anywhere you like. Mr. Bjorn should be with you soon."

With that, he left Julia in the library. She wondered why Mr. Bjorn was so concerned with security.

She walked around taking in the décor. Brown leather sofas and chairs were arranged in four separate seating groups. Each group featured two end tables and a butler's coffee table, all made of mahogany. The rich dark paneling complemented the wide wooden floorboards.

There were four Persian carpets, one for each section, all with different patterns in the same color palette of pine green and turquoise on a butter cream background. Tiffany lamps topped the end tables.

She recognized the paintings on the walls as originals by Monet, Renoir and Degas.

Just when Julia noticed the tiny cameras mounted in the bookshelves, the double doors to the library burst open and Thor Bjorn bellowed, "Hello, Julia!"

He walked to where she stood and took her hands in both of his. "I'm sorry to keep you waiting, Julia. How do you like what you've seen so far here at Thor?"

"Well, Mr. Bjorn, I'm very impressed with your library. Your interior designer seems to be enamored of the French impressionists, as am I!"

"I *knew* you had the eye of a professional, that's why I want *you* to work for me!"

He let go of her hands and said, "Let's sit, shall we?"

Thor led her to the oval conference table in the center of the room. He motioned for her to sit next to him at the head of the table.

There was a presentation folder in front of her. She wondered if it was for her.

Julia said, "I must admit, Mr. Bjorn, I'm a bit confused."

"Please, Julia, call me Thor, will you?"

"All right, Thor, you already have an interior designer, so why do you need my services?"

"Julia, I admire your frankness. If you open the folder in front of you, I believe you will come to understand why I want you for the position that I'm creating specifically with you in mind.

"Now, there is something I need to attend to elsewhere. I will leave you for a few minutes to read and formulate your questions."

"All right, Mr. uh…Thor."

He smiled and hustled out of the room.

Julia sat and stared at the folder. She had no idea what to expect. She held her breath, opened it and perused the summary page.

Loudly, she said, "What *is* this? It looks like a dossier - on *me!*"

Her instinct was to leave right then. Instead, she forced herself to read further. Her entire personal life was in that folder: who she was married to and how he died, the financials from Hamilton Interiors, who her friends and business associates were, places she'd lived, her college transcripts and even her medical records.

If all of that was not shocking enough, there was an entire section devoted to her Swedish heritage! Her Great Uncle Per was the main attraction of that section.

Julia flipped through to the end of the report, thirty pages in all and no mention of a job!

At that moment, Thor returned with another folder.

He sat and tried to get a read on Julia's thoughts.

Julia sat in stunned silence looking at the open file in front of her.

She disregarded her good manners altogether and blurted out, "What the hell is this about, Mr. Bjorn? You ask me here under the pretense of a job offer and then you bombard me with this...this exposé on myself! Just who do you think you are? This is an invasion of my privacy and I should report you to the FBI or the CIA or Interpol or or or..."

Julia stopped herself when she saw Thor's agitated expression.

"Miss Hamilton, are you quite finished? I assure you that you will want to hear me out. Will you listen now?"

"Yes, Mr. Bjorn, I will listen, but not much longer...make it fast."

He did not ask her again to call him Thor. He knew she didn't like him at that moment.

Thor put his hands on the folder he'd brought in with him and looked at Julia. He needed her to calm down so she would fully comprehend what he was about to reveal to her. It was important— to him and many others, even to her.

Thor cleared his throat.

"Julia, I know you're upset and I'm sorry for that. Perhaps I should have gone about this differently."

He tapped on the folder. "It was necessary to maintain the utmost secrecy regarding this department of my business. You see, the outside world knows me as a real estate developer. However, the top floors of this building are devoted to something entirely different."

He stopped and waited for some acknowledgment from Julia.

She nodded.

"I am Thor Bjorn, Jr., the son of Swedish shipping magnate Thor Bjorn, Sr. Sweden had business dealings with Germany involving transportation during World War II.

"My father had a deep hatred of the Germans. However, he was forced to cooperate with them due to agreements with the Swedish government. He found ways to fulfill those agreements and at the same time, to assist people who were trying to escape from the Nazis.

"There were a handful of people who knew what Thor Sr. was doing behind the scenes. Secrecy was paramount; many people were depending on him to save them.

"That all happened before I was born. My father wanted me to join him in shipping after I graduated from university, but I was hell-bent on capitalizing on the family properties and holdings worldwide. I went into real estate development and as you know, I've become quite successful."

Julia couldn't stand it a moment longer. She interrupted him. "Fine, you're very successful. *What,* may I ask, does that have to do with me?"

"I'm getting to that, Julia. Please be patient a little longer."

She sat back in her chair, crossed her arms and waited for him to continue.

"In 1990, my father became quite ill and needed constant care. My mother had died in an automobile accident years earlier and I was an only child, so it was up to me to see that he was taken care of. I went back to Stockholm, hired a staff to help and worked from there until he died in 1993.

"For the first year I lived with him, he was quiet and introspective. Then one day he asked me what I knew about Sweden's role in World War II.

"I told him the only thing I knew was that he was in shipping during the war.

"He said, 'Sit down, Son. This story will take a while to tell.'

"What he told me that day changed my life permanently. With great modesty, he told me about the people he saved from the Nazis, by picking them up from the shores of the Baltic Sea and delivering them to secret places along Sweden's shoreline.

"From there, underground organizations were able to give them safe passage to Canada or the U.S.

"He cried unashamedly when he told me about the families that he couldn't save—the ones left on shore in the dead of night as his ship slipped quietly away.

"I cried with him as he recounted meeting the Polish mothers whose children had been kidnapped by the Germans. As much as he wanted to help them, there wasn't anything he could do.

"As a boy, I *do* remember hearing those stories...the Nazi bastards took young Swedish girls too, and most were never seen again.

"After all that he told me, he didn't have to ask me to continue the work that he had begun during the war. I vowed to him that I would do everything in my power to find and reunite as many families as I could.

"He gave me his private logs containing names, dates and places he'd traveled to, in pursuit of saving people.

"I formed a private investigation division within my real estate development company and have been operating that portion undercover since 1993."

Thor said, "I'll stop talking now. What would you like to ask me, Julia?"

She did not miss a beat. She'd been listening, digesting and formulating her thoughts during his story.

"The most obvious question is why have you chosen me, Thor? What place do I have in your investigation company as an interior designer?"

"Ah, yes...the most logical place to begin. I've chosen you because of who you are, just as I have taken on this mission because of who I am. You see, you and I have a great deal in common, Julia. First and foremost, we are both from influential Swedish families.

"There is a good reason that you are interested in Sweden's role in World War II and it goes beyond your Great Uncle Per.

"The logs that my father gave me refer to Per Lundgren and others who worked with Swedish shipping and rail lines in order to save hundreds of people during the war. The logs also contain copious notes of a personal nature, rendering them a diary of sorts.

"And that, my dear, is how I found you. I wanted to find out what became of Per after the war and while I didn't locate him, I *did* find you.

"I understand that you are researching your uncle's war experiences and I would like to suggest that we work together to gather the pieces."

Thor paused to consider if he should tell her more and decided that he'd told her enough.

"What do you think, Julia? Are you prepared to join forces to discover what became of people who were saved by my father and your uncle?"

Her reaction thrilled and surprised him.

"Yes, yes and yes! When do I start?"

Thor smiled and said, "Just like *that*? You don't want to know how much I'm willing to pay you and where you will travel to?"

"At the risk of being indelicate, Thor, I know that money is no object to you, not to mention that I *am* the perfect person for this job. So how much *are* you willing to pay me?"

Julia leaned forward, put her elbow on the table, rested her chin on her hand and stared him down.

"I like your spunk, little lady! Indeed, you *are* the perfect person for this job; otherwise, you would not be here.

"Right here, in this folder, is my offer for your signature. I'll leave you to read it but first, I'll give you the highlights.

"Your sign-on bonus is $100,000. That will allow you to close up your apartment and your design firm."

He watched for her reaction; she showed none. *Oh, she is good!*

He continued, "I already set up a corporate account that you can draw from for any expenses whatsoever, personal or business-related."

Still no sign of a response from Julia. He thought, *Damn, she is going to do one hell of a job!*

"As for your salary, I'll start you at $150,000. We'll look at it again six months down the road. How does that sound, Julia?"

"That all sounds fine, Thor. The only question I have is when do I start?"

"I must say, Julia, I am very impressed with your enthusiasm, paired with your cool demeanor. You've confirmed in my mind that we will create some miracles working together—just as Thor Bjorn, Sr. and Per Lundgren did!"

He decided that she was ready to hear the whole story.

"You will want to know who you will be working with. Undercover, this is."

"I just assumed that it would be you, Thor. Who else would it be?"

With a sly grin, Thor said, "I recently hired the best international investigation firm there is. The CEO is Tom Pierson. Perhaps you've heard of him?"

Thor was aware that Tom and Julia were practically engaged. In fact, besides Tom's expertise, it was a primary reason for hiring him for this job.

Julia lost her composure. She was still recovering from her last encounter with Tom.

She blasted Thor, "Does Tom know that you expect me to work with him?"

She sat back in her chair again.

"I don't think this will work after all, Thor."

"Don't worry; I spoke with Tom the moment I knew that you and I would be meeting.

"Initially, he had the same reaction that you just had. After I gave him the overview of our mission and told him what you could bring to the table, he calmed down. He didn't go into a lot of detail, but he said he would be glad to have you back in his life.

"I hope you don't mind that the two of you will be working undercover…as Mr. and Mrs. White. You will join Tom in Canada."

"I don't mind. It will simply be part of the job. The only request I have is that you give me three weeks to close my apartment and enable me to see to it that my 5th Avenue client's design job is complete and ready for her annual ball."

"That will be fine, Julia. Ideally, I would like you to start right away, but I understand that you need some time."

"I appreciate that, Thor."

The intercom beeped and a male voice said, "Mr. Bjorn, the call you've been waiting for is on hold. Shall I have it transferred to the library?"

"No, I'll take it in my office."

Thor said, "Julia, I must take this call, please excuse me. Take the employment agreement with you. The last page has a private fax number for you to send a signed copy to me. I trust that you will agree with the details and sign it today."

They rose and Julia offered him her hand.

"Of course, Thor. I am looking forward to working with you. This is a worthy mission. Goodbye."

"I am, too. Goodbye, Julia."

Thor went out of the door and left it open for her.

The same security guard who had escorted her in was waiting to show her out. He greeted her by name this time and handed her a small manila envelope.

"Please open this after you sign the employment agreement, Miss Hamilton. After you remit the signed agreement to us, we will email you a security code that will enable you to open the enclosed thumb drive."

She was quickly becoming accustomed to the secrecy of Thor Inc.

"All right, thank you."

Once in the lobby, Julia stepped into the revolving door and exited onto the sidewalk.

She stopped and looked around. The sights that were so familiar to her seemed somehow more alive now that Thor had come bounding into her life.

Chapter Eleven

GOODBYES

Javier felt her presence in the lobby before he saw her. He turned, "Don't you look happy, Miss Julia!"

"I am enjoying this beautiful day, Javier!"

She was not ready to share her news with anyone yet, especially not with her dear friend.

Javier reached behind the desk and grabbed a long white florist box. He handed it to her.

"This arrived for you this morning, Julia."

"Thank you! I wonder who they're from. I love flowers!"

"Here, I'll press the elevator button for you. Do you need help?"

"No, thanks, Javier. I'll see you later."

Outside of her apartment, she put the box on the floor so she had a free hand to unlock the door.

The moment she was in the foyer, she dropped her purse and the all-important manila envelope. She picked up the big box and opened it to discover two dozen long-stem roses in the most fabulous shade of pink she'd ever seen. The tiny white envelope on top of the flowers held a card with one word on it: "Seth."

She had no idea what to think. This was a complication she certainly did not need—not with Tom back in her life and the new job.

Julia plucked her cell phone out of her purse and dialed Seth. She had to thank him right away…and let him down gently.

He was one of the people she would have to say goodbye to, and it looked like he would not make it easy.

Seth's line rang two, three, four times. Julia thought, *Great, I can just leave a message*.

However, Seth saw that Julia was calling and he interrupted his meeting to take her call. He stepped out into the hall and answered on the fifth ring. "Hello, Julia; I'm glad you called. Are you free for dinner at the Russian Tea Room tonight? I know it's short notice, but a guy I work with cannot keep his reservation and he asked me if I wanted it. Of course, I said yes. You know, you have to make a reservation at least six months in advance. Have you been there?

"I'm sorry, Julia. I'm not letting you get a word in edgewise. I'll shut up now."

Julia did some quick thinking. She would have loved to dine at the Russian Tea Room. But, she knew positively that she didn't want to be seen at another famous venue with Seth. The short notice for the date was her easy "out."

"Seth, that sounds fabulous! I really wish that I could join you, but I have a commitment that I cannot get out of."

It was only a little white lie...she had a lot to do since her meeting with Thor.

"I'm sorry that I can't go with you tonight. I wanted to thank you for the roses. They are simply gorgeous. Thank you very much."

Before he could comment on the roses and why he'd sent them, Julia said, "Let's have coffee one day this week. Do you want to call me when you're free?"

"Sure, Julia. How about tomorrow at our coffee shop? Shall we say one-thirty?"

"Absolutely. I'll see you then, Seth."

"Okay. Goodbye, Julia."

The sound of "goodbye" struck a nerve somewhere in her center. She set a reminder on her cell phone for coffee with Seth and then put him completely out of her mind.

With that done, she was free to review the employment agreement.

She found it to be straightforward and everything Thor had told her—the sign-on bonus, salary, an open-ended corporate account to draw from, and, oh yes, that she would be partnered with Tom. That last point was something she would never have thought would happen in a million years.

She faxed the signed agreement to Thor and anxiously waited for the email that would give her the code to open the thumb drive.

Only a moment later, her smartphone flashed, indicating an email had arrived from Thor, Inc. She jotted down the security code and opened the manila envelope.

Inside, she found a smartphone, a thumb drive and instructions from Thor that read as follows:

> Julia, the enclosed cell phone is to be used for communicating with Pierson International Investigations only. All calls, text messages, emails and photos between you and Tom Pierson are automatically forwarded to me.
>
> I will communicate with you only through Tom. And the only telephone number which you can receive calls from will be Tom's private cell number.
>
> As you can see, I've employed numerous security features to guard our work. There is more than one reason for that, most importantly, because both my father and your uncle worked outside of Swedish law during the war and their actions would be considered criminal, even after all these years. The Swedish government was aware of their covert actions but could not sanction them.
>
> I promised my father I would keep his work secret. To do otherwise could result in besmirching the family name for both of us and dishonoring the memory of two Swedish heroes.
>
> Many Germans have disavowed knowledge of the kidnappings of children during the 1940s in Europe. Our work is to find children, or their descendants,

who were stolen from Sweden, Poland, France and Norway, and then adopted or sold.

We have proof that wealthy couples from North America bought some of those children. That is why most of our work will be focused in Canada and the United States.

Presumably, the adoptive families were not aware that the children they were adopting had been kidnapped. As you might imagine, this will be a delicate situation, all the more reason for secrecy.

The enclosed thumb drive contains my father's logs along with his personal notes. You will need to spend time reviewing the documentation so when you team up with Tom, you will be prepared to get to work.

There is a voicemail on the cell phone in this package. It will inform you of when and where you will liaise with Tom.

Good luck, Julia and welcome aboard! Thor
P.S. Destroy this letter now.

The cross-shredder Julia recently purchased came in handy. She shredded the letter and powered up the new cell phone. The main screen had a bell icon that was blinking red – *hmm...that must be the voicemail.*

Hesitantly, she pressed the icon. Instantly, Tom's image appeared on the screen - the voicemail was a video message.

"Hello Julia, I've just spoken with Thor. In fact, you were at his office when I called."

She thought, *Oh, so that was the call Thor took in his office as I was leaving.*

"This message will be short. I will meet you three weeks from tomorrow at two PM on the Canadian side of the border, at the top of the New York State Thruway. You and I traveled to Montreal together last year so you will remember the trip takes about seven hours."

Up until that point, Tom had been all business. Then he stopped and smiled that special smile that he had always told her was *only* for her. The shell she'd placed around her heart began to dissolve.

He continued, "On the morning of our meeting, you will find a black BMW with New York State license plates parked on the street in front of your building. That is your rental car; the keys will be delivered to your door at six AM. If you want time to stop along the way, you should leave as soon as you get the keys.

"You have a lot to accomplish within the next weeks. Thor wants you to know he will send an assistant to help you if you like, and if so, to let him know, through me.

"However, knowing you, you already have the next twenty-one days all mapped out.

"I look forward to working with you, Julia. You know how to reach me."

Tom's image disappeared and was replaced by a notice that the previous video message was forwarded to an unknown party and then discarded.

Out loud, Julia said, "Wow, that's seriously impressive!"

She flipped off her shoes and padded to her favorite room—the kitchen. The walls were painted Sunrise Peach, a name she made up. The warm shade accented the terra cotta floor tiles. The radiant heat under her feet felt nice and toasty.

While the Keurig brewed French roast, she decided to listen to some music. She opened the corner cupboard normally used to store toasters and such, then turned on her SiriusXM radio. It was always tuned to "40's on 4." Immediately, she heard a song about laughing toes.. She wiggled her toes on the warm floor and smiled.

The next song was about a ghost. The laugh behind her sounded suspiciously like Uncle Per...*that would be just like him.*

She took her coffee to her desk along with the thumb drive and her iPad and prepared to review the logs and notes from Thor Bjorn, Sr.

Eight hours later, she realized it was past sundown, her coffee was stone cold and she was ravenously hungry.

As she'd read through the documents on the thumb drive, she felt as if she was a stowaway on a ship operated by Bjorn Shipping in the 1940s.

She imagined she could hear Thor Bjorn, Sr. and her Uncle Per talking about how to get their precious cargo to safety. She was excited and terrified to realize the risks they took to save people from the Nazis.

When she finished reading the last page, she felt confident that she was armed with all the information she would need to find at least a few of the family members of the children who had been saved and sent out of Europe.

She didn't expect to find children who would be eighty years old or more by this time, but maybe, just maybe they'd find their offspring.

The new life she was preparing for was exciting, not to mention intriguing.

Thankfully, she'd thought to stop by the Fresh Market that morning. She opened the refrigerator and took out the delicious fruit salad that waited for her.

To that she added sumptuous sesame dressing and sat at the kitchen table. The radio was still playing softly in the corner and she listened to "We'll Meet Again." Every word held the promise that the work of the newly formed triad of Bjorn-Pierson-Hamilton would be successful.

First thing the next morning, Julia dialed Mrs. Wellington's private number.

She answered on the first ring, "Hello Julia, I'm so glad you called. I wanted to let you know that my solarium is complete. I could not be more pleased, Julia! You are a master at your craft!

"I would like you to come by and put your stamp of approval on it. When can you come, dear?"

"Mrs. Wellington, I'm thrilled your design is complete. I'm free anytime this morning. Does that work for you, say in an hour?"

"Yes, of course, dear. I'll be waiting. I'm very anxious for you to see the finished product!"

"Great, then I'll see you soon, Mrs. Wellington."

On the cab ride over to Mrs. Wellington's, Julia looked at the invoice for the job. It had been a massive undertaking—her biggest job to date. She put the invoice back into her tote.

As she knocked on Mrs. Wellington's apartment door, she felt butterflies in her stomach. She was excited to see her completed project.

The housekeeper opened the door and welcomed Julia inside. "You have made Mrs. Wellington very happy, Miss Julia! She's waiting for you, go on in."

Julia heard Chopin's Fantasie Impromptu playing in the solarium. *How appropriate*, she thought.

Mrs. Wellington's voice drowned out all other sounds. "Julia! Julia! Come and see my paradise!"

Julia laughed as Mrs. Wellington grabbed her by the shoulders and gave her a great hug.

Julia did a turnaround and her eyes took in the entire solarium. "It certainly *is* a paradise, Mrs. Wellington!"

Mrs. Wellington babbled on, "And just look at my fountain with the sun shining on it, isn't it divine?"

"Yes, Mrs. Wellington, the contractors did a fine job. It's exactly as the plans called for, too. Does it remind you of your shop in Germany?"

"Remind me? It's *exactly* as I remember it. You transformed my vision into reality! I love to play Chopin's music, just as I did in my shop! Oh Julia, I could not be happier! The unveiling of my solarium will take place next month, at my annual ball. You remember—it's the event when I invite friends and acquaintances who are survivors of World War II.

"I'm sure that everyone will want to know who my designer is, and then you will have more work than you can handle!"

"Thank you so much for that, Mrs. Wellington. However, this is my last job for a little while."

Mrs. Wellington looked alarmed. "Oh my, you aren't ill, are you?"

"No, it's nothing like that. I'll be traveling with my uncle for the next few months. He's been asking me to take a trip with him for years, and I've decided that this would be a good time."

What she told Mrs. Wellington was somewhat true. Her travels *did* have to do with Uncle Per.

"Well then, I'm happy. You will surely have a fine time with your uncle. I will email you after my ball and tell you all about it!"

"Thank you. I would like that."

Julia handed her client the invoice and said, "You can pay the bill through the automatic deposit that we set up. There is no rush."

Mrs. Wellington looked very pleased with herself when she said, "I know what the final amount is, Julia. I've already deposited it into your account, along with a hefty bonus for a job well done!"

"Thank you, Mrs. Wellington. It has been a pleasure working with you."

With that, Julia threw her arms around Mrs. Wellington and said, "I will call you when I'm back in town."

"Yes, please *do*. We'll have tea when you return. Goodbye, Julia."

"Goodbye, Mrs. Wellington."

Before she knew it, it was time to leave for her coffee date with Seth.

They arrived at the same moment and Seth held the door open for her, "After *you*, pretty lady."

She smiled and said, "Thank you, Seth."

She intended to keep the conversation light, in other words, impersonal.

She said, "That was good timing, don't you think?"

He apparently did not share her idea for their meeting. He said, "We always have a good time, don't we, Julia?"

Seth led her to a small table for two in the back corner.

Oh, that's not a good sign, she thought.

Her butterflies fluttered again. She wanted to get this meeting over with. She didn't want to waste time; that might give him an opportunity to ask her out again.

He was about to say something when she interrupted him, "Seth, I have something important I need to tell you."

"Go ahead, sweetie, you can tell me anything. What is it?"

He is not going to make this easy on me.

He reached for her hands across the table and she managed to pull them back before he got a grip.

Seth reacted. He sat back in his chair and said, "Go on, Julia."

"I'll get right to the point." She stuck with the same story she had told Mrs. Wellington. "My uncle from Sweden has asked me to take a trip with him and I've decided this is a good time, now that my 5th Avenue job is done. I'm closing my apartment and I'll be gone for six to twelve months."

He didn't wait to hear more, "Your uncle from Sweden? Don't you mean Thor Bjorn? I *knew* that man was bad news from the moment we saw him at Central Park! Did he offer you a job? Are you traveling with him? He's an old man, you know! What the hell are you thinking, Julia?"

"Seth, control yourself. None of what you said is true."

She couldn't tell Seth the truth and she didn't like it, but it was necessary.

She continued, "I'm sorry; I know this is sudden. I'm not even sure exactly how long I'll be gone. My uncle is making the travel arrangements. I hope you're not upset with me, Seth."

Seth leaned across the table, "Upset with you? Yes, I'm upset with you! I thought that we had something together; that we were taking our relationship to the next level…you know, something of an exclusive nature."

He stopped talking when Julia sat back in her chair. It was obvious she was unaffected by his words.

"Seth, I'm sorry. I will let you know when I'm back. I hope you will excuse me. I have a great deal to do before I leave for my trip. Thank you for meeting me."

She couldn't wait to get out of the coffee shop.

Seth did not say anything at all, and he did not get up when she left.

Julia spent the rest of the day ticking off tasks from her voluminous checklist.

She quit working when the grandfather clock chimed five. She would miss that clock while she was away. It was a family heirloom, given to her by a distant cousin, Princess Olga of Sweden, when she learned that Julia's husband, Jed, had been killed in Iran. Princess Olga was her second cousin on Julia's father's side of her family.

Her chair seemed to rock in response to a breeze that wasn't there. Yes, she'd miss Aunt Margaret's rocker.

She thought aloud, "Now, for the most difficult goodbye. I have to talk to Javier before he goes home for the evening."

She got up and headed for the elevator and suddenly remembered she'd promised to let Javier read her journal.

She grabbed a copy of the most recent portion of her journal from her desk and went to tell her friend that she would not be seeing him for a while, perhaps a long while.

Javier was reading the newspaper when the elevator door opened into the lobby.

"Are you reading anything interesting, Javier?"

"No, just the usual political warfare, Julia. Is that your journal you have there? *That's* sure to be interesting reading."

"Yes, it's as complete as it will be for now."

He looked confused. She didn't wait for him to ask more questions that she could not answer.

"You see, Javier, in a couple of weeks, I'm going on an extended trip with a friend."

To tell him that she was going on a trip with her uncle from Sweden would just confuse him more—he knew about Uncle Per.

Julia continued, "I'm looking forward to traveling. We've decided to go to Greece, Italy, Germany, and France and maybe to Sweden."

She handed him the journal to break the tension.

"Julia, I am very happy for you. I hope you will send postcards along the way. I *do* hate the thought of not seeing you. You are family to me."

Javier embraced Julia as if she was precious to him, because she was. When he let her go, they both had tears in their eyes.

"Don't worry, Javier. I'll be back before you know it."

"I hope so, Julia."

Chapter Twelve

MISSION BLUE TANGO

It had been a busy day for Julia and she was glad to finally have a chance to put her feet up and enjoy a bowl of chicken soup from the corner deli.

She realized Javier needed more attention now that he knew she'd be leaving. So, when she ran out for groceries in the morning, she stopped by the deli and picked up a container of soup for each of them.

When she gave him the soup, he thanked her and said, "Julia, I read your journal and found it fascinating, as usual. Do you want it back?"

"No, Javier, you can keep it. I gave you a copy. I will let you read any other chapters that I may write while I'm still here, and if you like, I'll email chapters while I'm away."

"I would love to read whatever you write about your Uncle Per's adventures. I feel as if he's my family too, and I am most anxious to know what happened to him next during the war."

"I agree with you, Javier. Uncle Per is keeping me in suspense and I cannot wait for the next installment.

"Now it's time for me to get back to work. Enjoy your soup and I'll talk to you later."

"Thank you once again, Julia; you know how I love the chicken soup from Einstein's Deli."

"Me too! You're welcome, Javier."

She put her empty soup bowl on the coffee table, sat back in her easy chair and prepared for a ten-minute power nap.

While that was her plan, it was not the plan of someone else.

"Hello, Julia," Uncle Per said. "I understand you will be joining the company that Thor Bjorn, Jr. created. That is marvelous!

"Of course, you know that his father was my very good friend and we worked in concert during the war.

"It may sound strange to you, but we are once again working together, Thor Sr. and me. We will be feeding you information that will augment Thor's logs."

Julia blurted out, "Oh, great! This is just *great*...now I'm talking not only to *one* dead person but *two*! How do you think Thor Jr. and Tom will like *that*? Oh, wait...I know, I'll just tell them, 'I see dead people.' I'm sure they'll understand!"

"Don't worry, Julia; the information that will guide your work will be obvious to Tom because he's read the same logs that you have. He will simply think that you're a genius to come up with the clues, which, of course, you are! I haven't let you down so far, have I?"

"No, but..."

"All right then, just trust me. Let's get on with it, shall we? Your pen and your journal are right beside you."

"How did you, I mean, I didn't leave them here."

Julia decided not to try to figure it out. She picked up her pen and journal and listened to her uncle.

Three weeks after Raya and I parted in Stockholm, I joined her in Berlin and we attended our team meeting in the private conference room where my diplomatic talks had been hosted. We were to plan our first mission.

Hans got right to it, "We will refer to our missions as 'Blue Tango.' No one in Germany will think twice when they hear the name. Are we all in agreement?"

Will Bates was the first to respond. "From my point of view as a cryptologist, I think that referring to us as 'Blue Tango' is quite clever, especially since the newly renovated upper level of the club serves as a hotel for the military and it's the talk of the town.

Sometimes, the most obvious codes are the best. Yes, I agree with the name 'Blue Tango,' Hans."

"Thank you, Will. If you all agree, we'll continue."

Hans looked around the table, got an affirmative nod from everyone and went on. "Fine, let's get started then. Henrique, you will oversee communications. It makes sense as your field of expertise is intelligence. I'll come back to your duties later.

"Will, you'll formulate our mission strategies based on the timing and location that Wilhelm comes up with.

"We know that the Nazis rely on astrology for their strategy. Wilhelm can keep us ahead of their movements.

"Wilhelm, will you give us an example of exactly how your knowledge of astrology will aid us?"

"Of course. I will be happy to, Hans."

Henrique pointed to graphics on a pad that he had on the table in front of him.

"We know that Germany attacked and now occupies Norway. I have cast a joint astrology chart for Germany and Norway for the date of the attack and another one for two weeks prior to that attack.

"Hindsight is always 20/20. However, the timing of Germany's attack on Norway is evident within these charts.

"The value of this knowledge is that I can tell within hours when the Nazis will attack their next target.

"Their target location is not as easy to determine because there are so many possibilities here in Europe. But the good news is Henrique, Will, Karl and I have heard SS officers say that France is next.

"What we have also heard is that Germany wants the northern and western borders of France for access to the sea, and to Great Britain.

"So then, the next chart I cast was a joint one between Germany and France. That chart led me to know that Germany will begin their advance into France at sunrise exactly two weeks from today."

Wilhelm stopped and took note of the skepticism that was evident on the faces of all of us at that table.

He said, "It is not necessary for any of us to believe in astrology. We only need to know that it's what the Germans use to determine their military timing."

Hans said, "Thank you, Wilhelm; that was quite informative.

"Will, can we hear from you regarding the strategy you've worked out for us?"

"Certainly, Hans. As we now know, the attack will focus on the northern and western borders of France. So, our team will zero in on the small towns on the eastern border closest to Switzerland.

"Our sources tell us that German troops will travel through that area on their way to their targets.

"Based on how the Nazis operate, we are certain they will gather Jews and Catholics along their way, as well as anyone else they don't like the look of, and send them to camps where they will die in servitude or be put into gas chambers straight away.

"Our mission is to get to as many as possible before the Nazis arrive and get those people to safety.

"Our team will travel in Nazi uniform reflecting our usual ranks. We will be able to pass through Germany with relative ease.

"Per, I'm afraid that you too will wear a Nazi uniform, but only until we arrive in France. Then we will need you to dress in your civies and calm those who we will try to save. We don't want them to think that we're part of the Nazis who are there to capture them."

I interrupted Will, "I assure you that I will be most happy to take off the Nazi uniform. However, I must ask, what are these 'civies' that you refer to?"

When everyone stopped laughing, Hans said, "Sorry, Per, we forgot you are not military. Civies are your civilian clothes."

I admit I was a bit embarrassed, but it quickly passed when Hans said, "You're up, Per. You'll be in charge of arranging safe passage for those we can save. What are your thoughts?"

At that point, I stood and began walking around the table. I always found that I could think best as I paced.

It was rather comical to see all the heads following me as I got a grip on how I would respond.

I began. "My immediate assessment of our mission is that there are four main components. First, to get to France to save as many as we possibly can. Second, to convince those people that we are there to help them. Third, to get back through Germany undetected with our trucks full of people. And fourth, to arrange safe passage for those people.

"I am confident that I can assuage the fears of those we take to safety. I am equally confident that I can use my contacts in Sweden for safe passage. However, at this moment, I am not exactly sure how that will work."

Will said, "Understandable, Per. You've just heard what we're up against for this first mission. I can help you with that angle. Just let me know when you have your contacts lined up and we'll discuss strategy."

I said, "Thank you, Will. I will sit now so that you can give your necks a rest."

Raya giggled. She was the only one who understood my dry humor.

Hans took the floor again and addressed her. "Raya, you will remain here at the Blue Tango and keep the German officers entertained with your singing. Anything you hear may be of help to us and can be reported through Henrique. He, in turn, will get intel to our team in the field. I also will remain here in Berlin and keep an ear to the ground for Nazi rumblings."

Hans turned his attention to Karl, the former Polish Cavalryman, now a member of the SS intelligence.

"Karl, you will drive a supply truck for this mission. You will follow behind the lead supply truck, which Wilhelm will drive.

"Per goes with you, Karl; and Will rides with Wilhelm."

Hans continued. "That leaves three of us in Berlin: Raya, Henrique and me.

"Since the second level of the Blue Tango Club has been converted to hotel rooms, the Germans are using the rooms to take prostitutes to. When you mix men and alcohol with prostitutes, you often get informative pillow talk.

"Thus, our Henrique here has rigged the rooms with listening devices. Information gained in this way can be most beneficial to us. Henrique and Karl will work on a communication system between us here in Berlin and the four who will be in the field.

"It is imperative that we stay ahead of the Germans. Wilhelm's timeline gives two weeks until the Germans get to eastern France so we need to be ready to roll in five days. Do you all understand?"

Once again, everyone nodded in agreement.

Hans said, "Very well, go and make your plans individually and we will meet back here tomorrow at the same time. Thank you all."

We all got up and milled around, reluctant to leave after hearing about our first dangerous mission.

Hans and the others, except Raya, soon left for a meeting with top brass at the Reichstag.

The moment I was alone with Raya, she flew into my arms. It was as if we never parted, and time stood still...that is until we heard someone clattering around in the kitchen.

I released her and said, "I will go back to my hotel room and begin calling contacts for our mission. By the time you finish your evening performance, I will be finished. I will wait for you to join me in my room."

With a wink, I said, "And bring your toothbrush."

Raya did not need to say anything—the provocative swing of her hips as she walked away said it all.

As I walked to my hotel, I thought about our mission to France. It would be high risk for sure.

The Blue Tango team met the next day as agreed. Everyone was present, except Raya.

Hans answered my unspoken question when he announced that Raya had something to attend to and she would be late.

He continued, "So, gentlemen, I am most anxious to hear what you've come up with on the overnight. As of today, we have four days until we get underway.

"Wilhelm, since you will drive the lead supply truck, let's begin with you. What is your plan?"

As Wilhelm stood to his full height, I was reminded that he was an imposing figure of a man. With him in the lead, we were not likely to be stopped at the border. Obviously, that was why Hans put him out front.

He began. "I am most pleased to report that I met with the officer in charge of equipment and supplies after our meeting yesterday. I told him I was joining the contingent that was traveling into France and that my division would require two supply trucks full of provisions, each with a tag-along for additional supplies.

"*Of course, he assumed that I was talking about being part of the German troops headed to the coast of France and I did not inform him otherwise.*

"*He told me arrangements were in place for the troops to move out in four days and he would have my trucks and supplies ready with the others.*

"*He also apologized and said that because my requests were received last, that meant my trucks would be last in the formation.*"

Wilhelm finished with a smug grin. "*I told him it would have to do and that it was fine, given my late request. We know what this officer does not know—with our trucks at the back of the line, we will not be noticed when we detour away from the other trucks. It's perfect for us!*"

Hans applauded. "*That is excellent work, Wilhelm! Now let us hear from you, Will.*"

Will spoke from his place at the table; there were several maps in front of him.

"*I do have a couple of maps to get us to the eastern border of France from the military base, although I do not think we will need them. I do not expect any problems to crop up on the first leg of our journey. If we were to be stopped for any reason, we would not have people in our trucks at that point anyway.*

"*I've also worked out three routes to get us back through Germany after we make our rescues. One route takes us to the North Sea and two routes take us to the Baltic Sea.*

"*As we know, the tricky part will be traveling back through Germany with people in our trucks. The tag-alongs that Wilhelm ordered will hold provisions, while the back of the trucks will hold the people.*

"*I will have these maps ready, in the event we must take a different route. We will know that as the situation unfolds.*

"*The route we take on the way back depends largely on what transportation Per can arrange to get people to Sweden.*"

Hans said, "*Thank you, Will. Now then, Per, are you prepared to tell us what you came up with?*"

I stood. "Yes, I am. I was able to get in touch with an old friend in Sweden who runs his family shipping business.

"Bjorn Shipping has government contracts to transport goods and equipment primarily to Germany and Poland.

"Mr. Thor Bjorn is most interested in helping us rescue people from the Nazis. He said he has a shipment going from Malmö , Sweden to the Port of Danzig, which the Germans now control and refer to as Gdansk. That shipment is scheduled to reach Danzig in eighteen days.

"That means if we leave in four days, we should reach the eastern border of France easily in another four days. Then it will take us a day to gather all of the people who will fit in our trucks. We will then have nine days to travel northeast across Germany to the port. Berlin is between France and the Port of Danzig; however, we will need to steer clear of Berlin for obvious reasons.

"When we make it to Bjorn's ship, he will take the people we were able to save to Malmö. Wilhelm, Will and Karl will head back to Berlin with the trucks, and the Nazis will be none the wiser for our scheme."

Per paused before continuing. "I will travel to Sweden on Bjorn's ship. At Malmö, Bjorn will board us onto another ship to take us to Stockholm. All those people will be safe in the homes of volunteers in and around Stockholm until I can figure out how to get them to North America. A lot will depend on how many people we are able to save.

"I feel certain that our mission will be successful with the help of Thor Bjorn."

I sat and everyone clapped enthusiastically.

Hans announced, "Enlisting the help of Thor Bjorn is a major coup for our team, Per!"

He continued, "Will, can you alter your strategy to fit with Per's plan for our team to get to Danzig?"

"But of course. I am not called 'Strategist Extraordinaire' for nothing!"

Hans laughed and clapped Will on the back. "Excuse me for doubting your expertise, Will!"

It was a light moment...we all needed to have a brief respite from thinking about what we were about to do.

"We're done for now; we will meet again in three days. That will be the day before our field team leaves...same place, same time. Good day, gentlemen."

After the others left, Hans grabbed my arm. "Per, a word?" He looked very serious and I had no idea what to expect. "There is something you should know about Raya."

My mind jumped to a million conclusions. "What? What's happened? Where is she? Is she all right?"

With a steadying hand on my shoulder, Hans said, "Yes, she is all right. You see, she went to see a doctor this morning. I know that she didn't tell you...she passed out while she was on stage last night."

I panicked. "But I was with her after the show last night. She seemed fine and she did not mention that she fainted. What did the doctor say? Is it serious?"

"No, Per, it is not serious. The doctor told her to get some rest and see him again in a month."

Hans looked at me with the hint of a smile on his lips. "Well, old boy, I'm sure that Raya will...here she is now. Raya, I was just telling Per that you visited the doctor today. I shall leave you two alone. I will see you later."

Raya didn't look ill; in fact, she looked radiant. Then it dawned on me why she fainted and why the doctor wanted to see her in a month.

I went to her and scooped her up in my arms. "We're having a baby, aren't we, my love?"

Raya kissed me so sweetly that I thought I would melt. "Yes, Per...do you mind very much?"

I said, "Do I mind? No, I am thrilled beyond words and I could not be happier."

"I am very relieved, Per. Now, will you please put me down?"

We laughed. We were happy.

The last meeting before our mission to France came all too soon. We went over every detail of the plans again and again, until all of us knew what to expect and how to react every step of the way.

Henrique reported that the listening devices had already rendered useful information from the German officers who had bedded women in the upper rooms of the club.

He could now confirm the timing and the locations of the German attacks on France—just as Wilhelm had predicted.

Hans stood at the head of the table and spoke to us as if it might be the last time he would see any one of us, or all of us. "This is our first mission of mercy. It will be difficult, but I have every confidence in the plans we've formulated as a team."

He looked at those of us who were headed to France in the early hours of the next day. "I expect to see you back here in twenty-one days, except you, Per. We will be in contact with you by telephone as soon as you reach Stockholm."

I looked at Raya. Her sad face was almost more than I could bear to look at. I wanted to say something to lighten her mood. "Don't worry. I plan to be back in Berlin in twenty-two days and after that, you'll all be sick and tired of seeing me!"

Raya's face brightened a bit at the thought of me being back a day after our mission was complete.

Hans said, "I think I speak for all of us here when I say that we would never tire of seeing you, Per.

"Now we should all go and get plenty of rest.

"We will be tracking your progress from the command post 'Blue Tango.' Good luck and God speed."

Chapter Thirteen

TO FRANCE!

Julia put her pen down, stretched her legs and said aloud, "I cannot focus. I need a break…a snack and a cup of coffee."

Uncle Per responded with his signature chuckle. He said "Right. I'll join you for that coffee."

Aunt Margaret's rocker tipped forward as Julia passed it. She looked at the rocker and said, "I know you must be enjoying Uncle Per's story, Aunt Margaret."

Julia shook her head and thought, *Now I'm sure I'm a bit left of center!*

She stood at the coffeemaker and waited for a large cup to brew. There was not a thought in her head at that moment.

Something lightly brushed her cheek; she heard her Uncle Per say, "Julia, I'll give you some background regarding our first mission while you're relaxing."

"That will be fine. It will give my writing hand a rest."

"Excellent. You just sit back and listen, my little chickadee."

Julia pulled a chair up to the kitchen table, added some lavender honey to her coffee, ripped open a protein bar and listened.

I slipped out of Raya's apartment well before dawn, without waking her.

Hours earlier, we'd had a tearful goodbye. Raya fell into an exhausted sleep. I watched her until it was time for me to leave.

Before sunrise the next morning, the four of us who were traveling to France waited for Hans to pick us up in front of the Blue Tango Club. Each of us was dressed in Nazi uniform.

We passed other vehicles carrying military men along the roadway to Kaserne Krampnitz in Potsdam. It was a military motor transport base and training facility about thirty miles from Berlin.

We got through the main security gate with time to spare. Of course, everyone other than me had been to the base many times. I was sitting up front with Hans. He looked at me and said, "Quite an impressive facility, is it not, Per?"

"Yes!" I was in awe of the huge buildings that seemed to stretch on for miles. And the entire property was behind high security fencing.

"I'll drop all of you in front of the main building, which houses a most amazing art piece in the ceiling of the center hall. I'm sure that your fellow Nazis will be more than happy to accompany you, Per. Isn't that right, gentlemen?"

A joint groan was heard from the back seat; however, it was in jest. Wilhelm piped up, "Sure, Hans. It will be sort of an initiation for Per, since it's his first day as a Nazi and all!"

That got a laugh from everyone, including me.

Hans stopped the car in front of the main building. As I stood on the sidewalk and watched Hans drive away, I felt as if I was a miserable child being left at summer camp.

I shook off the feeling when Karl said, "Okay, let's go look at the masterpiece!"

He led the way to the foyer and I looked up. What I saw on the ceiling was the most fabulous mosaic that I had ever seen. It was a picture of the Nazi Eagle perched on a swastika; all done in brilliant mosaic tiles and it was enormous. Of course, I abhorred what it stood for, however, I had to admit that it was impressive.

Will nudged me and said, "Let's get out of here, there are some officers who just came in and we don't want to see them right now with you here."

Wilhelm and Karl spotted them at the same time and headed for the door too.

We met outside and walked alongside the line of jeeps and trucks that were set to roll within the hour. We knew our trucks were last in line. We walked all the way to the end.

"Now then, Julia, if you are ready to begin the writing again, we'll pick it up from here."

"Oh yes, I am most anxious to hear about your mission!"

Wilhelm waited for the dispatcher to call his name. I stood beside him with Will and Karl, ready to hop into the truck with Karl.

We were all feeling anxious but so were the other troops who were waiting to be dispatched.

Wilhelm leaned in and said, "Per, you make a good showing in the Nazi officer's uniform. Let us hope that none of the real Nazis address you directly."

I had a response for his smart remark on the tip of my tongue; however, just then the dispatcher approached our group and shouted, "WILHELM WEBER! SPEAK UP!"

Wilhelm snapped to attention, saluted and replied, "Captain Weber present here, SIR!"

"Right, Weber...here are your papers." He handed him a batch of crisp documents.

The dispatcher had a prickly disposition, presumably due to the early hour. He halted in front of me and looked me up and down while I did my best to appear calm.

He finally looked back at Wilhelm and snapped, "If these are your men, get them to your transportation at the end of the line and wait until everyone moves out ahead of you!

"You will find keys in your trucks. While you wait, and I am happy to inform you that it will be a very long wait, you will go and find the tag-alongs and hook them up to your trucks. I have no idea how you rate the special treatment of receiving the tag-alongs in the first place!"

He abruptly turned on his heel and walked toward the front of the line. The four of us looked at each other, glad to see him leave.

"I've seen that guy before. He's always looking for a fight. I thought for a minute that he was going to harass our good Nazi officer here," Karl said, pointing to me.

I was far too tense to see the humor in Karl's cajoling.

Karl headed for the garages. He said, "Let's find the tag-alongs, hook them up and see if we can rustle up more provisions to store without being noticed."

No one was at the supply garage. All personnel that morning were in their vehicles waiting to move out.

We quickly located the tag-alongs and chose the best two of the lot. As we dragged them to our trucks, I spotted a large wooden toolbox, just inside the garage, off to the side.

Karl saw it too. I understood his head jerk to mean "bring it with us."

I looked around, saw that the coast was clear and grabbed it. But when I picked it up, it was much heavier than I anticipated. I dropped it and it fell open. Still, no one was around to notice so I hurried to throw all the tools back into the box.

Karl saw what happened, dropped the trailer he was pulling and ran to help me.

It was then that we discovered just why the toolbox was so heavy. It had a false bottom that dislodged when I dropped it and three bars of gold dropped out.

I said to Karl, "Maybe we'd better leave the box where I found it and the gold, too."

Karl spoke through clenched teeth to control his reply. "Are you a lunatic, man? We can use this gold and no one will know who took it. Let's put it back into the box and throw it in the back of Wilhelm's tag-along. Come on, get a move on!"

It took both Karl and me to tote the box to where Wilhelm was hooking up the trailer to his truck.

He gave Karl an inquisitive look and said, "What's this you have here, boys?"

Karl snapped, "Just open the tag-along so we can put it in, Wilhelm! Does this thing have a lock?"

Wilhelm produced a padlock from his jacket pocket. "Sure, here it is."

We nearly fell into the trailer with our newfound treasure. Karl slammed the door and attached the lock.

By this time, Will was wondering what was going on, too.

Karl was about to tell Wilhelm and Will that we had stolen what was found in the toolbox when he said, "Don't look now but here comes that asshole dispatcher again."

All of us turned to greet him. He said, "So I see that you have managed to commandeer our best trailers! I suggest you get into your trucks and wait your turn to be sent to your destiny, girls!"

He laughed to himself as he swaggered away.

Every one of us would have liked to take a swing at that monkey.

Wilhelm put up his hands to signal "stop" and said, "Let's just get into our trucks. Forget about him."

I hurried to the last truck and jumped up into the cab and waited for Karl. He was talking to Wilhelm and Will with animated gestures.

After a minute or two, both of them laughed and clapped Karl on the back. They seemed amused at whatever Karl had told them.

Karl jogged over to the truck and hopped up into the driver's seat. I asked him why he seemed so pleased with himself, and what he had said to Wilhelm and Will to amuse them.

Karl responded. "Wilhelm wanted to know what was so all-fired important in the toolbox we stashed in his tag-along. So, of course, I said our good Per stole three bars of Nazi gold and I told him we should leave it there!"

I said, "I was the one who wanted to put the box back if you recall, Karl!"

He put on a look of feigned astonishment and just sat there glaring at me. That's when I realized he was making fun of me. Again. I was such an easy mark under those circumstances.

"Don't worry, Per—those two know me and they didn't believe for one second I would leave the gold for the Nazis!"

I mock-punched his shoulder and said, "You're a knucklehead. You had me going there for a minute!"

Shortly thereafter, the rumble of jeeps and trucks filled the air as the convoy began to drive out of the yard.

The papers Wilhelm was given stated the convoy was to set out for Cologne, then through Brussels to the French coast just south of Dunkirk.

Before we left, we agreed our trucks would not be missed when we headed south toward Leipzig, instead of west to Cologne with the rest of the convoy.

We purposely did not keep up with the trucks in front of us and by the time we reached the first bend in the road, we were out of their sight completely.

From Potsdam, we passed through Leipzig, then Gera and Nuremberg. Outside of Nuremberg, we stopped at a country inn for the night. The innkeeper treated us like royalty.

We dined on wiener schnitzel, spätzle and red cabbage and we drank Jägermeister to our heart's content.

We turned in at sundown to get a fresh start at daybreak.

Karl was able to transmit a brief message to Heinrich regarding our position.

The reply was equally brief. "Copy."

I wished I could talk to Raya, but I knew Heinrich would convey our message to her. That would have to suffice.

The innkeeper insisted we be fed a hearty meal before we left in the morning. We gratefully obliged; we planned to drive until dark that day without stopping to eat.

The day's route took us southwest to Stuttgart, then almost due south to Basel, Switzerland.

We were ahead of schedule. We'd allotted four days to get to France and it looked as if we'd arrive in France in only two.

We stopped for fuel just before crossing the German border into Switzerland. At the last second, Wilhelm noticed a military jeep being fueled. It was unlikely that we could pass without being noticed, so we pulled in.

All the pumps were busy so we parked our trucks off to the side. Wilhelm walked to the truck that Karl and I were in and said, "I'll speak to the officers in the jeep and see if I can ward off curiosity about where we're headed."

As he approached the jeep, the two junior officers jumped out and saluted Wilhelm.

He said, "At ease, lieutenants. Where are you headed?"

The taller of the two seemed suspicious of our presence. He slouched against the hood of the jeep and said, "We've been called back to Berlin. I'm surprised you and your men didn't get the same orders. Looks like you're headed to Switzerland."

In a cool tone, Wilhelm responded. "Our orders are to proceed to the western coast of France through southern France."

Wilhelm pointed to our trucks. "We're transporting provisions for the troops that were dispatched through Cologne."

He decided to cut short the explanation, "We will be back in Berlin next week. Good day, officers."

As the jeep pulled away, the one who had questioned Wilhelm looked over his shoulder and gave a nod, which said, "I intend to report you."

Wilhelm quickly walked over to Karl, who was in the driver's seat. "That guy spells trouble. Let's fuel up and get the hell out of here!"

Karl jammed the gearshift into reverse and backed up to the pump and said, "You got it, boss!"

Twenty minutes later, we crossed the Middle Bridge over the Rhine at Basel. The Alsace region of France was on the other side of the bridge and it was fabulously beautiful. The air smelled of lavender at that time of year and added to the visual charm of the area.

I would have loved to share that trip with Raya, under different circumstances, of course.

Alsace has plenty of forested land, so we decided to find a secluded area while it was still daylight and make camp for the night.

After we were settled in, Will dug out the ration supplies for dinner.

I broke open a pack of dried meat and for some reason, it struck me funny. "Ooh, this wiener schnitzel is dee-licious!"

Karl joined in the fun and added, "Yes, and I have bratwurst. Pass me the sauerkraut, please."

Will and Wilhelm laughed until they nearly choked on whatever they were munching on from their ration pouches.

We finished our camp dinner, and Will popped out from behind a truck with a bottle of beer for each of us. He said, "At least we have real beer for dessert!"

I said, "Good man, Will. I knew we brought you along for some reason!"

We drank our beer in silence. The reality of what the next day would bring was sobering.

Karl belched, tossed his beer bottle on the ground, turned to Wilhelm and said, "Well then, do you think those wise guy Nazis at the fuel stop will cause trouble for us?"

Wilhelm gave a great sigh. "I'd be lying if I said no. When they get to Berlin, they will probably report that they came across two trucks with tag-alongs near Switzerland. The dispatcher will be contacted and he will know it was us.

"The next thing that will happen is the military police will come looking for us. So we had better get to a small town near here at first light and see how many people we can rescue before we ourselves require rescue!"

We chose our sleeping spots in the truck. Each of us with a single wool military-issue blanket. Karl left the front seat of the truck for me. He found a slot in the back of the truck for himself after moving boxes of supplies around. Will and Wilhelm made the same arrangement in their truck.

No one got much rest.

The next morning, we carefully picked up and covered over all traces of our presence in the forest.

The town that we headed for was only fifteen miles to the north. We arrived within thirty minutes.

As we drove into town on the main road, we were horrified to find that the Nazis had ravaged the buildings. There did not appear to be any signs of life, not even a chicken.

Wilhelm was still in the lead. He stopped his truck in the middle of the deserted main street and shut the engine.

Karl followed suit and we met Will and Wilhelm in front of an old apartment house.

Wilhelm said, "This may have been where those Nazis at the fuel stop were coming from. We must have missed the trucks carrying townspeople to the camps. There does not appear to be anyone here for us to rescue but we should check out these few apartment buildings just in case.

"Karl, you and Will take the other side of the street. Per and I will check out the four buildings on this side. We will take the chance of going further into France after we're done here."

I knew when Wilhelm said, "mach schnell" he meant "move your ass" and that's just what I did.

The interior of the first apartment I entered was completely destroyed. The furniture was broken, mirrors smashed, drapes torn and china cabinets open and empty. The scene was very disturbing and I hurried to check all the rooms for survivors—not a soul.

I walked out onto the street and saw Wilhelm leave a building and go into another one. That left one more apartment building for me to check. My greatest fear was that I would find a dead body. The top apartment in the building looked a lot like the one I had just come out of, but the floors were littered with glass. There must have been a terrible struggle there.

I was spooked. I thought I heard people screaming and crying. I wanted to get the hell out of there. I ran upstairs to check the last bedroom. I took the stairs three at a time and banged my head at the top. I swore loudly.

I stopped to rub my head and glared at the ceiling that caused my pain. An opening in the wall at knee level caught my attention. I peered into the hole and there I saw a small boy crouched under the eaves. He was crying softly.

I gasped and backed up so as not to scare him more than he already was. Obviously, his family had been taken and he'd managed to hide.

It was all I could do to rein in my emotions. The thought of what he must have seen and heard in the past days brought tears to my eyes.

I heard Wilhelm yelling. "Come on, Per...we're leaving!"

I did not answer him and I knew that I had to work fast so he did not come barging in before I had a chance to console the boy. I saw a small, hinged door under where I had banged my head. Very slowly, I squeaked it open and crept inside to where the boy was.

He did not seem to know I was there. I sat next to him and put him on my lap for just enough time to know he was not afraid of me. I'm sure he was in shock.

I carried him out of his hiding place, down the stairs and out into the street.

Karl said, "Thank God you found him, Per. Put him on the seat between us. He doesn't look too good. Wilhelm and Will are just ahead of us; we will catch up to them."

I gingerly placed the boy on the front seat and ran to the back to grab a blanket. I wrapped him in the blanket. Soon, he leaned on me and stopped shivering. He slept.

We caught up to Wilhelm's truck and Karl said, "We will soon be at the next town. Let's hope that we get there and find that the Nazi bastards have not been there ahead of us!"

I nodded.

The roadways were in bad condition on the way to our next destination, presumably due to the heavy rains and Nazi trucks going in and out of the area.

When we finally got to what had been a quaint little mountain town, we found that all the buildings had been set on fire and some of them were still smoking.

Slowly, we rolled down the main road. It didn't look as if there was anyone left to rescue. Karl was looking to the left and I was searching to the right. Suddenly, he jammed on the brakes, nearly sending me through the windshield. I managed to keep our little friend from sliding forward and he continued to sleep.

Karl shifted the truck into neutral and yanked the handbrake up. Excitedly, he said, "I think I just saw a man open that cellar door over there and go underground. Stay here, I'll signal Wilhelm and Will to go with me."

I watched as they cautiously approached the cellar door, guns drawn. I wondered why they needed their weapons and decided that whoever was hiding might be armed, so it made sense.

The three of them were stationary outside the cellar door. Wilhelm turned in my direction and signaled for me to join them.

Gently, I leaned the boy off of my side, got out of the truck and jogged to where I was needed.

Karl whispered to me, "We will need you to calm whoever is down there...you're the only one not wearing a uniform."

I nodded and waited for the door to open. We had no idea what we would find.

Will stepped forward and opened the door ever so slowly. We all looked in from the sides of the opening.

Wilhelm whispered that I should speak to whoever was in there.

I spoke loudly in French, "We are here to rescue you. We are not Nazis. Please come out and we will take you to safety."

There was complete silence—no voices and no movement.

I continued, "We know you are scared. There is nothing left for you here. Send someone out to talk to us...please...it's not safe for us here. Send someone out."

It was difficult for me to keep desperation out of my voice—that would only serve to intimidate whoever was in there.

Then a male responded in French. "Move back and we will come out."

I said, "All right, we've moved back. Please hurry. We must leave."

I motioned for our team to move back and to keep their guns out of sight. They quickly complied.

The one who had spoken for his group emerged. He wore charred clothing and walked with a limp. He said his name was Franz and that he had managed to hide his family and some friends after the fires had been set by the Nazis. He said that the people who were shot and burned were thrown into a truck and that the live people were captured and taken away in another truck.

After he was satisfied that we were not Nazis, he ducked his head into the cellar doorway and said, "It's safe, you can all come out now. God has sent us angels."

The first one out was an elderly woman about seventy years old, then a younger woman, maybe her daughter, then a string of six children all under the age of seven. They were followed by a young couple; the wife was carrying a baby wrapped in a tattered blanket.

That made five adults, six children and a baby.

I spoke to Franz, "Is that everyone?"

"No, my father-in-law is gathering all that he can. Here he is. Come, Papa."

So then we had six adults, six children, a baby, plus the little boy asleep in the truck.

The old man was weighed down with pillowcases full of who knows what. I guessed it was all they had left in the world. He was barely able to get himself up the stairs with all he carried.

As he passed by me, he said, "Bless you, young man, bless you."

I tried to help him but he refused. I understood it was all he could do for his family now and he needed to do it himself.

I joined the others who were making space for our passengers in the back of the trucks.

We repacked the tag-alongs with all that would fit from the trucks, leaving some of the boxes in the trucks that could be placed side by side for sleeping when they were not used for seats while we drove.

While all of this was going on, our little passenger in the front seat woke up and realized he was alone in a strange place. He was crying.

I started to go to him and was stopped by the mother of the six children. She opened the passenger door of the truck, got in and picked up the boy. She rocked him in her lap and sang him a French lullaby.

She pulled a piece of candy out of her apron pocket and gave it to him and I saw the first smile from him. I breathed a small sigh of relief.

She told me that her name was Marie and that she couldn't stay with the boy because her children needed her to ride with them in the back of the truck.

When Marie started to leave him, he screamed for her. I was helpless but she knew just what to do. She took him with her to the back of the truck; that made him happy.

Wilhelm closed the back of his truck and Karl closed the back of ours.

With our precious cargo, we headed back toward Switzerland.

Julia jumped up from her chair and ran to her OfficeJet to make a copy of what she'd just written.

Minutes later, she rushed to the lobby and saw Javier putting his coat on to go home.

She stopped just outside the elevator and stared at him.

He rushed to her and said, "Julia, what's wrong? You look as if you've seen a ghost!"

She was too excited to speak. She thrust the pages into his hand and managed to say one word. "Read."

"All right, Julia, I will read it right now. Go ahead and sit behind the desk over there. This must be very important. I've never seen you like this before."

Julia watched as he read. His expression changed from interest to surprise and then to shock.

His tears flowed like rain. Finally, he knew who the kind fair-haired man was who rescued him all those years ago.

Chapter Fourteen

PERFECT FOR THE JOB

Julia sat at her desk and reviewed the pages she had given to Javier.

"Uncle Per, are you here?"

"Yes, Julia."

"When did you know Javier was the little boy you rescued in France?"

"Well, Julia, when you ran out of here like a bat out of hell with a copy of those pages, I put it together.

"And so, you see, *you* are the perfect one to work with Thor Jr. and Tom to find families of those rescued from Europe during the war.

"You know how to find clues that others may never find. Add to that your intuitive skill set and voilà, the results are magical."

"I appreciate your confidence in me, Uncle Per, really I do, but *you* were the one who found little Javier and saved his life."

"Yes, and if not for you, Julia, Javier would never know who saved him. It was very important to him that he should find out."

"I suppose that's true," she said. "He *did* tell me that he thanked the man who saved him, in his prayers every night, and he wished to know who the man was."

"Julia, I am as thankful to you as Javier is. I did not give up looking for survivors in that apartment house in France, and you have not given up listening to my story.

"I was not able to finish my work during the war, but now, through you, I can complete work that is very important.

"I cannot thank you enough, Julia. I know what you're doing and what you will do, will not be easy. At times it will be tiring and frustrating and may even take you into harm's way. I am confident Tom will keep you safe, he's a good man.

"You will undoubtedly encounter those who will not welcome your findings, and others who will not believe what you tell them.

"That is another reason you are cut out for the work you are about to undertake. You do not question what you know to be true. You can cut through extraneous details and get to the heart of any situation or issue. I do admire that about you, Julia. We certainly could have used you during the war!

"But, you will help the descendants of those my team helped. And *you*, are worth your weight in gold!"

"As much as three bars of gold, Uncle Per?"

"Oh, much more than three bars, three *hundred* bars of gold!"

Julia enjoyed a laugh with her uncle.

She looked pensive for a moment and asked, "Why were you not able to finish your work during the war? Were you killed, or were you captured by the Germans?"

"Always with the questions you are, Julia. That, my dear, is a story for another day. We've done enough for one day. For now, I will say good evening."

Julia sighed. "Good night, Uncle Per."

As Julia dressed for bed, she said aloud, "Well, it doesn't hurt to ask."

Then she heard the familiar chuckle.

Julia grinned and shook her head. Yes, they had done enough for one day.

Chapter Fifteen

COMPLICATIONS

Julia jolted from sleep…a phone was ringing, ringing, ringing. She rolled over and reached for her cell and managed a groggy "Hello."

"Good morning, Sunshine. It sounds like I woke you up. Do you know what time it is?"

"Good morning. Seth?"

"Yes, it's me. I picked up lunch at the corner deli and I thought maybe I could come by and we could eat together."

She rolled her eyes and was glad they were not on a video chat. "Where are you now, Seth? What time is it? Aren't you working today?"

"Jeez, you have a lot of questions. I'm outside of the deli, it's eleven-thirty and I'm not at work because I've given myself the day off. I was hoping to spend some of today with *you*."

Wow, could this guy be any more presumptuous? I have so much to do. Well, I suppose I must eat anyway.

"Okay, Seth, but you have to stay in the lobby for twenty minutes. Talk to Javier while you wait."

She realized she sounded abrupt and added, "Lunch sounds great, Seth. I'll see you shortly."

"All right, Jules. It will be nice to see Javier again."

When did he start calling me Jules?

Seth walked the short distance to Julia's. He loved people-watching and Manhattan was one of the best places to do that.

He waited for the signal to change to "Walk" at the corner of 5th Avenue and 72nd. As he looked across at the people waiting to cross, there in front of the crowd was an old man dressed in a tweed suit and a top hat. He looked as if he belonged to another century. The man tipped his hat, looked directly at Seth and poof! he disappeared.

Aloud, Seth said, "What the hell?"

He looked at people on both sides of him to see if anyone else saw the old man…no.

The crossing signal changed and Seth moved with the crowd. He searched people walking toward him—no evidence of the old man.

He arrived at Julia's apartment building. Javier opened the lobby door and greeted Seth with a hearty handshake.

"How are you, young man? It's nice to see you again."

"I'm very well, thank you, Javier. Do you mind if I talk to you while Julia gets ready for this fine lunch I have here?"

"Of course, I'd be delighted! The last time we met, you and Julia were off to the Central Park festivities. Did you enjoy it?"

Seth hesitated for a moment. *That was the night Julia met Thor, and now she is leaving to work with that bastard.*

He smiled, "Yes, the tour through the park was enlightening. It's quite a place, right in our backyard."

Javier eyed the white paper bags that Seth carried. "Is that soup from my favorite deli?"

"If your favorite deli is Einstein's, then yes. Would you like some?"

"I've had my lunch already. Thank you, anyway."

Javier thought about what to say next. It was obvious that the young man was enamored of Julia. "It looks as if we will soon lose our Julia to the big world. She's off on an adventure. I'm sure you know."

Seth kept it light. "Yes, it's very exciting for her. That's why I brought a farewell lunch. I'm sure she will keep in touch with you, Javier." *And I'm sure she won't keep in touch with me.*

The lobby phone rang. Javier answered. "Yes, Julia, I'll send him right up."

Javier smiled at Seth. "Go ahead, young man, and enjoy your farewell lunch."

"Thanks, Javier."

Julia opened the door before Seth knocked. "Hi, Seth. Oh, lunch smells great. I just realized I'm famished. Come on in, we'll sit in the kitchen alcove."

He followed her to the kitchen and put the bags on the table.

Julia had already set the table with soup bowls, luncheon plates and coffee cups. A long-stem pink rose in a bud vase was the centerpiece.

Seth knew the rose was from the two dozen he'd sent to her.

She noticed he looked at the rose and said, "Isn't it a beautiful shade? It's the last of the roses you sent."

There was an uncomfortable pause. Seth could not say what he wanted to—not with her leaving in just a few days to parts unknown, at least unknown to him.

"Yes, it's very pretty, Julia."

Then he changed the subject and commented on the 1940s music coming from the radio in the kitchen corner. "I like your choice of music. Most people our age don't appreciate music from the war years. But I suppose it's not surprising that we history buffs love this music."

Julia stopped dishing up their lunch and said, "You know, you're right about that. Sometimes I feel as if I was born into the wrong era. History comes alive through music."

As if to illustrate her point, the radio played a swing song.

Seth jumped up. "Let's boogie!"

He didn't give her a choice. He easily lifted her from the chair, set her bare feet on the warm tiles, grabbed her right hand and twirled her around.

Julia laughed and got in time with the beat. She loved to jitterbug. By the time the song ended, they were both out of breath and laughing.

Before she knew it, she was in his arms, slow dancing.

It seemed so natural for her to walk him to her bed and make love to him.

Afterwards, Seth stroked Julia's cheek and said, "This is not at all what I expected when I called this morning."

He quickly added, "But I'm not complaining, believe me!"

Julia smiled, then a sad look came over her face. "Seth, I'm sorry to be leaving you. I hid my feelings from you, even from myself. Now I realize what we have is special. I don't think it will disappear, even if I'm away for a few months. Do you?"

He was silent for a long moment.

"Jules, I know your heart was broken when your husband was killed. That's one of the reasons I tried to take things slow with you. Then when I met your boyfriend, Tom, I thought I'd taken things too slowly and I tried to make up for lost time. I invited you to the museum, Central Park and out to dinner…and I sent roses.

"Today I wanted to see you to apologize for pushing you and for my reaction at the coffee shop when you told me you were going on a long trip."

He smiled and whispered in her ear, "I never dreamed we would be lying here like this."

She kissed him softly. "If we don't get out of this bed now, we may stay here forever."

She tickled his ear and jumped away before he could change her mind. She grabbed her robe and ran away. "Come on, let's have lunch! I'll meet you in the kitchen."

They thoroughly enjoyed lunch. Julia brewed coffee while Seth cleared the table.

He walked up behind her and put his arms around her waist. "This is nice, Jules."

She turned to meet his eyes. She started to speak and he put his finger on her lips and said, "I'm in love with you, Julia. That's the long and the short of it."

"Seth, I'm at a loss for words. This is all so new to me. Tom and I broke up only a short time ago, and my life is complicated right now."

He kissed her gently and said, "Don't you worry. I intend to be here when you get back from your travels. I want you to know you can call me any time for any reason. Count on me. Understood?"

With a smile, she said, "Yes, it's understood. Now let's drink our coffee. How about one of my cupcakes?"

"Yes, ma'am! I would not pass up one of your cupcakes!"

Suddenly, finally, they had so much to talk about, and now, so little time.

Julia's cell phone chirped—the phone she shared with Tom. She bolted to attention.

"Go ahead and take the call, Jules."

"No, he'll leave a message. I'll call him later."

Seth thought, *It's probably Tom calling. She did say she'd call 'him' later.*

"You probably have work to do, Jules. So I'll leave you to it."

She looked disappointed.

He got up from the table and kissed her for all he was worth, as the song that played in the background was "I'll Be Seeing You."

"I'll show myself out and call you later, Jules."

With that, he was gone.

Julia stood alone in her kitchen. She grinned and shook her head. Aloud she said, "What an amazing day this has been! I'm in love— with an amazing man!"

In jest, she said, "Don't you agree, Uncle Per?"

"Indeed, I do, Julia. I like that boy for you!"

"Uncle Per! How long have you been here?"

"Don't worry, my little chickadee, I have only been here since you addressed me just now."

"Oh, then how do you know you like that boy, as you call him?"

"Well, I confess, I have your best interests at heart and I peeked in every now and then—only to the kitchen, though."

"I should hope so. In the future, I would appreciate it if you would not interrupt my personal life."

"You're right, Julia. I apologize. Will you forgive me?"

She imagined her uncle looking ashamed as he asked for forgiveness. "Yes, I cannot stay angry with you, Uncle Per."

"Very well. Are you ready to pick up where we left off in the writing, Julia?"

"Sure, let's go!" She sat at her desk and listened.

The journey out of France, through Switzerland and across Germany to Danzig promised to be difficult.

Our trucks were weighed down with passengers and we knew they were very uncomfortable riding in the back without windows, heat or real seats.

It was a long trip. We traveled only thirty to thirty-five miles per hour to avoid jostling our passengers overmuch.

We ate breakfast before driving each day. We stopped only for fuel. When we stopped for the night, we prepared dinner. Thankfully, Wilhelm had stocked the tag-alongs with plenty of "borrowed" rations.

An obstacle came within the first hours of our journey—at the Swiss border as we left France. A border guard motioned for us to pull to the side. Wilhelm hopped out of the truck and spoke with the guard for quite some time.

When they finished their discussion, Wilhelm waved Will, Karl and me to the front of his truck.

Wilhelm said, "The Feldjager directed the Swiss border guards at France and Germany to apprehend us if we tried to cross either border. We would then be escorted back to Kaserne Krampnitz."

He continued, "The guard was most sympathetic to our plight. He said if he allowed us into Switzerland, he would have to report us. He suggested that if we turned around and traveled back through France, he would never have seen us.

"That is our only option now. It will add at least two days to our trip, but we gained two days getting to France and we allowed nine days to get to Danzig, therefore, we still have enough time."

He looked at Will. "Do you have an alternative route for us, for travel through France?"

Will replied, "Yes, I planned for many possibilities, especially after we met up with those Nazi bastards at the fuel stop. I know it seems counterintuitive to drive west when our destination is northeast, but here's what I worked out."

He pulled a map out of his well-worn canvas folder and pointed out the route as he explained. "We're here just across from Basel, Switzerland. We will go west to Dijon, France, then northwest to the outskirts of Paris."

Karl interrupted, "But Paris is under siege by Germany. Is that the best idea for us?"

Wilhelm answered, "That's the beauty of Will's strategy, Karl. We will blend right in, driving German military trucks, and we'll be in uniform, of course."

Wilhelm patted Will's shoulder. "Continue, Will."

"Yes. We will pass on the east side of Paris and head northeast to Reims. Then, our best route will be east into Germany at Saarbrucken.

"We won't start heading north toward the Baltic at that point because it would take us on the same road we traveled en route to France." He added, "The Nazis will be on the lookout for us along that corridor."

I said, "That's a long way to get to the sea, Will. When will we begin to head northward?"

"I agree, Per. It is very long. However, I feel it's the safest way to get to Danzig. And so then, we will be going southeast to Stuttgart, through Ulm, Augsburg and Munich.

"By the time we reach Munich, the Nazis will not be looking for us that far southeast of the base, so we can head north into Czechoslovakia.

"It will be a short distance northeast from Prague to Wroclaw, Poland. Germany occupies both countries, so we can travel without attracting attention. Once we enter Poland, we will take the most direct route north to Danzig."

Wilhelm said, "Thanks, Will. Now let's get on with it. Karl, do you and Per understand Will's directions?"

We both nodded. Wilhelm said, "Let's go!"

However, we didn't drive away quite soon enough. The Swiss border guard who had spoken to Wilhelm approached him again.

The guard waited beside the truck while Wilhelm unlocked his tag-along, took out a package and handed it to the guard.

The guard seemed satisfied with his gift and waved us on.

As we drove away, Karl said, "It doesn't take a genius to know that the guard asked for something to maintain his silence. Now we have two gold bars left."

I said, "Yes, and even if he does report us, the Nazis would never think we would take the route Will mapped out. They won't find us. They don't know our destination anyway."

We got on our way. Thankfully, our passengers had been quiet at the Swiss border.

We stopped for fuel at Troyes, France and decided to take a shortcut and head north toward Reims and turn eastward toward Saarbrucken rather than chance going toward Paris, where there was so much military activity.

We were relieved to get out of France. Nazis were swarming everywhere; it was unnerving.

Outside of Saarbrucken, Wilhelm led us off the roadway into a forested area to camp for the night. We helped the elders out of the trucks. The children popped out like jack-in-the-boxes and ran around the trees, happy to have been released from their temporary prison.

I saw the little one I'd rescued from his hiding place; he was standing alone. I went to him and asked his name. He whispered, "Javier."

He looked so sad. I asked what was wrong.

Through tears, he said, "I want my mommy."

I sat in the leaves and put him on my lap. In my best French, I said, "Don't worry, Javier. I'm sure your mommy is looking for you right now."

He giggled and said, "You talk funny."

Then, in a more serious tone, he said, "Do you really think my mommy will find me?"

I lied and said, "I'm sure she will."

I thought, sometimes hope is all we have and so I allowed this little boy to hold on to his hope.

I said, "Now, go play with the other children."

He skipped away to play. I was left with a heavy heart for the losses that he was not fully aware of yet.

It would be nice to say that we cooked dinner over a campfire but all we had to eat was packaged military rations.

No one seemed to mind, and the children were amused to eat their meal from a package.

Marie tended to her husband's knee which had been badly bruised during the Nazi attack. Karl was a trained medic. He took a look at Franz's knee and said the contusions had caused ecchymosis—and it looked much worse than it actually was. He recommended elevating the leg, adding that it should heal on its own.

After dinner, and after the children had expended their excess energy, we gathered the blankets and rearranged the back of the trucks for sleeping. Everyone found a place to rest for the night.

Morning came all too soon. During the night there had been a torrential downpour. It was miserable. Everyone was cold and cranky, including the four of us who were responsible for the mission.

The roads were in poor condition, to say the least, made worse by the heavy rain. Visibility was next to nothing.

On the fourth day, we finally made it to the Czech border. We'd assumed that because it shared a border with Germany, we would pass right on through the border.

However, that was not the case. The border guard in charge approached Wilhelm's truck with a sickening grin on his face.

Karl said, "Damn! Looks like big trouble! Do you think the Nazis have a bulletin out on us here, too?"

We watched the interaction between the guard and Wilhelm. I said, "I'm sure Wilhelm will know what to do."

Sure enough, Wilhelm once again unlocked the tag-along, took out a rectangular package and handed it to the guard.

Wilhelm turned toward us and gave a thumbs-up signal. Karl and I had to keep our heads down as we passed the guard so he would not see us laughing.

We were on our way to Poland with only one bar of gold left. I said, "Well, it looks as if the gold is going back to the Nazis where it came from, eh, Karl?"

"Right you are, Per. It's a good thing that you pilfered those bars. I can't imagine what we would have done without them." We had a good chuckle over it.

Along the way, we spent another three nights camped just off the main roadway. The rain continued; everyone was cold and dirty.

Will complained about the conditions as we set off for the final leg of our journey, to which Wilhelm replied, "I will remind you that this is war, and we are on a mission!"

That shut him up.

On the sixth day, we made it to the north of Warsaw and were turned back because a bridge had been washed out.

Will checked his maps and said, "It looks like the only possible road will be west to Poznan, then we can turn north to Danzig. But it's getting dark and we've been driving all day through this muck. How about if we find a place to spend the night?"

A male voice was heard from the back of the truck. "Yes, we're all tired in here!"

Loudly Wilhelm said, "All right, that's just what we'll do then!"

Thankfully, the rain stopped long enough for us to eat dinner under some trees and stretch our legs a bit.

Marie found a stream nearby and filled a canteen with water to wash the children.

Karl said, "I'm going to that stream to get cleaned up."

I said I'd join him and off we went. We sat on a rock at the edge of the stream, dangling our tired feet in the water.

I thought Karl looked worried and asked if something was bothering him.

"Well, I'm not concerned about getting to Danzig. We still have time to meet Bjorn's ship, and we should get there without any further problem.

"But, I'm very worried about how we get back to the base without getting caught by the Nazis. We know they are on the lookout for us. They don't know why we didn't stay with the convoy as ordered, and if they give us a chance to explain, we will have to come up with a plausible story."

I said, "Yes that's true. I'm sure that Will, our strategist, along with Wilhelm, our mission leader, already have the story that will be acceptable. The bars of gold we used for bribery will likely be an additional issue for you to deal with back at the base. By now, the original owner would have discovered them missing and the news would have spread like wildfire around the compound.

"I wish I could be of help but I'm better off in Sweden for a day or so. It will be left for the three of you to explain my absence, as well as why we didn't stick with the convoy."

I changed the subject. "Have you been able to get a message through to Heinrich in Berlin?"

"No, I tried, but I think communication lines are down with this damn rain. I'll try again before we leave in the morning. I'm dog-tired. I'm going back to the truck for some shut-eye. Good night, Per."

"Good night, Karl." I knew he'd be fast asleep by the time I turned in.

I enjoyed a few minutes of solitude by the stream—to daydream about Raya and the baby we would share.

I decided to ask Inga to plan a simple, yet elegant wedding for us in Sweden, as soon as possible.

I hopped off my perch and walked back to the campsite. I found that all our passengers were bunked down for the night.

Will and Wilhelm were dousing the campfire and clearing our site in preparation for an early exit the next morning. I helped them, and it was my opportunity to ask about their plan to get themselves back to the base.

Wilhelm said, "That's the easy part, Per. The more difficult part will be to explain your absence. If we say that you are dead and then you show up with us in Berlin later, they'll be sure to kill you. Will and I have discussed it ad nauseam and you will not like what we came up with."

My stomach did a flip. "What are we talking about here, Wilhelm?"

They looked at me as if they'd lost their best friend.

Then it hit me. "Oh my God! No! You're saying I can't go back to Berlin?"

Will said, "I'm sorry Per, that's what we're saying."

"But what about Raya?"

I almost said that Raya was pregnant but thought better of it.

Wilhelm looked somewhat confused that I was so upset about not seeing Raya. Apparently, he had not noticed what was going on between the two of us. But then I guess Hans had kept our secret as promised.

He said, "We can send her to you in Stockholm. We will use the excuse that she is scheduled to perform for the King of Sweden. How will that be, Per?"

I brightened at the thought of Raya joining me in my home. "That's a fine idea! Now then, what's your plan to get back into the base? What will you tell the Feldjager?"

Will responded, "That's my area, this is positively ingenious; we will arrive with only one truck and no tag-along. Our story will be that the trucks got stuck in the mud after we lost track of the convoy.

"Then we'll say we got one truck out of the mud but not the tag-along, and that the other truck was so deep in the mud that the axle got broken and we had to leave it somewhere near the Swiss border.

"So, we will arrive three abreast in the front of Wilhelm's truck. It's a good story, don't you think, Per?"

"It's a damn good story and I think it will work. But what if word of the missing gold bars has gotten out?"

Wilhelm answered, "That's when that third bar will save our bacon. It will be our payment for ignoring the case against us. Perfect, eh?"

I breathed a big sigh of relief. "Well, gentlemen, congratulations. You've figured out how to outsmart the Nazis once again! I am very pleased and most anxious to get on that ship to Sweden with our passengers."

Wilhelm stood up, "Yes, I would say we can count this mission a success. We should arrive at Danzig early tomorrow afternoon and, if our luck holds, Bjorn will already be in port. Let's catch a few winks. Good night, Per."

I replied, "Good night to both of you."

Chapter Sixteen

DANZIG!

The next morning, Karl had no better luck getting a message through to our team in Berlin.

We prepared to get back on the road. Everyone was bone-weary, but there was a festive atmosphere in the air despite it. We were so close to a successful end to our mission—at least for those we'd saved.

We drove west. The rain had let up but the roads were still in rough shape. It took longer than we expected to reach Poznan.

Wilhelm pulled over and stopped just after we passed through Poznan. He walked back to our truck.

Karl opened his window and said, "What's up, boss?"

"We'll stop for fuel at the next station. It doesn't look like we will get to Danzig today unless we drive for five or six hours more. Will and I agree that we should stop for one more night. Do you and Per agree, Karl?"

Karl looked at me and I nodded. Karl said, "Yes, but you know we're running low on meal rations. I think we have enough to feed only our passengers."

Wilhelm replied, "That's all right. After we drop off our passengers, we'll be free to stop at an inn for some home-cooked food. Man, does that sound good!"

My stomach rumbled at the thought of hot food.

We drove another hour, refueled, and found a wooded area that looked safe and secure for the night.

No one noticed we had been followed from the time we left the fuel stop. The lone officer sent by the Feldjager approached our campsite after everyone was out of the trucks.

Wilhelm saw the officer walking toward the children playing in the grove.

Wilhelm went into overdrive. He grabbed my sleeve and spoke in an even, hushed tone, "Get everyone in the trucks...now!"

I felt his energy as if I'd been struck by a bolt of lightning. I motioned for Will and Karl to help me while Wilhelm walked up to the officer with all the confidence of the Commandant.

Karl and I were able to distract all the children from the danger and get them into our truck...that is, all except little Javier, who stood motionless, staring at our would-be captor.

I called for Javier to come to the truck. He didn't hear me.

I looked past him and saw that the officer and Wilhelm were engaged in a heated discussion about twelve feet from where Javier stood.

The officer saw Javier and waved to him. I was terrified to see that Javier walked toward him.

Wilhelm spun around and saw Javier and yelled, "No! Go back! Go back!"

The intruder pushed Wilhelm aside to get to the boy just as I got to Javier and scooped him up.

Javier sobbed as I carried him away from harm. Thank God he did not see Wilhelm shoot the officer. I left him with the other children in the truck and ran to help Wilhelm. We dragged the body as far as we could into the woods, where it wouldn't be noticed for a while. We were out of breath as we walked back to where the officer's jeep was parked.

Wilhelm said, "This changes our plan. We cannot stay here tonight. We will have to drive until we reach the port—tonight. You wait here until Karl and I drive the trucks to you and then you drive the jeep a few miles from here and dump it. We'll follow and pick you up. Got all that, Per?"

I was dazed. I rubbed my forehead and said, "Yes."

I went to the jeep and stood beside it. I didn't want to sit in the driver's seat any longer than necessary.

When the trucks rumbled toward me, I had no choice but to jump into the jeep, make a fast three-point turn and head to the road. I stalled the engine twice, just as I had when I drove my Volvo. My heart was practically thumping out of my chest by the time I drove out of the woods.

My sense of direction was excellent. I knew to turn left and drive north. Driving that jeep was like riding a bucking bronco - I ground the gears with every shift—until I remembered to use the clutch pedal instead of the brake!

Finally, I saw a dirt road ahead on the right. I pulled into a grove of pine trees, shut the engine, jumped out of the jeep and ran to Karl's truck.

Karl had a silly grin on his face and said, "Can I assume you have a driver in Sweden, Per?"

I smiled and said, "Can I assume you don't want me to drive?"

We laughed. Karl said, "An excellent assumption, Per!"

It was hours after sunrise when we arrived at the Port of Danzig. We could see the water before we spied the docks. I said, "It would be great if Bjorn was in port waiting for us, but we've arrived early. It's too much to hope for."

We got closer to the docks and saw there were three ships in port and a fourth one coming in. That one flew the blue and yellow flag of Sweden. The letters on the side of the ship were BJORN.

Karl and I both yelled, "Look, it's here! The ship is here!"

Wilhelm parked. He walked to the back of his truck, moved the canvas door aside and said something to those who were inside.

He then walked to our truck and said, "We need to figure out how to get these people onto Bjorn's ship without being seen by the German guards. I'm fresh out of ideas. How about either of you?"

Karl said, "The only thing I can think of is to use our last gold bar to bribe the guards."

"We need that bar to save us when we get back to the base. What else can you suggest?"

Wilhelm looked at me and said, "Per, any ideas?"

I grabbed my duffle, hopped out and met Wilhelm in front of the truck.

I said, "I need to get out of this damn uniform first. Then I'll meet Bjorn and tell him my scheme. As a Swedish diplomat, I will convince the guards that Bjorn Shipping has orders to pick up Swedish citizens and take them to Stockholm."

Wilhelm said, "What is your answer when the guards ask why Swedish citizens are being escorted by the German military?"

"I'll figure it out as I go along. Right now, I will duck behind a tree and transform back into a Swede."

Two minutes later, I boarded the pride of Bjorn Shipping. Thor saw me and dropped his bills of lading. I gave him a bear hug and said, "Thor, old man! You cannot know how glad I am to see you! Thanks so much for helping us!"

"No problem at all, Per. How did your mission go? Any problems?"

"I'll tell you the whole story after we're underway. Right now, I need you to confirm the story I intend to tell the guards so we can get six adults, seven children and a baby on your ship without question."

He looked intrigued, "Sure, Per. What's the story?"

I leaned in and spoke so that no one else would hear. When I finished, he said, "You're going to use the name of the Fuhrer? Holy Mother of God, Per! That will work like a charm!"

I'll admit, I thought I was clever, although somewhat daft.

I said, "If you're ready, Thor, I'll go to the guard hut."

"I'm always ready to pull a fast one over on the Nazis. You go ahead. My crew will finish the offload and get ready for your people."

I squared my shoulders and walked off the ship toward the guard hut, ready to do what I do best. It would be assumed that I arrived with Bjorn, as I was pretty sure I'd not been seen getting out of the German truck.

I knew German guards were required to learn English and it was my preferred language. I greeted the two guards, "Good day, gentlemen. I am Per Lundgren. I represent the Swedish government in its relations with Germany.

"By now you must have the orders from Berlin to allow transport of Swedish citizens from here to Stockholm."

They looked at each other and shrugged. The senior officer said, "We have no such orders. Do you have them, Mr. Swedish?"

I paused to show my aggravation. I stood toe-to-toe with the senior officer and said, "Are you questioning my authority? Because if so, I assure you that you will regret it. Would it make any sense at all for two German military trucks to bring people to your port to be shipped out, if it was not by order of your Führer? For God's sake, Man, why else would I be here to take those people to Sweden?

"Are you aware that Germany and Sweden have friendly relations? Perhaps you two are willing to jeopardize those relations?"

I could see they were starting to fold. I poured on the coal to seal the deal. "I would like your names for my report to your headquarters."

I pulled a pen out of my breast pocket along with an official-looking notepad.

The junior officer looked at the other and said, "That will not be necessary, will it, Helmut?"

Helmut replied, obviously aggravated that the guard had used his name, "Of course, we will do our utmost to assist you, Mr. Lundgren. Wait here while I give the German drivers permission to let their passengers aboard the ship."

I watched Helmut speak to Wilhelm and Karl. He came back to the hut and said, "Now you see that we are being most cooperative. Please go and take care of your passengers and have a pleasant journey."

I gladly walked away from those guards. I wiped perspiration from my brow and went to help our French friends onto the ship that would take them to safety.

Javier was standing alone, so I took his hand and walked him to the ship. He perked up considerably when he realized that he would get to ride on the big boat, as he called it.

The guards did not seem interested in the Bjorn ship. They simply let Will, Karl and Wilhelm load the passengers.

I had precious little time to say goodbye to my teammates and we wanted to appear impersonal to onlookers. Will and Karl waved as they walked off the ship and back to the trucks.

I shook Wilhelm's hand and said, "Take care, Wilhelm. It has been an honor to serve with you."

He replied, "Likewise, Per. We could never have done this without you. These people owe you their lives. Now you take care of yourself and we will send Raya to you very soon."

"Thank you, I appreciate that. Goodbye, Wilhelm."

After dinner that night, Thor asked me to meet him in the Captain's cabin for a nightcap. He broke open a bottle of Swedish potato vodka. I filled him in on all that had happened since we left Berlin.

When I told him that Wilhelm shot an officer of the Feldjager, his eyes got as big as saucers and he shouted, "Let's toast to that! Dead Nazis are my favorite kind!"

We clinked our glasses together and I continued my story.

Thor asked about the little boy that I brought onto the ship. He said that the boy didn't seem as if he was related to the other people.

I said, "You're right, Thor. He's not related to the others. I found him hiding in the eaves of his home in the Alsace region of France after his family had been taken by the Nazis. It's very sad, but I hope that because he is so young, he will be spared the horrible memories."

Thor agreed. "On a slightly different topic, Per, I have made a connection with an old friend in Copenhagen who has agreed to see that the people you rescued are safely transported to North America by way of Nova Scotia.

"This friend asked to remain anonymous for his protection and for the protection of the steamship line. He has helped to save people from the Nazis in the past, and he will continue to do so for as long as he's needed.

"You understand secrecy is very important for all of us involved here, Per."

"Understood, Thor. I must ask about the logistics of travel arrangements. How soon do you think your friend will be able to pick up our people? I can still house them in private residences near Stockholm if necessary."

"That's the good news. The steamship is waiting for our arrival in the western harbor of Malmö as we speak.

"It will not be an easy crossing to North America. Steamships have to dodge the German naval vessels these days, but the accommodations will be much better than those we have here on my ship. Hopefully, their crossing will take no longer than ten days."

I said, "Thor, I don't know how you managed it. You are a miracle worker."

"Oh, nonsense. I just do what I can.

"On a different note, we're passing by the Pearl of the Baltic— look out the starboard porthole. You can barely make out the light on that church steeple on the highest hill of Ronne."

I jumped up and squinted through the porthole to enjoy the sight. Bornholm Island, aka the Pearl of the Baltic, has high cliffs on its western shore, and so at night the church atop the cliffs appears to be floating in space. It was quite a delight.

Thor continued, "Our course will keep us in the shipping lane that passes Trelleborg on the southwestern tip of Sweden. There will be no more sights to view from the sea until we get to the Port of Malmö. Then you will see Malmohus Castle. Have you been there, Per?"

"Indeed, I have been there. And when I was studying at Uppsala, I wrote a paper on the hidden history of the castle."

Thor laughed and said, "Now that sounds like something worth reading!"

I agreed to send him a copy.

The engines began to reverse and Thor left to oversee the docking.

I went to find Franz and Marie to let them know what their travel arrangements would be. I found the whole group huddled together on benches next to the engine room, where it was warmest.

Franz limped over to me before I reached the group and said, "Per, I can never repay you for what you have done for us."

I shook his hand and said, "No need, Franz. I'm happy to have helped. You kept your family safe until we found you."

I then told him about the steamship that would take them to their new life.

He looked fearful.

I said, "Don't be afraid. The ship is waiting and there are many Scandinavians already on board. You will find them friendly and helpful. You'll be together, heading for your new life. Immigration Services will assist you and your family, Franz, and you will meet others who will become part of your community."

He looked at his family and back at me. With tears in his eyes, he said, "If that is what you say, then I believe it is true. Thank you, Per."

He gave me a great hug and went back to sit with his family.

It was then that I noticed little Javier holding onto Marie's apron, smiling at me.

I got down on one knee and motioned for him to come to me.

He looked up at Marie and she nodded her consent. He ran to me and sat on my knee.

I hugged him close and he took my hand and kissed it. It was his sweet way of saying thank you.

It was a moment I will never forget.

As promised, the Danish steamship majestically rested in port and waited for its newest passengers.

Thor was first off as soon as we docked, so he could liaise with his Danish friend. He came back shortly and instructed two of his crew members to assist the passengers onto the other ship.

He then pulled me aside and said, "Bad news, Per. Word has it that the Germans are looking for you. My friend has offered his Chris Craft so I can get you to Stockholm quickly. Get your duffle, we leave immediately."

The 42-foot Chris Craft cabin cruiser and the steamship carrying its precious cargo left Oresund Sound, headed in opposite directions.

I couldn't help but wonder what was in store for them, especially for little Javier.

My mind was also on the members of my team. If the Germans were looking for me, they'd surely be looking for Wilhelm, Karl and Will too.

Chapter Seventeen

RAYA

Stockholm is breathtaking. It's built on fourteen islands and that is why it's called "the city that floats on water." I marveled at its beauty as we motored into the harbor.

Thor docked the cabin cruiser in the only empty slip at the Port of Stockholm as the sun slipped into the horizon.

I hopped off the bow onto the old wooden dock and grabbed the front rail to guide the boat far enough in to tie onto a cleat.

Thor shut the engine and said, "Per, I need to be going and get back to my ship. I suspect when I get there, the Germans will be snooping around looking for you. What do you want me to tell them?"

During the boat ride to Stockholm, I had plenty of time to think about exactly that. I carefully weighed all the options and decided on the one that was safe for Thor and for the members of the Blue Tango Team, especially for Raya.

I hopped back onto the boat and we sat in the galley. I said, "You will not like what I am about to say, Thor, and don't try to change my mind. I want you to tell the Germans that when you realized that I was smuggling people out of Germany, you refused to take them to Sweden, but I forced you at gunpoint.

"You also say I held you in your cabin until the ship reached Malmö and the smuggled people were loaded onto a steamship headed for North America.

"Then add to your story that you overpowered me, took my gun and shot me."

Thor looked at me. His mouth hung open.

I continued. "When they ask what you did with my body, tell them you stole a cabin cruiser and drove out into the Baltic and dumped my body. They will see you drive the cabin cruiser back to Malmö, so it won't be hard to believe."

Thor's face was ashen. "You're right, I don't like that story one damn bit! However, I don't have the energy to argue about it or to think up a better story. It's been a grueling couple of days."

"I know, Thor. You have accomplished what no one else could have. Thank you."

"I suppose you will have to go into hiding in Sweden, Per?"

"Yes, that is a simple matter for me in my position. Only two of my staff members will be aware that I am alive—the two whom I trust implicitly. That would be Inga, my assistant and Sven, my driver. Whatever I need can be provided by them in secret.

"Thor, I must ask you to help me with one more thing."

He laughed, "Of course, since I am going to shoot you, it's the least I can do for you!"

I laughed along with him. We needed a moment of levity, however brief.

"Ask away, my friend."

"Wilhelm promised to send Raya to me. Can I count on you to help him?"

"Yes, but how do you think I can help with that?"

"My entire team in Berlin will be under surveillance after our mission. I don't think she should try to go to the airport. I thought if one of the team could get her to the coast north of Berlin, you could then get her to Malmö on one of your ships. From there, I could have Sven pick her up and drive her to Stockholm. What do you think, Thor?"

"I think it's doable, Per. In fact, it's a damn good plan. About ninety miles north of Berlin, there is a major shipping port at Szczecin, Poland; it's at the top of the Oder River. I am in and out of that port often with shipments of ball bearings to Germany.

"I recommend that Raya catch a small boat on the Oder, which will take her directly to the port. I will coordinate with your man in Berlin to pick her up."

"Great, Thor. Once again, I greatly appreciate your assist."

"You're welcome. I want you to know that if your team can save more people from the Nazis, I will do whatever I can to help. Actually, because I am so often at Szczecin, if there is a next time, we should make that my pick-up point. From there, Malmö is a short distance. And I'm sure that my Danish contact will offer help also."

He got up and gave me a bear hug. "Good luck to you, Per. Please keep in contact with me when you can. I must be getting back to Malmö now. Goodbye."

"Goodbye, Thor. Safe journey."

I untied the boat and gave it a shove out into the harbor. I stood on the dock and watched until I could no longer see the lights of the Chris-Craft.

I walked the mile to my office. No one was in. It was Saturday evening.

I shut the door, lay on the leather sofa and drifted off to sleep.

The sun was warm on my face. I woke up and for the life of me, I had no idea where I was for a minute.

I got up and turned on the heat...how wonderful it felt to have heat. I went in search of coffee. I had relied on Inga to bring me coffee, so I wasn't sure where it was kept. But this was an emergency and I figured it out after a while.

Under the cabinet, I found a stash of cigarettes. I lit one while I waited for coffee to brew. A fresh cigarette was just as welcome as heat.

With coffee and a cigarette in hand, I went to my desk to begin my work.

I didn't dare to call Raya. Any communication with her or with my other team members would put us all in jeopardy.

First, I called Sven, then Inga. I asked them both to meet me at the office in an hour and to tell no one that I was in Stockholm.

Inga arrived, looked at my coffee cup and said, "Good morning, Mr. Lundgren, may I make another cup of coffee for you?"

"Good morning, Inga. Thank you for coming and yes, please make me a decent cup of coffee."

She came back with three cups of steaming coffee on a tray and set them on the conference table.

Just then, Sven showed up dressed for work. He wore his uniform with a white shirt and a driving cap.

I said, "Thanks for coming, Sven. Inga has brewed coffee, help yourself."

"I don't mind if I do. It must be important for you to call both Inga and me here on a Sunday, Mr. Lundgren".

"Yes, it's very important." I explained in detail about our Blue Tango mission and why I needed to be presumed dead.

I ended the discussion with, "From here on, I will work out of the lower level of my home. I ask that both of you communicate with me in person, after normal working hours - after dark."

An hour and a half went by before I finished talking. I said, "Do either of you have questions?"

Sven said, "I understand the need for secrecy, Mr. Lundgren. May I suggest that you relocate your office to somewhere outside the city? My home is not elegant, but it's secluded. I live about thirty minutes from the city."

"That is an excellent idea, Sven. You can use your private vehicle to drive me where I need to go with no questions asked. No one will think of looking for me at your home if they suspect that I'm not dead. Thank God my parents are no longer alive to be told that I'm dead."

I continued, "I asked Thor Bjorn to contact Raya and the team to tell them that I'm alive but in hiding, and that Thor will help Raya get to Sweden.

"Sven, that will be all for now. If you will pick me up with your personal car, I'll be ready in about thirty minutes."

"Yes, Mr. Lundgren. I'll come back for you."

I said, "Inga, please stay."

She looked surprised. "Yes, Mr. Lundgren."

Sven closed the door and I looked at Inga. She said, "It's about Raya, isn't it? I can see it in your eyes. Before you say anything more, I want to assure you that it will all work out for you two. I'm certain of it."

"Inga, I hope you are right. I thought you and I would be having a very different conversation right now. I wanted you to make the

arrangements for Raya and me to be married here in Stockholm. I wanted a big church wedding with a grand smorgasbord reception after. Clearly, that cannot happen until I can come out of hiding.

"If need be, she and I will go to North America and get away from danger altogether. For now, I will be happy to get her and the baby here safely."

Inga gasped, "You have a baby? Why, that's wonderful! Is it a girl or a boy?"

"Hold up, Inga, we don't have a baby yet. Raya is due to deliver in a few months."

She looked positively crestfallen, but said, "I'm glad Raya and the baby will be close by. I will help—I love babies."

"There is much to be done and the first thing is to get me situated. Will you please gather what I will need to work in my office annex?"

She got up and said, "Yes, I'll get right to it...and Mr. Lundgren, I'm glad you're back safely."

"Thank you, Inga. I am too."

Sven and I met Thor's ship at the Port of Malmö four days later. I had to wait in the car and stay out of sight.

I watched as Sven shook Thor's hand and then Thor led Sven up the gangplank.

It seemed like hours before I finally saw Raya. How radiant she looked dressed in pink. I wondered if it was a sign that our baby was a girl.

She waved goodbye to Thor as she walked to the car. Sven carried her suitcases and opened the back door for her.

To onlookers, we looked like business associates, nothing more. I wore a hat and glasses to disguise myself, which Raya thought was quite comical.

She sat next to me. I looked at her and said, "Sven, get us away from prying eyes!"

Sven looked at me in the rearview mirror. He said with a smile, "Yes, Sir!"

Raya talked nonstop for the entire trip. I hung on her every word. She had the voice of an angel, whether she spoke or sang.

When we arrived at Sven's, he parked the car in the garage. He said, "I'll get Raya's suitcases, you two go in and rest. I will cook dinner for us. It will be ready in about two hours."

We both said, "Thanks, Sven."

I took Raya's hand and led her to my quarters.

We missed Sven's dinner. Some things were just more important than food.

The next morning, I awoke before Raya and tiptoed to the kitchen. Sven was at the table. He said, "Coffee's hot, have a cup."

I poured a giant cup, lit a cigarette and joined him at the table.

He gave me a sly grin. "Salmon is just as good for breakfast as it is for dinner."

I smiled and ignored the obvious implication. "That sounds really good. I'll go see if Raya is awake."

The three of us enjoyed salmon, creamed potatoes with onions and asparagus for breakfast.

Sven was the only one to talk. Raya and I were far too hungry to talk.

For the next many weeks, Raya and I enjoyed the Swedish summer. We walked down the lane and talked about everything under the sun.

On weekdays, I wrote my diplomatic papers, which would be unveiled after my release from seclusion.

Raya spent her days reading about Swedish history and traditions, and sometimes she would knit a few rows on the rainbow-colored blanket for our baby.

Inga visited us most evenings. She cooked dinner with Sven; they had a friendly competition to see who the best chef was. After dinner, I would do some office work with Inga while Raya and Sven washed the dishes.

Inga kept us stocked with toscakaka, which is Swedish almond cake. It was our dessert often.

The four of us became very close during that time. It was a wonderful diversion from the war that raged on in other parts of the world.

One evening after dinner, Raya said she was feeling tired, so she went to bed.

A few minutes later, I went to check on her. Her water had broken and she was hysterical. I helped her into bed and tried to calm her.

She said, "It's too soon for the baby; it's not due for two more months!"

Inga and Sven watched from the bedroom doorway.

Raya moaned, "I think the baby's coming now!"

Inga took over; she shouted orders to Sven and me. "I need a pot of hot water, white towels, a sheet, a large blanket and a small blanket!"

We rushed for the ordered items.

Inga leaned over Raya and said, "I've delivered babies before; you and your baby will be fine. You just listen to me and I'll tell you what to do."

Raya needed Inga's confidence. She said, "Thank you, Inga. I'm so glad you're here."

I wasn't sure how many towels would be needed so I grabbed twenty or so. Inga gave me a strange look when I handed them all to her. Then she promptly dismissed me. I was doing my level best; I was truly out of my element.

Sven got everything else that Inga asked for and then she said, "Now you two wait outside while I help Raya birth her baby."

I didn't have to be asked twice. Sven and I went to the kitchen. We waited.

We waited through that entire night. At one point, I knocked on the bedroom door and Inga yelled, "Go away!"

I had been in some pretty tight spots in my life. Those situations were like a walk in the park compared to waiting and worrying about Raya and the birth of our baby.

I saw a rosy, pink sunrise more beautiful than I had ever seen. At the same moment, I heard our baby cry.

I ran to the bedroom...there was Raya holding our baby girl. Inga was smiling down on them like a proud Swedish grandmamma.

I said, "Raya, our baby girl looks just like you. She's beautiful." I kissed them both ever so gently.

I looked at Inga, "She's so small, do you think she's all right?"

"Oh, yes, she's a feisty little one and she was most anxious to be born!"

The following weeks proved Inga to be correct. Our little girl quickly grew from 4 to 6 pounds.

Our little family was deliriously happy—along with Uncle Sven and Aunt Inga.

I asked Sven to deliver an invitation to Thor to come visit us and see the baby. We also wanted Thor to contact Raya's brother, Hans, and invite him.

A week later, Sven arrived home with Thor and Hans in tow.

Raya greeted them while I held the baby.

Hans hugged his sister. "Don't you look happy and healthy, Raya! Now, where is my niece? Oh, I see—her Papa has her."

I got up from the rocking chair and shook his hand. "Hans, it's good to see you!"

"You too, Per. Let me hold that little lady!" I handed her to Hans, and he seemed to know just how to hold her.

I hugged Thor and said, "We are so very glad that you are here."

"Well, I could not wait to see your baby. She's beautiful just like her Mama!"

I said, "Time's up, Hans, it's Thor's turn to hold his goddaughter."

"Did you call her my goddaughter?"

"Yes, Thor. Raya and I hope that you will accept."

"You bet I will accept—it's an honor!"

Thor held the baby as if she was a treasure from the gods. He said, "What have you named this precious child, Raya?"

Raya came and stood next to me. She smiled and said, "Per, why don't you tell Thor what we named our little girl?"

With my arm around Raya, I said, "Her name is Thora."

Thor got a big grin on his face. He looked down at Thora and said, "Do you know you're named after an old sea captain? Just you wait, you and I will take many sea voyages, and maybe Mama and Papa can come along too!"

Thora chose that moment to display a huge smile for her godfather. She knew he was special.

Raya put Thora down for a nap and joined Hans and Sven in the kitchen for some catch-up time.

Thor and I sat in my office. He said, "Hans told me about a new mission Blue Tango has in the works. But first, I will let him tell you what happened when Wilhelm, Karl and Will arrived back at the base after the first mission."

That evening, Hans, Thor and I went to my den to talk. I said, "Hans, how did it go with Blue Tango after I left? Did Wilhelm's plan to use the last gold bar work out?"

"It absolutely did, Per. It was their saving grace. The three of them showed up with only one truck and told the story they'd concocted to get themselves out of trouble. Thankfully, there was only one officer who oversaw their interrogation so when they offered the gold, he accepted without anyone else knowing about it.

"However, there is something else that you need to know, Per. By the time they reached the base, information about your involvement with the French people's escape was common knowledge. The only way to handle it was for Wilhelm to blame it on you and say that ultimately, he had to shoot you. Otherwise, there was no reasonable explanation for the three of them having driven the people to the port using military trucks.

"The officer who questioned them did not understand how they got involved with you, Per. And, he did not know that you fooled the guards at the port into letting you put the French people on Thor's ship. However, when he eyed the gold bar, his questioning ended and our team was released. So now you see that you cannot show up in Berlin, or anywhere else for that matter."

I said, "I understand it was the only way to keep the rest of our team from being thrown into the brig. It's a great advantage that the officer who accepted the gold bar probably would not have written in his report what Wilhelm told him about me because those details would raise too many questions. Especially the fact that Wilhelm shot me."

Hans looked at me in surprise. "Why is that, Per?"

I said, "Thor knows why...that's the story he told the German investigator who questioned him about my whereabouts. He said he shot me and dumped my body in the Baltic because I forced him at gunpoint to transport the French people on his ship. That's very funny; shot dead twice! I don't think I could survive a third time!"

We all laughed, and Hans said, "Yes, we will be sure to keep you away from the Germans, Per. But seriously, it means you cannot have a hand in our next mission."

I said, "I'm sure I can find a way to help, behind the scenes."

Hans said, "As the leader of Blue Tango, I cannot and will not have you involved in any way, Per. I'm sorry but that's how it is. This mission promises to be riskier than our first one. You need to stay on this side of the Baltic. If the Germans get their hands on you, they'll throw you in a prison camp, or worse."

I said to Thor, "Do you agree with Hans?"

"I'm afraid so, Per. You have Raya and Thora to consider now."

I said, "Of course, I would never do anything to jeopardize them. However, I do not agree that I should remain in Sweden while my team undertakes a mission without me."

I looked at Hans, "You need me Hans, and you know it! I easily pass for a Nazi when I wear their uniform."

I could see the decision was made, without input from me.

What neither of them knew was that my decision was also made. I would assist in the next mission—without their consent. I had no idea exactly how I would manage it, but I had every confidence I would figure it out, as I always had. Figuring things out was what I did best.

Thor looked at me with squinty eyes. He seemed to know what I was thinking.

Chapter Eighteen

TOM/SETH

A young man dressed in a Pierre Cardin suit stepped into the lobby of Julia's apartment building and spoke to Javier. "I'm here to see Julia Hamilton."

Javier ignored the man's demeanor, which illustrated his disdain for 'the help.' "Who shall I say is here?"

He admired himself in the mirror behind Javier as he spoke. "Tell her Mr. Bjorn's Executive Assistant wishes to see her immediately."

Julia answered her house phone and thought, *I'm not expecting anyone.*

She said, "Yes, Javier. Is there another flower delivery for me?"

He stepped into a side room and whispered into the phone. "Julia, there's a man here who says he's Mr. Bjorn's Executive Assistant. He's quite demanding. He wants to see you right away. What should I tell him?"

"It's all right, Javier, send him up."

As the man stepped from the elevator outside of Julia's apartment, she opened her door.

She recognized him as the secretary who had interrupted her meeting with Thor in the library to announce an important call. He'd apparently given himself a promotion from secretary to Executive Assistant.

She spoke first. "Is everything all right with Mr. Bjorn?"

"Well, Miss Hamilton, Mr. Bjorn sent me personally to ask *you* that same question. He said Tom has been unable to reach you on the secure cell.

"Both Tom and Mr. Bjorn were concerned that something had happened to you."

Oh, no . . . I forgot to return Tom's call when Seth was here!

She lied. "I received a message from Tom and called him back and left a message but I didn't hear back from him. I assumed he'd call again today."

Coolly, she said, "Is there something I need to know? Have my travel arrangements changed?"

He seemed agitated. "I am not privy to that information. I'm simply here to make sure that you are all right. Now that I can see you're fine, I'll report back to Mr. Bjorn. I would suggest that you call Tom right away. Good day, Miss Hamilton."

"Please thank Mr. Bjorn for checking on me. Goodbye."

With that, she closed her apartment door, looked out the peephole and watched until he got into the elevator. She didn't like the man in his fashion suit with the prissy attitude.

She sat at her desk and looked at the secure cell phone. She'd avoided Tom's messages longer than she should have. It was time to face the music.

This would be so much easier if I didn't have to work with Tom and pretend to be his wife. Oh, this is a sticky wicket!

She pressed #1 on the cell. Tom answered before a complete ring.

"Julia! Are you all right? You didn't return my calls!"

"Yes, Tom, I'm all right."

She didn't make excuses. She didn't tell him she purposely did not answer the phone when he called because Seth was in her apartment.

"Tom, I will get right to the point. Since you broke up with me, I've been seeing Seth, my architect friend."

She was careful to remind him that *he* had broken up with *her*.

"Yeah, I know who he is. That didn't take long, did it, Julia?"

"You're not being fair, Tom. The last time I saw you, you made it clear that we were done. And to use your words, I am free to see anyone I like. Do you remember that?"

"Yes, I'm sorry, Julia. You're right. You had no way of knowing that I was protecting you when I broke up with you."

He continued. "At that time, I had no idea Thor would hire you to work with me. If I'd known that, I would have simply told you I was going on a business trip and I wouldn't be able to see you for a while. Then we wouldn't be in this situation—you with Seth, and also with me."

"I'm sorry, Tom, but that's not exactly how it is. I'm with Seth now. You and I are strictly business. I hope you understand."

"You're expecting an awful lot from me, Julia. Next week we'll be in Canada together, sharing a hotel room as husband and wife. How will your boyfriend like *that*?"

"I have no intention of sharing a hotel room with you, Tom."

"And just how does that work? We'll be checking in as Mr. and Mrs. White."

"That's easy, Tom. Reserve a room for Mr. and Mrs. White, and I'll reserve a single room for myself."

"That will be just fine, Julia."

He changed the subject. "Have you had a chance to read Thor's father's logs?"

"Yes, and I found them very interesting. Tom, I'm sure when we put our talents together that we will find some of the people who've been missing since the war."

Julia continued. "I've designed a chart of names and relationships along with dates of crossing to North America. It's shaping up pretty well. I think I have a few promising leads."

"I've done the same, Julia. When you get here, we will combine our charts. It will be an excellent beginning.

"How is your move coming along? You'll be on schedule to meet me next week, Julia?"

"Absolutely; I'm ahead of schedule. Tom, I'm excited about the work we'll be doing. I had no idea until I read the logs that my uncle teamed up with a shipping company to save people during the war."

"Yeah, your uncle sounds like quite an amazing guy. It's a mystery how he died, though. Thor's logs didn't have anything to say on that topic. Do you know what happened to him?"

"No, I always wondered how he died. Maybe we'll find out during our investigation."

I expect Uncle Per will tell me in an upcoming session.

Neither knew what to say. There was a long pause.

Finally, Tom said, "If you come up with anything interesting about our work, give me a call."

He couldn't resist a final jab. "And next time I call you, either answer the phone or at least call me back within the hour."

Julia grimaced. She knew his ego was wounded. "Will do. Bye, Tom."

"Goodbye, Julia."

Julia talked to the rocking chair that sat next to her desk. "I'm glad *that's* over with. I think Tom's really mad at me, but I don't think it's fair. Do you?"

No reaction from the rocker.

Seth had called earlier in the day and asked if she was free for an interesting evening date.

"That sounds mysterious, Seth. Of course, I'm available for *you*. What time, where, and what is the suggested attire?"

"I enjoy being your man of mystery, Jules. I will tell you only the time and place. You wear whatever your intuition tells you to wear.

"I will meet you at the Central Park entrance closest to your apartment, at six PM sharp. See you there…goodbye." Click.

Julia laughed and looked at the phone in her hand.

Hmm . . . I wonder what I should wear? Oh, I know!

Seth laughed to himself when he spotted Julia as she walked toward him at the appointed time. She was dressed in jeans, sweatshirt and sneakers, with a bright bandana covering her hair. She figured they were going bicycle riding in the park.

He balanced a bike in each hand and had only his lips to greet her with. He kissed her and said, "I love that you know me so well that you figure me out. Here, hop on your bike. We'll ride along 5th Avenue. If you're hungry, we'll stop at the Dancing Crane Café at the zoo."

She said, "I *am* hungry. I forgot to eat lunch today. Come on, I'll race you to the zoo!"

Seth lost the race. "You're in better shape than I am, Jules." He grinned.

"I know you let me win, Seth. You play racquetball three mornings a week. There's no way that I won fair and square!"

He laughed and kissed her.

"Stay with the bikes, I'll go and buy gyros and iced tea for us."

"Okay, Seth." Julia happily leaned up against the bike rack and waited.

They enjoyed the rest of the evening together. They stopped often to see again the sights they'd seen on their tour during the park festival.

At dusk, they returned the bikes to the rental shop. As they walked toward Julia's apartment, she said, "Seth, let's sit on this bench for a minute."

"Sure, what's up?" He looked concerned.

"I feel like our relationship is on a good path."

He said, "Oh-oh. But what?"

She put her hand on his arm to reassure him. "I want to be completely honest with you."

Seth looked her squarely in the eyes. "Go ahead, Julia."

"You know that a few weeks ago, Tom and I broke up. Just after that, you invited me to the Central Park festival. That's when you introduced me to Thor Bjorn. Remember, Seth?"

"Yes, I remember." He felt his gut tighten.

"As you know, I was offered a job with his company, but not as an interior designer."

Seth looked perplexed.

She continued, "What I am going to tell you must stay between us. You'll understand why in a minute."

He nodded.

"Thor Inc. is an umbrella company for a private, and I mean *very* private, investigation company. The sole objective of that company is to find people who escaped from Europe during the Second World War and then came to North America.

"There are reasons to keep details of those escapes secret—in part, because Thor Sr. broke laws and ignored agreements between Sweden and Germany."

She was about to tell him more, but he interrupted.

"That's very interesting, Julia, but what does that have to do with you?"

"That was exactly my question to Thor. As it turns out, my uncle and Thor's father worked together to help people escape from the Nazis. My uncle, Per Lundgren, was a Swedish diplomat charged with mediation between Sweden and Germany. That put him in contact with a German underground group named 'Blue Tango.' He joined that group.

"Well, Blue Tango arranged missions to rescue people from the Nazis, right under the noses of the German military.

"Thor Sr. operated a Swedish company, Bjorn Shipping, and had government contracts to deliver materials to Germany—mostly ball bearings."

Seth interrupted, "And all of this involves you, how?"

She leaned over and kissed his cheek. "I'm getting to that."

He leaned back on the bench.

"I became interested in my Swedish heritage and started a journal detailing my Uncle Per's experiences during the war."

Julia paused for a long moment. She was not sure if he was prepared to hear the truth about her journal. She decided to put her faith in him.

"The night we went to Central Park, you heard me tell Javier, the doorman, that I would give him the next chapter of what I was writing. You asked me if I was writing a book. Do you remember, Seth?"

"Yes, I do remember. Javier seemed very anxious to read what you had written. It definitely piqued my interest."

"My journal is not from my research about my uncle. It's being *told* to me by him."

"Who's telling you? What do you mean?"

"I'm intuitive. I have the ability to communicate telepathically. My uncle is also intuitive and is able to send me information that I write in my journal. He's giving me information about the people he and his team saved, and about the assistance of Thor Sr.

"Thor Jr. has his father's logs and hired Tom's investigation company to find people named in the logs, if they still exist. Thor knew about me and that I am Per Lundgren's niece. He could not believe his good fortune when you introduced me to him.

"The fact that Tom and I were involved personally was icing on the cake, so to speak, to Thor's way of thinking. He hired me and asked Tom to work with me to find people Thor has been looking for. His idea is that Tom's talents and mine will be a good match to get the job done."

Julia continued. "I agree, and so I'm headed to Canada next week to begin to work with Tom."

Seth seemed distracted by his thoughts.

"Seth? What do you think?"

Now it was his turn to pause. He cocked his head from side to side as if to access memories.

Finally, he said, "That *does* explain some weird happenings, Julia."

"It does? How so?"

"On the way to your apartment with lunch, I thought I saw an old man wearing a top hat and a tweed suit. He tipped his hat to me. No one else seemed to see him. Then poof! He disappeared.

"I didn't mention it to you, but I thought somehow the man had something to do with you. Crazy, huh?"

Julia was delighted. "Seth! That was Martin...you saw Martin! I thought I was the only one who saw him—in my dream, anyway."

She continued, "I called you to help with my client's indoor fountain. You never asked me how I knew there was a brook running under 5th Avenue."

"Now that I think about it, I *did* wonder how you came up with it."

"I often dream when I have a problem to solve. My dreams give me answers. I was trying to figure out how to place an indoor fountain in Mrs. Wellington's design and Martin—the Martin you described—appeared in my dream and told me about the brook. The next morning, I raced to the City Clerk's office to check out the property records and found that it was true."

"Wow, that's cool, Julia. But why would I see this Martin fellow?"

"I'm not sure. Maybe he likes our association?"

"Maybe. Then there was the day when we were dancing in your kitchen. I thought I saw a man out of the corner of my eye—just a fleeting glimpse."

He laughed. "I chalked it up to being deliriously in love with you!"

"Seth, it seems that you have some intuitive abilities of your own. I'm impressed."

"Possibly. I still think it was delirium.

"All right, Miss Julia, let's go to your apartment and I'll let you cook me an omelet. Then I'll have one of your famous cupcakes."

"Gladly, Seth. Let's go."

Chapter Nineteen

ANOTHER MISSION

The clock radio next to her bed clicked on to music at eight AM. Julia rolled over and expected to touch Seth. Then she remembered he left at dawn to play racquetball before work. He said he needed to keep his routine in preparation for when she was gone.

She said she understood. She really did, but she felt sad.

Aloud she spoke to no one. "Maybe Tom and I will finish our work in a few weeks rather than a few months."

"Yes, Julia, let's try for that. Meanwhile, you will leave in a couple of days and there are some things that I need to tell you before then."

"Uncle Per, you always surprise me! It's coffee time for me, and then I will listen and write. I'm all for anything you can tell me to help us locate people rescued from the Nazis.

"By the by, naming your baby girl Thora was very touching. I suppose you will *not* tell me if you and Raya got married."

"You suppose correctly, my little chickadee. There is a reason for everything and you will soon understand everything."

Julia sighed and smiled.

Twenty minutes later, she was dressed and at her desk, ready to add to her nearly full journal.

One month later, I was still undercover. Raya and I were not free to marry or to have Thora baptized in the church. We decided to ask Thor, in his capacity as Ship's Captain, to perform both services privately, even though we would not be at sea.

I spoke to Thor on a secure line that Sven had rigged up for me. Thor was delighted with my request and said, "You will be married and Thora will be baptized in the eyes of the Lord. I will come to your home as soon as you tell me you're ready."

"That will be fine. Raya suggested that two weeks from Sunday will give us enough time to prepare. Does that work for you, Thor?"

"Yes, I will be back from a meeting with the Blue Tango team by then, Per."

"I presume that meeting will be about the next mission. I hope you will discuss it with me when you're here, Thor."

"You know I will, Per. Hans was very definite about you not being involved. But if it's any consolation, I believe as you do—the team needs you."

Just then, Raya brought Thora into my office.

I swiftly changed the conversation. "Yes, Raya will be happy to hear that you will perform our ceremonies. We'll see you here two weeks from Sunday. Thanks, Thor."

I hung up and went to hug my girls.

Raya smiled. "I am happy that Thor has agreed to perform our wedding and Thora's baptism.

"I'll put Thora down for a nap. You can ask Sven to get a message to Inga. She can help with the menu, the decorations and the Swedish traditions, of course. This will be wonderful for us, Per."

"Raya, sweetheart, I know this is not the wedding we envisioned, but I promise you that we will throw the biggest bröllop celebration that Sweden has ever seen, just as soon as we are free to marry in the church. You will wear a garland of myrtle to signify your innocence."

She proudly said, "I know what a bröllop is...it's a Swedish wedding. I also know that I will be your brud and you will be my brudgum - and, my bouquet should be very smelly to ward off trolls!"

I laughed and said, "Yes, that's right. You can never be too careful here in Sweden - those trolls are a nasty lot!"

Two weeks later, on Sunday, Thor arrived dressed in his captain's uniform. He marveled at how Raya and Inga had decorated the living room to look like a church altar.

There was an arch of flowers for Raya and me to sit under. On Raya's chair was a garland of myrtle leaves that Inga had made.

Traditional Swedish weddings have only two attendants—a bridesmaid and a best man. Inga and Sven served as our attendants and our only guests.

I dressed in coat and tails. I wanted our ceremony to be as authentic as possible.

Thor said, "It looks like you're ready to get married, Per. Where is Raya?"

"She's trying to settle Thora down. She's fussy today and won't take a nap."

Sven ducked his head out of the kitchen and said, "Is it time?"

Thor said, "Yes, please let Inga know we're ready to begin and that Raya can follow in a minute."

Inga appeared carrying the baby. "Thora wants to share in the wedding ceremony of her parents."

The baby smiled and gurgled, happy to be included.

Thor took his place on the makeshift altar and I sat under the arch. Sven stood at my side.

Inga held Thora and stood next to where Raya would sit.

Everyone was quiet while we waited for the bride to enter.

Raya appeared like a vision out of a dream. All of us were completely mesmerized. She wore the wedding dress Inga's mother had worn when she married. It was a full-length gown of white taffeta with an overlay of delicate lace. The hem swept the floor as she walked. It looked as if she floated to my side.

Her smile lit up the room.

Raya sat next to me and Thor began. He had added words to the ceremony-at-sea verbiage, just for us. What he wrote was magical and lovely.

He then asked if we'd written our own vows. We both said yes. We faced each other.

I read my vows first and it was a good thing that I'd written them, because I was so emotional that I would never have remembered what I wanted to say.

Next, it was Raya's turn. She did not need to write her vows because she'd memorized them. Before she began, she took my hands in hers. Then...she sang her wedding vows to me. She sang through her tears of joy as she wiped away my tears.

When she finished, not a sound could be heard. I looked at Inga, Sven and Thor. Each had a wet face.

Thora broke the silence with her gleeful and well-timed screech. We all laughed.

Thor pronounced us Man and Wife and said, "Per, now you may kiss your bride."

Sven announced, "Time to eat!" He had prepared a smorgasbord fit for royalty.

We began with a rose hip soup, then the cold dishes were served: fresh fruits, cheeses, Baltic herring and fresh rågbröd which is rye bread.

The hot dishes were served next: roast beef, köttbulla; that's Swedish meatballs, salmon, boiled potatoes, onions in a cream sauce and glazed carrots.

Dessert was almond cake—everyone's favorite.

Thor sat back in his chair and rubbed his stomach. "That was the finest smorgasbord I've ever eaten, Sven. Thank you!"

Sven said, "You are most welcome. I'm glad you enjoyed it."

I said, "Raya, why don't you get Thora dressed for her baptism. And while you do that, Thor and I will take a walk down the lane."

"All right, she should be awake by now."

Inga said, "Sven and I will wash the dishes."

Thor and I walked outside. We each lit a cigarette. I said, "Thor, thank you for all you're doing for us."

"You don't have to thank me. There isn't anything I wouldn't do for you and Raya, and for Thora."

"We feel the same, Thor. Now then, let's talk about our next mission."

He laughed. "What do you mean by 'our' next mission? I'll tell you about it, but I don't think you will be involved."

"Laugh as you will, I'll be the judge of how I will be involved. Now, let's hear the plan."

"All right, all right. We know that the Nazis have kidnapped thousands of Polish children to be Germanized. They separate them into categories for processing. The children who are rejected for not having sufficient Aryan traits are sent to labor camps or prison camps.

"Believe it or not, labor camps are a good deal for those kids, compared to the prison camps. At least at the labor camps, they are fed enough to sustain them to be able to work. At the prison camps, doctors conduct medical experiments on those poor children until there's nothing but a shell left of them.

"Because Karl, your driver for the first mission, was born in Poland and taken by the Nazis to be Germanized, he's heading up this mission.

"Henrique is still monitoring the listening devices he set up in the second level of the Blue Tango Club. Recently, the team learned from those recordings that two groups of children were rejected by the Nazis and are being moved from a facility in northeastern Germany to various camps.

"We have only two pieces of intel that Will and Hans are currently building on. First, the groups of children include approximately twenty boys and ten girls, all between the ages of twelve and fifteen. The second bit of intel is that the transport will take place within the next month.

"Wilhelm is casting astrology charts to determine the time when the Nazis will move the children. He will then be able to project the most opportune time and place to intercept the transport. The team will be waiting with an enclosed truck to grab the kids."

I said, "That is an ambitious and worthwhile mission, Thor. All the team members have a role in carrying it out. That is, everyone except me and Raya.

"I presume the facility where the children are being moved from in northeast Germany is near the sea. You will be available to pick them up and take them by ship to Sweden?"

"Yes, that's right. I know how you feel about not helping, Per. Maybe you can assist me at the Port of Malmö."

I reluctantly agreed to the small part I would be allowed to play. "Thanks, let me know how the plans progress, Thor. Right now, you have a baptism to perform."

"Indeed I do. Let's rejoin the party."

Thora saw us walk into the living room and screeched with delight.

Thor laughed and picked her up. "Don't you look beautiful in your little white dress? Now, I don't want you to be mad at me when I dip your head in water."

She started to fuss and Raya said, "I'll take her. Let's get the head dipping over with, shall we?"

Inga said, "I have a pan of nice warm water ready."

As suggested, Thor kept the ceremony short. Raya and I together held Thora while Inga held the baptism bowl and Thor dripped water over the top of Thora's head. She was so taken with us hovering over her that she barely noticed the water.

Afterwards, Thor said, "I have a gift for my goddaughter."

He reached into the breast pocket of his uniform jacket and withdrew a tiny package wrapped in pink ribbons. He handed it to Raya and asked her to open it.

"Gladly." Raya untied the ribbons, opened the box and took out a sterling silver locket with a pin on the back, rather than a chain. Attached below the locket was a tiny sterling silver bow no bigger than one-quarter inch. She said, "It's exquisite, Thor. Thank you so much."

"I had it crafted by a jeweler in Stockholm. Open the locket."

Raya opened the locket, read what was engraved inside and handed it to me. It read 'To Thora' on one side and on the other, it read 'Angels keep you safe. TB'.

I said, "It's perfect, Thor. Thank you."

Raya pinned it on Thora's christening dress and we all admired the thoughtful gift.

Soon, evening was upon us and it was time to continue our wedding celebration. We gathered around the kitchen table.

Sven said in a loud voice, "As best man, I propose a toast! Inga, the champagne, please!"

She reached beside the chair where she sat and said, "I have it right here!" She proceeded to pop the cork and poured each a glass of the bubbly. Then she said, "Okay, Sven, toast away!"

He stood. "I am honored to have been chosen as the best man for a man whom I have come to consider my brother."

He laughed and added, "Never mind that I am the only man, other than Thor, who is available. But seriously, I am truly honored and blessed to have you and Raya in my life, Per. I wish you many happy and healthy years."

Sven raised his glass and shouted, "Skoal!"

Everyone raised a glass and sipped. I stood and said, "Sven, if I had a thousand friends around me, I would still choose you as my best man. You are a loyal friend and I too, consider you my brother. You have protected us in your own home all these many months. I trust you with the lives of my wife and our daughter. We look forward to many years of happiness with you, Sven. Thank you."

Glasses were raised again and all shouted, "Skoal!"

Thor broke open a bottle of potato vodka and Sven led us in the singing of Swedish folk songs into the wee hours.

Raya and I wandered off to bed around four AM. We left the others to fend for themselves as to sleeping arrangements.

By eight AM, Sven had reheated a hearty breakfast of smorgasbord leftovers and was gone to drive Thor back to Malmö.

Inga left sometime before Raya and I made it to the breakfast table.

While we ate, I told Raya about the team's next mission.

She said, "That sounds wonderful. I hope they can save all the children and get them to Sweden without mishap. Will Thor be able to connect with his Danish friend to get them to North America?"

"Yes, he thinks so."

I hesitated and looked at Raya.

She said, "Oh, no, Per! You don't intend to help with the mission, do you? It's far too dangerous for you to be seen. Everyone thinks you're dead!"

"*Raya, you know me. I'm careful. I promise you I will not take unnecessary risks. Besides, I'll be in disguise; I will not be recognized. I intend to stay in Sweden to be on hand when Thor docks at Malmö. He will need help with thirty or more children who've been traumatized by their experiences.*"

"*I do know you, Per, and I know your mind is made up. I will not argue with you.*"

I kissed her. "*Thank you, my darling. I will not be in danger and I will be gone only for a day or two, at the very most. Inga will stay with you and Thora. Sven will drive me to the dock.*"

Thora then made herself known and Raya went to nurse her and get her ready for the day.

I was left alone to consider the possible ramifications of my involvement with the next mission.

Sven and I waited for hours until we finally saw Thor's ship pull into port. It was a rainy day, so my hat and trench coat served as the perfect disguise.

I said to Sven, "*I hope everything went all right in Germany. Thor's ship was expected hours ago. I'm very anxious to hear about the mission.*"

"*You won't have to wait much longer. Thor is running down the dock right now.*"

I jumped out of the car and met Thor at the end of the dock. His uniform was torn and dirty, and he looked as if he'd been on the front lines of the war.

I grabbed him by the shoulders and said, "*Thor, what happened? Do you have the children? Are they all right?*"

"*As God is my witness, Per, I've never imagined anything so horrible! Somehow, the Nazis got wind of our plan to rescue the truckload of children and they...they...*"

Thor wept uncontrollably. I shook him and yelled, "*Thor! Tell me what happened! Get hold of yourself, man!*"

Sven came up behind us and suggested that we move to the car.

It took Thor a few minutes to compose himself enough to tell what happened.

He began slowly. "*I docked the ship at the designated place and there was no sign of the team. I arrived early, so I was not concerned with the wait. I wasn't there long when a German military truck roared into the dockyard with a second truck in hot pursuit.*

"I instructed my First Officer to be ready to leave port as soon as he saw me come back on board.

"I ran to my quarters and got the gun I keep loaded.

"I raced down the dock toward the trucks. As I ran, I saw Karl get out of the driver's side of the first truck. Hans got out of the passenger side.

"Karl took cover beside a rock wall and began to shoot at the Nazis who had jumped out of the second truck.

"Hans helped the children out of the back of the first truck and funneled them to me.

"There were so many Nazis. There were too many for Karl to hold off. He got shot, but not before he killed at least six of those bastards!

"Hans managed to get eight of the kids to me before he also got shot.

"Per, it was a nightmare. Kids were screaming and crying...and kids were lying dead.

"I motioned for the tallest boy to get the kids to the ship. I was able to kill the last of the Nazis. We ran down the dock to the ship."

Thor broke down again and I had all I could do to keep my mind on the task at hand. There would be time to grieve later.

I said, "Thor, where exactly are the children you rescued?"

"They're in the galley of the ship. My crew is feeding and consoling them the best they can. Children should never have to endure what they've been through."

"All right, I will go to the galley and see what I can do for the children. You see if you can find out when the steamship will arrive to take them to North America."

I walked into the galley and saw five boys and three girls huddled together on the floor. My heart felt as if it would burst with sorrow. I got down beside them on one knee. In English, I said, "You're safe now. We will see that you get to a new home in North America."

I got no response at all. One of the crewmen said, "They don't understand, sir. I think they speak Polish."

I repeated what I had said in French.

An older boy replied, also in French. "We want to go back to Germany and get our friends who were with us on the truck. Will you take us there first?"

I clutched my heart and exhaled loudly. Apparently, there had been so much commotion at the port that they did not know the others in their group had been shot. Thor had been able to shield them from the murders as he hustled them aboard the ship.

I realized it wouldn't help the children to know the others were dead.

I said, "We will go back for them. Meanwhile, you eight will get a trip across the Atlantic to a new, safe home. Will that be okay?"

The boy translated to the others in Polish. He then said to me in French, "That will be okay with us, sir. Thank you."

Thor called from the upper deck, "Per, the steamship is in port, come on up."

I patted the shoulder of the boy who was my translator and he gave me a half-hearted smile.

I met Thor, and he said, "I want to get the names of the children before they leave. I presume they speak Polish?"

"Yes, but one boy speaks French. I'll get the names from him."

I got the names of the eight and of several of the children who had been shot.

When I returned to the captain's quarters, I found Thor writing in his log.

He put the quill pen down and looked at me with sad eyes. "I'll write the names of the children here. This log may be of use in the future."

Slowly, he wrote each name in perfect penmanship. When he was done, even the quill pen looked spent.

"Thor, why don't you come home with me to recuperate for a few days?"

"Thanks, but after this, I just want to be alone. I'm going home."

"All right, I'm going home too. I need to see Raya and Thora to regain some peace."

Thor looked shell-shocked, which of course he was. I said, "I'm sorry I wasn't in Germany to help. Maybe I could have saved Hans and Karl and the other children."

He seemed at a loss for words. He got up and hugged me for a long time.

Finally, he said, "Take care of my goddaughter and Raya. Goodbye, old friend."

"I will, and you take care of yourself, Thor."

If I thought the worst was over, I could not have been more wrong.

As we neared our home, Sven said, "Who the hell are those guys on the front porch?"

I grabbed the gun from under my trench coat and jumped out of the car even before it stopped. I ran toward the uniformed men as fast as my legs would carry me.

They both stood firm. I realized they were Nazis. One said, "Stop right there, Mr. Lundgren."

I was nearly out of my mind with panic. I shouted, "Where are my wife and child? Let me into my house!"

The other Nazi said, "Don't worry. We'll take very good care of them."

I rushed them. I didn't care if they had guns—my gun was pointed at one of them.

Suddenly, the Nazi that I was not aiming at jerked backwards and fell off the porch. Sven had come up behind me and shot him clean through the heart.

I pulled the trigger and shot that other bastard right between the eyes. He dropped to the ground, giving me a clear path to the door.

I tried to jump onto the porch. I had to get to Raya and Thora.

I could not move.

Sven grabbed me under my arms from behind and said, "I've got you, Per. Don't try to move, you've been shot."

The Nazi I killed got a shot off at the same time I did. There was so much adrenaline in my body that I did not even feel the bullet that penetrated my chest.

I looked down. There was a pool of blood at my feet. Sven gently helped me as I collapsed on the grass. The front door flung open and Raya ran to me.

I heard her sobs as the life poured out of my body. And then nothing.

Chapter Twenty

PER

I was in a coma for two months. Raya, Inga and Sven cared for me at home. I could not go to the hospital because it was still not safe for anyone else to know that I was alive.

The Nazis on our porch had apparently followed us from the Port of Malmö and reached our house before we did. Because we killed them, it was unlikely that any others would come looking for me, at least not anytime soon.

Raya told me she sang to me every day while I lay sleeping. Later, I told her I heard her voice and that's what kept me breathing.

Miraculously, Thor showed up on the evening I was shot. He'd reconsidered my offer to spend a few days with us. That may have been what saved my life; he had some basic medical knowledge, at least enough to know how to clean, stitch and dress my wound. He said the bullet passed clean through my middle without touching major organs.

Inga got tape to wrap the ribs that the bullet had broken. She also got an IV setup from her sister, who was a hospital nurse. Inga's sister never asked questions, a good thing, especially in this situation.

I opened my eyes for the first time one sunny afternoon, and for a moment I simply watched Raya as she sat by my bed engrossed in a book.

I became aware of tubes and bandages and severe pain in my midsection. I tried to sit up but only managed to move my left arm.

Raya saw the movement, jumped out of her chair and came to my side. "Per! You're awake! Thank God you're awake!"

I winced with pain as she gently leaned on the bed.

"I'm sorry, you are in pain. I'll get Inga. She can give you pain medicine."

I managed to whisper, "No, I don't want pain medication and I don't want to sleep. Where is Thora? Please bring her to me."

"Yes, yes. I'll get her right away."

Raya held our precious child next to my bed so I could see her. The two of them were the best medicine.

Inga stood in the doorway with tears streaming down her face. She sniffled, and Raya said, "Look, Inga, our Per is awake!"

Inga hesitantly approached my bedside. "You gave us one hell of a scare, but you fared a whole lot better than those dirty Nazis did!"

I started to smile at her humor but I was suddenly struck with the horrible memory of Nazis on our front porch when Sven and I returned from Malmö.

It had been a recurrent nightmare while I was deep in the coma. I realized it wasn't just a dream. The shock of recall was too much to bear. I passed out.

When I woke again, it was dark outside and Raya was still at my bedside. She said, "Everything is all right, Per. Just relax and listen while I sing to you."

I did exactly that. I relaxed while I listened to my angel's voice. I drifted off into peaceful sleep and when I woke the next morning, I felt much better.

I became healthier with each passing day. I enjoyed the sounds of Thora's giggle when her jack-in-the-box popped, and the smells of Sven's cooking, although I was not ready to eat solid food right away.

Finally, I was strong enough to get out of bed and sit in a chair. It was painful but oh so wonderful to be out of that bed.

That was the same day Thor came to visit. Raya had told me he visited every Sunday while I slept.

When I heard Thora's gleeful screech, I knew Thor had arrived. He plucked her out of her playpen and brought her in to see me.

He took one look at me and said, "You look like you've been run over by a steamroller, Per!"

I laughed weakly. "Thanks, it's nice to see you too, Thor!"

That's how we were with each other. Thor and I took great pleasure in banter.

"Seriously, Thor, it's wonderful to see you. Raya tells me you visited every week. Thanks for that. You're our rock."

Raya came in and said to Thora, "Miss Lundgren, you're going for a nap and your godfather and Daddy can talk over old times."

Raya took the baby from Thor and stuck a biscuit in her mouth before she could protest.

After they left, Thor pulled his chair close to mine and said, "Per, I thought you were a goner, but you've pulled through like a champ!"

"If not for my team right here in this house, I'm sure I never would have pulled through. I'm a very lucky man.

"Thor, I don't remember much about getting shot, but I do remember the last time we saw each other. It was when you returned from Germany with the children."

Thor hesitated. "Per, are you sure you're ready to talk about the mission?"

"Absolutely. Have you met with Blue Tango since Karl and Hans were killed? Does Raya know that her brother was shot?"

Suddenly, I felt an intense pain in my stomach. I leaned forward until the pain subsided.

Thor said, "Let me help you back into bed."

"Maybe that's a good idea, thanks."

I said, "Sometimes I get spasms, I'm fine now. Tell me, does Raya know about Hans?

Then I got the surprise of my life. I heard Hans say, "Does Raya know what about me?"

I was speechless. He came to my bedside and gingerly touched my arm. "It would appear that you and I are not so easily killed, Per!"

I laughed and cried at the same time. "But how did you survive, Hans? Thor saw you get shot."

"Well, I'll tell you...there sure was a lot of commotion and a whale of a lot of bullets flying as I got the kids hustled to Thor at the end of the dock.

"I'm sure it looked as if I'd been shot. Actually, I tripped as I ran back to the truck and I fell on a rock. I was knocked out cold for a couple of hours, as near as I can figure.

"When I came to, Thor's ship was gone and I saw dead kids and dead Nazis all over the dockyard. I stumbled to the truck, that's when I saw Karl lying beside a stone wall...dead."

Hans continued to talk, seemingly unaware of the tears rolling down his cheeks. "Karl was one of the best human beings I've ever known. He was strong and brave and loyal. It was important to him to head up the mission for the children, especially because they were Polish like him. He would be happy to know that we saved some of them."

I said, "You're right about Karl, he was a good man. He endured so much loss at the hands of the Nazis, but he came out on top. In the end, he outwitted the bastards, as he always had. I miss him a lot."

We were silent for a moment.

Thor broke the silence. "Hans, tell Per how you got back to Berlin from the port."

"Well, that's almost funny. I was the only one left alive. I stumbled to our bullet-ridden truck; all the tires were flat. I had no idea how I would get back to Berlin.

"I sat on the end of the dock with my head in my hands. I had a terrible headache from hitting my head on the rock.

"Suddenly, a military truck sped into the dockyard right toward me. There was only the driver, no passengers. He stopped two yards from where I sat.

"He ran to me and said, "I came as fast as I heard that you guys needed help. It looks like I'm too late."

"It didn't take me long to figure out he thought I was one of the Nazis who was transporting children to the camps.

"I went along with him. I pointed to the truck that Karl and I were in. I said, "There were two guys in that truck—they stole the kids we were taking to the labor camp. We followed them here, and

then they started shooting at us. We killed them but only after they killed all our guys... except me."

The Nazi looked around the yard. "There are a lot of dead kids. Is this all of them?"

"I answered flatly, as if I didn't care, 'Yes.'"

"Then he said, 'You poor devil, come on. I'll take you back to the base. Let someone else clean up this mess.'"

"As we drove into Berlin on the way to the base at Potsdam, I said, 'Drop me on the corner here, I want to let my mother know I'm safe.'"

"He said, 'Sure, I understand. It's nice of you to think of your mother.'"

"He stopped the truck and I jumped out like my ass was on fire. I heard him yell, 'Hey! Wait! I didn't get your name! I need your name for my report!'"

"I ran around the corner and was out of sight before you could shake a stick!"

Thor and Hans laughed heartily. I stifled my laughter as much as I could; it hurt my stomach.

Hans said, "I almost feel sorry for that dumb Nazi. I can't imagine what he told his superiors when he got back to base!"

I said, "Nicely played, Hans!"

He continued. "By the time I walked the two miles to the Blue Tango Club, Henrique and the others had already heard via the grapevine what happened with our mission. They thought both Karl and I were dead. They were happy to see me and I didn't have to be the one to tell them Karl was dead.

"The rumor mill did not have our names, but of course, our team knew who was being talked about, judging by the details being bandied about.

"I don't know where I'd be right now if not for that young lieutenant being dispatched to find out what happened to the truckload of kids."

Raya said, "You, my dear brother, have a team of guardian angels looking out for you, just like my dear Per!"

Hans grinned. "I suppose you're right, Raya. You're lucky to have us!"

She ruffled his hair. "Sven has dinner for us. Go find a seat at the chef's table."

She looked at me and said, "I'll bring you some mashed food, Per."

It was bittersweet. I was happy Hans and Thor were with us, but unhappy that I could not join my friends at the dinner table.

Thor brought his dinner, along with the mush I had to eat, to my room and we ate together. We joked and laughed our way through our meal.

A short time later, Sven appeared at my bedroom door and said, "I hate to break up this party but Hans needs to get back to Berlin, and since he's going on your ship, Thor, you might want to come along."

"Right you are, Sven. I'll be right there."

"Per, I cannot tell you how happy I am that you're on the mend. We all need you, old boy!"

Hans was in the doorway. He smirked and said, "I say the same, old boy! Goodbye!"

I heard their voices outside and then the car doors closed. I listened as the car drove down the lane.

Inga and Raya were laughing and singing in the kitchen as they washed dishes.

I fell asleep smiling.

The next afternoon, Raya came to my bedside, leaned over and kissed me. "Sven is taking me to buy food for the week. Would you like anything special, Per?"

"Yes, I would love some of Sven's Swedish meatballs, mashed, of course. Please ask him to buy what he needs to make almond cake, too."

"Okay, I'll tell him. Inga is taking Thora for a little stroll down the lane. It's such a beautiful day. Maybe you and I will sit in the sun after I get back."

"That would be wonderful, Raya. I'll see you when you get back. I'm going to enjoy some light reading. Inga brought me the Diplomatic Gazette!"

She laughed that beautiful, lilting laugh I loved so much. "All right, sweetheart, see you soon."

An hour and a half later, Inga had not come back with the baby and Raya and Sven had not returned either. I was concerned about what could have happened.

I felt helpless. I could barely walk five feet without sitting down. There was no one that I could call for help...at least no one close by.

I called out for Raya...no response. I found my cane and shuffled to the living room to look out the front window and see down the lane.

What I saw sickened me beyond belief. Sven's car was in the driveway, the engine was running and the car doors were wide open.

Sven was walking toward the house carrying Inga. Raya, obviously in shock, was walking alongside, pushing Thora's empty stroller.

I flung the front door open for Sven. He came in and gently placed Inga on the couch.

Raya burst through the door and found her voice. She screamed at Inga, "What happened? Where is Thora? Who took her? Answer me NOW!"

Sven said, "Raya, give her a minute to recover herself, she's hurt."

Inga had a nasty gash on her forehead. I did the only thing I could think to do—I got a wet towel for her head.

Raya was out of her mind with panic and I admit I wasn't much better.

Sven took over. "Inga, can you tell us what happened to Thora?"

She was overcome with emotion and could barely speak.

Sven consoled her, "Take your time, Inga."

She sobbed. "I walked to the end of the lane with Thora—you know, where the dairy farm is."

Sven urged her. "Yes, go on, Inga."

"A milk truck drove toward us and I moved the stroller off the lane to let it pass."

She looked at Raya, "I'm so sorry, Raya."

Raya screeched as I had never heard. "What happened to my baby, Inga?"

Inga looked terrified and grief-stricken. "The truck stopped right beside me. The driver jumped out and hit me on the head with a wooden bat. I fell and when I looked up, I saw him take Thora out of her stroller and hand her to a woman who was in the front seat of the truck. Then the man who had hit me, drove the truck away."

Raya jumped up and ran to Inga. She began to shake Inga by the shoulders.

Sven grabbed her and said, "Raya, Raya, listen to me. We will find Thora, I promise. Please sit down so we can decide what to do next."

Raya knelt in front of my chair and put her head in my lap. Her voice was unrecognizable as she grieved aloud for our baby.

I gathered my strength, gently moved Raya aside and got up from my chair. I threw my cane across the room and stalked to my office. I slammed the door and picked up the secure phone line.

I dialed Thor's number. He answered. I said, "Thor…"

I choked up.

He said, "Per? Is that you? Is something wrong?"

"Yes." I swallowed hard. "Thora has been kidnapped. She's gone."

I will not tell you all of the words Thor used. Suffice it to say he was very angry. He said, "I'm coming up there right now. We'll find her, Per. Hold tight."

I hung up the phone and put my head on the desk. Tears of frustration and fear flooded my eyes.

Suddenly, I sat upright. Raya and Thora needed me to be strong and I would not fail them.

I stood as straight as I could and walked back to the living room. I announced that Thor was on his way to help us find Thora.

I added, "And when he gets here, we're going to the authorities to report Thora's kidnapping. I cannot afford to stay in hiding when our daughter is missing. By tomorrow, everyone will know my name and that I'm very much alive! By God, we will find the despicable people who've taken her!"

Raya quietly said, "Per, please don't do that. I can't lose you too."

"I know you're scared, Raya, but it's the only way we will be able to find Thora. I have to go to the police. The longer she's missing, the less likely it is we'll find her. Please, Raya, trust me."

"All right, Per." Her voice trailed off, *"We'll find you, little Thora."*

Thor came bounding through the front door two hours later. I was ready to go with him to the local authorities.

He looked at Raya who was sitting in a heap on the floor. He picked her up and hugged her close until she stopped shaking. He didn't need to say anything. He slowly walked over to the couch and sat her down next to Inga who had calmed down somewhat.

Thor said, *"Let's go, Per. Sven, you stay with Raya and Inga. We'll be back as soon as we can."*

Sven nodded. *"Count on me."*

At the precinct, first we had to explain why I had been in Stockholm for many months living in seclusion. We left out the part about the Nazis that Sven and I shot on our porch.

When the officer in charge learned that our baby had been kidnapped, he was not completely surprised.

He said, *"Mr. Lundgren, I'm sorry to hear that your daughter has been kidnapped. We have been in pursuit of a gang of kidnappers for many months."*

That sounded at least a little bit hopeful. I said, *"Then you must have some leads. What can we do to help?"*

He thought for a long minute. *"I will ask you to go home and write every single detail you can think of that relates to your daughter's disappearance. Your case is high priority due to your government position, Mr. Lundgren. I intend to call a conference of the Sergeant, the Inspector, the Chief Inspector in charge of our city station, the Chief Superintendent who has been overseeing the investigation of the kidnapping ring, as well as the National Police Commissioner.*

"When I have everyone assembled, I want you two to come back and give us the details of your case. I'm sure the Chief

Superintendent will have helpful information that will lead us to your daughter."

He ended the interview. "I will send word to you later."

Thor said, "Come on, Per. We have a report to write."

Back at the house, we found Raya in a catatonic state, still on the couch next to Inga. I sat down next to Raya and tried to get her attention, to no avail.

Sven asked what we learned from the police. I said, "There is an active kidnapping ring in operation. A meeting of high-ranking officials is being called. Thor and I will join them once they are gathered.

"Meanwhile, Inga, please come into my office and tell Thor and me everything you can remember about Thora's kidnapping."

Inga got up. "Of course. Do you think Raya is all right without me?"

Sven moved close to Raya. "I will be right here. Go ahead Inga."

Inga had an amazing recall of minute details regarding Thora's abduction.

Thor questioned her while I wrote her responses. After he asked the last question, he said, "That is very helpful, Inga. That's all we need for now. Thank you."

"I'll go take care of Raya now." She looked at me and said, "I would give my life for your child, Per."

I dropped my pen and went to her. I hugged her for a long time. When I let her go, I said, "This is not your fault, Inga. I do not blame you."

She breathed a sigh, then left us to review what little we knew.

No one slept that night. In the morning, Raya was still sitting on the couch. I finally got her to lie on the bed, where she fell into an exhausted sleep.

I went back to the living room.

Thor said, "A policeman just came by—they're ready for us. Let's go, Per."

We were whisked into a large conference area the moment we arrived at the precinct.

The National Police Commissioner got up from the table and introduced himself. He said, "Mr. Lundgren, I want to assure you that we will do everything in our power to find your baby.

"Please...sit. We will update you. Mr. Bjorn, you may sit next to Mr. Lundgren.

"Now, Mr. Lundgren, have you written what you've learned about the kidnapping?"

I handed him my notes. "Yes, I hope this helps."

He read my notes out loud. There were ten officials at the table. When he finished reading and looked up. "Now that we've heard the facts of the Lundgren case, I will ask the Chief Superintendent to summarize his findings from all the current kidnapping cases."

The Chief Superintendent stood and addressed me directly. His manner was matter-of-fact. "I regret to tell you, Mr. Lundgren, that what we know about this kidnapping ring is quite little. In the past eighteen months, there have been twenty-four kidnappings similar to the kidnapping of your baby.

"The children are always taken when they're away from their home—at a playground or a store, usually when their caretaker is momentarily distracted, like in your case."

I stood and interrupted him. "I beg your pardon, but my baby girl's caretaker was NOT distracted. She was hit on the head with a bat and then my baby was taken from her stroller! If you had paid attention to the notes just read, you would know that!"

Unaffected by my outburst, he said, "Now, if I may continue, in all the cases, other than the Lundgren case, the kidnapper was not seen. All the children taken were under the age of two. That leads us to believe that this ring of criminals is connected to another group that specializes in illegal adoptions.

I interrupted him again. "Have any parents been contacted for a ransom?"

"No ransom requests, Mr. Lundgren. Thank you for meeting us. We will keep you updated."

Obviously, we'd been dismissed but I was not convinced I had adequately impressed upon that pompous ass the importance of finding Thora right away.

*Still standing, I was not ready to leave. "Now you listen to
ME..."*

*Thor grabbed my arm. "Per, let them do their job. We should go
home."*

I looked at the Chief Superintendent and back at Thor.

"I suppose you're right, Thor. Raya needs me."

Thor drove me home—to the house with the empty crib.

*Raya was not the same as she'd been before Thora was taken.
The light was gone from her eyes and she lived in a fantasy world.
She talked to Thora all day.*

*On the day Raya's breast milk dried up completely, she walked
outside, fell on the grass and suffered a massive heart attack.*

*I had a funeral for her in the church I had attended as a child—the
church where I had intended to marry Raya. I was desperately
bereft.*

*There never was any evidence that led the police to find our beloved
Thora. It was presumed she was adopted by a couple out of the
country, most likely Canada or the United States.*

I was still weak and had not recovered from the bullet wound.

*Sven said, "Per, now that you don't have to stay in hiding, you
should go to the hospital for medical treatment."*

*I agreed. I wanted to recover completely so I could find Thora.
I underwent many tests at the hospital to find the cause of my
continued weakness.*

*I was referred to a surgeon. He told me I needed surgery to
attempt to repair the damage in my abdomen.*

I asked what the odds of success were.

*He said, "You have a ten percent chance of surviving the
surgery, given your current condition."*

"How soon can the surgery be done?"

*"It can be scheduled this afternoon. Are you sure you want to
take this chance?"*

"Yes, I'm sure. I have to take any chance there is."

*In my mind's eye, I can still see the faces of my friends as I was
wheeled into the operating room.*

Thor, Sven, Inga and Hans watched as I disappeared behind the swinging doors.

During surgery, my heart stopped beating. I too, died of a broken heart.

Chapter Twenty-One

SURPRISES

From the time Seth knew Julia would be going to Canada, they spent every night together.

Seth had a special plan for their last evening. As he left for work that morning, he said, "Jules, don't cook tonight. I made dinner reservations for us."

"That's a great idea, Seth. Are you going to tell me where we're dining?"

"Don't you want to be surprised?"

She kissed him. "I love your kind of surprises. Don't tell me. I'll guess!"

He laughed and kissed her in return. "You'll never guess this surprise! I'll see you after work, Jules."

"Okay, sweetheart. See you later."

Julia sat at her desk to re-read, for the tenth time, the last parts of her journal. It seemed strange that there was nothing else to write.

She cried every time she read about the innocent children who were shot, just before being rescued by Thor.

She sobbed for her uncle's loss of his soulmate and their beloved Thora.

She thought aloud, "It's so unfair that Thora was kidnapped when the Blue Tango team worked so hard to save other people's children."

A wistful sigh wafted through the air. "Yes, Julia, it was unfair. Sometimes life is not fair, especially during war.

"Now you know why it was important for me to finish my story before you and Tom begin your investigation."

"Uncle Per, maybe we will be able to find the family who adopted Thora!"

"That's very unlikely, Julia. But if anyone can find where she was taken, it's you.

"You also have Thor's log with the names of the Polish children our team was able to rescue. Those children were old enough to say where they were from and who their parents were.

Julia said, "While we're on the subject of Thor's log, I thought maybe Thor Jr. would like to read my journal."

"I'm sure he would, Julia. My relationship with his father was, as you know, a special one. Tom really should have access to the information in your journal too."

"But Uncle Per, how can I let them read my journal without telling them I got the information from my dead uncle?"

"You can say that in the process of closing your apartment, you found a journal written by me. How does that sound?"

"That's a great idea! You're a genius, Uncle Per!"

"And you, dear Julia, soothe my soul just by being you. Now go make copies of our journal."

She gathered up the precious journal with its dog-eared pages and made copies for Seth, Tom and Thor Jr. She remembered to make a copy of the pages Javier had not read yet.

While her copier worked, she thought about the reaction each of the recipients would have. Undoubtedly, they'd become emotional, especially about the suffering of the children. But they would each deal with it differently.

Thor Jr. would feel great pride for his father's role during the war; Javier would relate to the children because of his own experiences; Tom would use his anger to fuel the fire already lit toward the Nazis. And Seth, dear Seth, would be amazed that Julia channeled the events he would read in the journal. If Javier suspected that was the case, he probably wouldn't be surprised.

Julia called Thor's office and left a message with his haughty secretary saying she'd like an hour of Mr. Bjorn's time that afternoon.

The secretary's response was, "Do you mean *this* afternoon? Because if so, you're out of luck. Mr. Bjorn is very busy today. I'll let you know." Click.

Julia hung up the phone and rolled her eyes. She wondered why Thor would keep such an unpleasant person on his staff.

In the next instant, her phone rang. It was the secretary. "Mr. Bjorn will see you as soon as you can get here. You should hurry, Miss Hamilton." Click.

She buzzed Javier in the lobby. "Yes, Julia, what can I do for you this fine day?"

How I'll miss this wonderful man.

"Javier, I have the last portion of my journal for you to read. Can you come and pick it up when you have a minute?"

"Of course, I'll be up directly."

When Javier arrived, she threw her arms around him.

"What is this about, Julia? What's wrong?"

She let go of him and stepped back. "I will miss you, Javier. But don't mind me; I just have cold feet about leaving tomorrow. Here is the journal. I won't keep you from your work. Thank you for everything, Javier."

"Thank you for sharing with me, Julia. But I must ask you, why have you stopped writing your journal?"

"Just read it, dear man. You will understand."

"All right then, have a pleasant trip, Julia."

She closed the door and thought, *I hate goodbyes!*

Next, she wrapped Seth's copy in a map of Central Park, she thought it was appropriate. She taped a note on the top, "Do Not Open Until Tomorrow." She didn't know why, but she didn't want him to read it until after she was gone.

Tom's copy fit in an outside pocket of her suitcase.

Lastly, she lovingly wrapped her original journal in pink and blue tissue paper and then tied it with pink ribbon. She remembered the christening gift Thor Sr. gave to baby Thora—it too, was wrapped with pink ribbon.

She sighed deeply and thought of the baby ripped away from her family and sold to people who knew nothing about her.

A wave of sorrow swept through her heart and into her gut, where it transformed into anger like none she'd ever felt. Julia realized this level of emotion could only be due to her compassion and empathy for her Uncle Per and Raya. Those emotions would be tools to use to discover what happened to Thora.

Julia quickly dressed in a black business suit softened with a rose-colored silk scarf and pink diamond earrings. She chose flats rather than heels. She could walk faster that way.

Thor met her in the hallway outside the library where they had their first meeting. He was wearing an overcoat and carrying a fat briefcase.

"Julia, I'm sorry I can't stay and talk with you. I've just gotten word that there's a problem in one of my satellite offices. I'm flying out right away. Tell me what you want to talk about, as we walk."

She followed him into a private elevator. "Thor, I found a journal written by my Uncle Per and I thought you should read it. There's a lot of information about your father's involvement in helping to save children during the war."

She handed the journal to him.

"Really? You just found it now?" He gave her the same squinty look Thor Sr. had given to her Uncle Per when he agreed not to be involved in another mission.

"Yes, really." She said it without an abundance of conviction.

"Julia, you are a gem! I will read the journal on my way to Canada. Thank you."

He hugged her and then rushed off to catch his limousine.

"You're going to Canada?" He didn't hear her question.

She wondered if it was a coincidence that Thor was headed to Canada when Tom was already in Canada and she would be there the next day.

Her thought was interrupted by the chirp of her cell phone. Seth said, "I just wanted to make sure you remember that we're going out to dinner tonight, Jules."

She laughed and said, "Of course I remember, silly. I'll see you later. Thanks for calling!"

Her mood immediately uplifted as she thought about Seth.

By the time she got back to her apartment, Javier had gone home for the day. She imagined him sitting in his easy chair, reading the journal and wiping his eyes occasionally.

It was time to get dressed for dinner. She walked into her dressing room and opened the double doors to her closet.

She smiled as she chose black palazzo pants and a matching bolero jacket. Next, she went to her scarf drawer and picked out two scarves—one casual, the other dressy.

Julia stood in front of the mirrored wall and switched it to evening light. Either scarf would do nicely. She folded the casual one into her Hermes bag and wrapped the more formal one around her neck.

Seth rang her intercom at six PM. "Hi, Jules, if you're ready, come down to the lobby. I'll hail a cab."

"Okay, I'll be there in a jiffy."

When the elevator opened into the lobby, Seth stood in front of her. He kissed her and presented an orchid corsage. "Let the surprises begin, Jules!"

"Oh, Seth, it's beautiful, thank you!"

"You're beautiful, Jules. Now, come along with me, your carriage, I mean your cab, awaits!"

They got into the cab and the driver turned onto 5th Avenue without waiting for instructions as to where they were going.

Julia looked at Seth for an answer and he grinned like a Cheshire cat.

She smiled at him, "Looks like I'm the only one who doesn't know where we're going!"

"That's right, Julia...you'll see, just sit back and enjoy the scenery."

And so, she did just that. They rode through Central Park on the 79th Street Traverse Road. As they passed Belvedere Castle and Delacorte Theater, they reminisced about the festival where she met Thor.

She thought how different her life was now and how happy she was with Seth.

The cab crossed over Central Park West and came to a stop. Seth looked at her. "This is where we get out, Jules."

She waited at the curb while he paid the fare. She looked in every direction and could not imagine where the restaurant could be.

Then Seth put his arm around her shoulders and led her into the lobby of the Haydn Planetarium. He said, "Wait here for a minute, I'll be right back."

Julia was surprised for sure. The planetarium was not open and no one was around.

Seth held the door to the theater open. "Come on, Jules, let's go in."

He led her into the planetarium. The only light came from a flashlight Seth shined on the floor to show the way. They walked onto a stage in the center of the theater. Seth said, "Sit down on the blanket, Jules."

"Blanket? What?" She could barely see the large, fluffy blanket spread out on the wooden floor.

She sat. Before she could ask what was happening, she heard the click of a projector.

Seth said, "Look up...look up at the sky."

The sight over their heads was awe-inspiring. Seth sat next to her and they lay on their backs to take in the entire view.

She whispered, "Seth, this is a wonderful surprise!"

He kissed her. "Shhh."

The planisphere on the huge overhead dome began to revolve slowly.

Seth said, "There's the Orion constellation...see, its stars have different colors. That's because they're different temperatures. The blue ones are hot and the red ones are cooler."

She listened with interest.

"The map being shown now is the spring sky." He pointed out Ursa Major and Ursa Minor in the northern sky. "And over there is the Leo constellation. Look for the double star just at the back of the lion's neck. Can you see it?"

"I don't think so. No, I don't see it."

In the darkness, Seth put his arm around her and put his face right next to hers. He pointed toward the double star and said, "Now look past the tip of my finger."

"I see it! I see it!"

"Okay, good. Now look at me."

She turned her face to his and he kissed her again.

She said, "That was an unexpected delight."

He turned back toward the night sky and said, "There are more surprises to come tonight."

Seth took great joy in teaching Julia about the stars and the constellations. He explained that the Virgo constellation contains as many as 2,000 galaxies. "One of the largest galaxies known is M87, in the core of Virgo's galaxies. The cool thing about M87 is there's a black hole in its core and it's about six *billion* times bigger than our Sun!"

"That's amazing! What exactly is a black hole, Seth?"

"Well, scientists disagree about what a black hole is, but most define it as an object with intense gravity that does not allow light to escape from it, thus the term black hole. When material is ejected from a black hole, it travels at almost the speed of light."

Julia said, "Is that the constellation Libra over there past Virgo?"

"Yes, it is."

"Oh, and there's another double star. Do you know its name, Seth?"

"*That* is Izar and it's actually in the Boötes constellation, sometimes referred to as Boo for short. It's interesting to note that stars, like people, don't live forever. The low-mass stars are red or yellow and on their way to dying. The higher mass stars, or blue stars, are brighter and have a longer life."

"How do you know so much about astronomy, Seth?"

"I took a course at Columbia. The professor who taught the course got a kick out of introducing students to the 'wonders of the night sky' as he put it."

"I took an astronomy course too," she said. "But it was a long time ago and I don't remember much."

"Well then, it's a good thing you have me. I'll tell you anything you want to know. Ask away, Jules."

She thought for a moment. "Okay, here's a question: What was formerly the largest constellation before it split into three constellations?"

"Hmm...can I have a hint?"

"All right, one hint, it's in the Milky Way."

"Ya got me on that one, Jules. What's the answer?"

"Argo Navis," she announced proudly.

Seth laughed and said, "Oh, are you referring to the discovery by the French astronomer Nicholas Lacaille, who named the three constellations that Argo Navis split into? I believe the names are Vela, Carina and Puppis."

She poked his arm, "Oh, you! You knew the answer all along!"

He pretended to be hurt by the poke. "Now look what you've done, Julia. You made me knock over our dinner basket!"

Julia hadn't seen the wicker basket beside the blanket.

"Oh! We're having a picnic here under the stars? Seth, how did you manage all of this?"

"The manager is a personal friend. I designed his family compound in the Poconos and he wanted to repay me. I told him all about you, Julia, and why tonight was so important to me...to us."

Julia sat up. "Because I'm leaving tomorrow?"

"Sort of." He kneeled in front of her. "Julia Hamilton, will you marry me?"

Without hesitation, she said, "Yes, I will marry you, Seth!"

He handed her a small black velvet box.

She thought, *I won't be able to see my engagement ring.*

However, it *was* a night of surprises. When she flipped the box open, a tiny light illuminated the most incredible diamond ring she'd ever seen.

Tears flooded her eyes. "Seth, it's truly beautiful...I love it."

"When I saw this ring, I knew it was yours. The jeweler told me that it's a one-of-a-kind cut and setting. It was designed by a Swedish craftsman; 'LL' is engraved inside - that's his mark."

"It's perfect, Seth. I will cherish it always. I love you."

He kissed her. "And I love you, Julia. Are you hungry? I sure am, let's eat!"

He pulled a little flashlight out of the basket and produced a bottle of champagne.

Julia said, "Wow, you thought of everything!"

He popped the cork and said, "Quick, look up!"

She looked up and saw a brilliant meteor shower. "How did you do that?"

"I can't give away all my secrets. I'll just tell you that *this* meteor shower has never been seen until now, and the name of it is 'Jules.'"

She kissed him and said, "You make me happy."

Seth laughed. "That's my plan. Let's eat, drink and be merry!"

They watched the Jules meteor shower as they enjoyed Swedish meatball sandwiches on rye bread.

Seth poured more champagne. "Did you know there's a Swedish deli right around the corner from your apartment?"

"No, but apparently you did. These meatballs are *de*-licious!"

When they finished their sandwiches and the bubbly, Seth said, "We'd better get out of here before it starts to rain. Come on, Jules, I'll pack up the basket while you fold the blanket! Hurry!"

"What are you talking about? It's not going to rain inside! You've had too much bubbly, Seth!"

Just then, she touched her nose. It felt like a raindrop fell on it. Then her cheeks got wet.

Seth quickly packed the basket.

She began to believe him and picked up the blanket.

Seth said, "Here, you'll need this."

He handed her a full-length hooded rain slicker and she gladly put it on. He already had a rain slicker on—the lemon-yellow color glowed in the dark.

Seth was practically beside himself with glee. He put the squirt gun back into his pocket.

They exited the planetarium into a spring rainstorm. They giggled like children in an amusement park.

"Now I know you can make it rain, Seth, but can you make it stop?"

"That surprise is for another night, Jules."

They stood on the corner and kissed in the rain.

Julia said, "Let's go home, I have something for you."

"You'll get no argument from me. I'll hail a cab."

Julia poured them both a cup of French roast decaf. She sat next to Seth at the kitchen table.

He took her hand, "Julia, I want us to be married as soon as you return from Canada. Do you agree?"

"Yes, of course I do, Seth. But be prepared because I have a few surprises of my own that I will unleash upon our wedding celebration!"

"I would expect nothing less, Jules. It sounds like fun! Now, you said you have something to give me?"

"Yes. I'll get it."

She came back with the package that was wrapped in the map of Central Park. "You can open it after I leave tomorrow."

He took the package from her. "Thank you." He had a pretty good idea what he held in his hands.

The last thing Seth said as he left that night was, "Leave your diamond in the safe here, but don't forget that you're engaged to marry *me*!"

"Don't worry, sweetheart. I would never forget!"

Their last kiss was searingly bittersweet.

The next morning, Julia picked up the car keys that mysteriously appeared outside her apartment door. She locked the door and listened as the deadbolt clicked into place.

She took a moment to make sure she had everything she needed. The secure cell phone was the most important item. She patted her coat pocket to confirm that it was there.

The black BMW was parked exactly where Tom said it would be. She stashed her luggage in the trunk, then got behind the wheel, started the engine, and pulled away from the curb.

"We're off!" she said aloud.

Chapter Twenty-Two

THE INVESTIGATION BEGINS

Julia knew the route from Manhattan to Montreal was pretty much a straight shot. However, she encountered a construction detour in Yonkers that led east to the Cross County Expressway instead of north to the New York State Thruway.

The good news was that the rush hour traffic was headed in the opposite direction.

Two hours later, she crossed the Tappan Zee Bridge over the Hudson River. She traveled as slowly as she could, to catch a glimpse of the spires of Lyndhurst Mansion over the treetops. She knew Seth would admire the fabulous Gothic Revival architecture of the mansion. *Maybe we'll tour the Lyndhurst sometime,* she thought.

It was a clear day and she could see the Catskill Mountains in the distance. She smiled as she remembered the vacation she and her husband, Jed, enjoyed before he was deployed. They'd rented a cabin on a lake near Monticello. She recalled the scent of the pine trees—intoxicating and fresh. Every evening, they sat on the old wooden dock and watched the sunset while they wiggled their toes in the water.

Julia's daydream of days gone by was cut short when her secure cell phone rang. She pressed the speaker button. "Hi Tom. How are you today?"

"I've been better, Julia. We have a change of plans. Thor and I are working on a situation in Montreal and I won't be able to meet you at the border. You'll have to drive to the hotel."

"No problem, Tom. What's the address of the hotel? I'll find it."

He explained the directions from the border and across the bridge to Montreal, then to the Hotel Julien.

Since she didn't have to meet Tom at the border, Julia decided to slow her pace and stop for breakfast at a service area outside of Albany.

She wanted a meal, so she went to the one restaurant with a cook and a wait staff. She ordered a spinach omelet, rye toast and a fresh cup of hot coffee.

Someone left a copy of USA TODAY at the table next to her, so she got up to get it and noticed a man watching her closely. He had light hair, a medium build and dressed casually. He glared at Julia as if she'd murdered his dog.

She then sat with her back to him and focused on the newspaper.

The waitress brought her breakfast, leaned close and said, "Excuse me, Miss, but do you know that man sitting behind you over there?"

She knew who the waitress referred to. She said, "No. Why do you ask?"

"Only because he keeps staring at your back. He's kind of scary if you ask me."

"Oh, he's probably mad at someone who looks like me. I don't think there's any reason to worry, but thanks for mentioning it."

"No problem, Miss. Here's your check. Just let me know if you want anything else."

"Thank you," Julia said.

Julia was no longer comfortable being alone. She ate quickly and drank only half of her coffee.

As she got up to leave, she noticed the "watcher" was gone.

She thought how silly she was to worry about a stranger looking at her. She leisurely walked through the parking lot. When she got in her car, she saw the man again. He was behind the wheel of a black Crown Victoria, like the New York State troopers used to drive before they upgraded to the Ford Taurus.

"Who *is* that man?" she wondered aloud. She watched as his car entered the Thruway and headed north. She waited fifteen minutes before heading in the same direction.

For the next four hours, she was on the lookout for the Crown Vic. She didn't relax her guard until she reached Canada.

From the Champlain Bridge, she could see her destination. The Hotel Julien was one of the tallest buildings in downtown Montreal.

She drove into the underground parking garage. She glanced in the rearview mirror as she rounded the first bend. The coast was clear.

Her cell phone chirped. "Hi Tom, I just parked in the hotel's garage."

"Great, leave your luggage in the car and I'll get it later. Thor and I are in the lounge. You can find us there."

"All right, I'll see you in a minute."

Julia checked the perimeter and the interior of the elevator before she stepped in.

Tom saw her enter the lounge and stood to greet her. Immediately, she felt a knot in her stomach. The last time she saw him replayed in her mind—when he left her apartment in a rage. She smiled and shook his hand.

Tom's smile disappeared with her impersonal greeting. He led her to a corner booth.

Thor got up and hugged her. "Julia, I'm glad you're here. Have a seat; we'll get to the matter at hand. Look at the man sitting at the bar facing us, but don't be conspicuous."

She turned slightly to look at the man, then abruptly turned back to Thor and Tom. "*That's* the man who was watching me! Who the hell *is* he?"

Tom jerked forward, "What do you mean he was watching you?"

"He sat staring at me in the restaurant that I stopped at outside of Albany. Even the waitress mentioned him to me. Who *is* he?"

Thor answered. "He is a member of the Nazi party."

She looked at Tom. "That's right, Julia. His mission is to assure no one finds the children who were kidnapped by the Nazis during the war and sold to couples in North America."

"That doesn't make sense. Those children would be more than seventy-five years old by now! What interest could they possibly have?"

Thor said, "The Nazi party is active all over the world. Baby marketing is a prime source of financial stability. Our informants tell us that this is the same organization of kidnappers that was in operation throughout the Netherlands and Europe in the 1940s when Thora was taken.

"The man who followed you is very dangerous, Julia. He's part of a team sent to make sure that we do not expose their operation. We believe that the man who is sitting right over there is second in command. He'll stop at nothing to protect his corporation. Tom heard about the team from his confidential informant here in Montreal. That's why I'm here.

"It will take all three of us to break through the invisible walls that have been built around their corporate structure and maybe find where Thora was taken."

Thor continued, "I read your journal, Julia. I felt as if my father was telling me that we're very close to finding her."

Tom added, "Don't forget about the eight Polish children Blue Tango saved, Thor. We may find out where they ended up on this side of the pond."

Julia said, "How did you know about the Polish children who were saved, Tom? I haven't given you a copy of the journal yet."

"Thor handed me his copy the second he laid eyes on me. He said I should read it right then. When I read it, I felt as if your Uncle Per was speaking in the present. It was a little bit eerie."

Julia heard her uncle's signature chuckle. She thought she was the only one to hear it. Although Thor hesitated for a moment.

She said, "I know exactly what you mean, Tom. As I wrote the journal, I felt it all…the suspense, the intrigue, the glory of missions accomplished and the extreme sense of loss, especially regarding the children.

"I never met my Uncle Per, but I know he would want us to finish what he began…to find the children the team saved from the Nazis. However, he would also want us to find where his baby was taken. If by chance she's still alive, we will be able to tell her about her real parents."

Tom was skeptical. "That's 'pie in the sky,' Julia."

She smiled. "We'll see."

Thor agreed. "Indeed, we will. Now let's make a game plan. Julia, that Nazi will continue to follow you, so tomorrow you visit the World War II museum and lead him there. Tom and I will follow up on the leads he's been working. We will meet back here at one PM and compare notes. Tom, do you have anything to add?"

"No, you covered everything, Thor. What do you say we get out of here and find a restaurant for dinner?"

Julia grinned. "Maybe we'll find a French restaurant."

They all laughed.

Thor leaned in between Tom and Julia and whispered, "There's a French restaurant next door to the hotel. If we hurry, we'll lose the Nazi. We'll walk out together and take the elevator to the parking level. Even if he sees where the elevator takes us, he won't see us make a quick left and duck into the restaurant."

"Good plan. Let's do it," Tom said.

Their five-course dinner was served on Limoges china. To begin, they shared a fromage platter, and then they each had French onion soup followed by a goat cheese salad. The main entrée consisted of poulet topped with lemon and caper sauce for Julia, steak tartare for Thor and mussels Provençal with tomato, garlic and basil sauce for Tom. The side dishes of ratatouille, mashed potatoes and steamed vegetables were served family style.

By the time they reached the final course, they were too full for dessert. Julia ordered a plate of fresh berries to share.

Thor ordered Benedictine brandy, and being a world traveler, he told them all about the brandy. "There are only three people on earth at any one time with the complete recipe. It was created by a Benedictine monk, Don Bernardo Vincelli, in 1510. It's reported to contain twenty-seven plant extracts and spices."

"I've never tried it before, but I like it, "Julia said. "It tastes sweet like cognac."

Julia took advantage of a lull in the conversation. She looked at Tom and said, "Seth has asked me to marry him and I said yes."

Tom's face dropped. He looked as if she spoke a language that he didn't understand.

"Why, that's wonderful news," Thor said. "I *like* that young man, Julia!"

"Thank you, Thor."

They looked at Tom for a response. He gulped down the last of his coffee and got up from the table. "Congratulations, Julia. I'm going back to the room. I'll see you two later."

Julia was silent until Tom walked away. "I never meant to hurt him," she said.

"I know, Julia. He'll get over it. I think he was surprised to hear that you're getting married so soon after you two broke up."

"I'm sure you're right, Thor. I had to tell him before he got the idea that he and I would pick up where we left off. I hope our working relationship won't be affected."

Thor touched her hand. "Everything will be fine, Julia. Tom needs some time, and he'll be too busy to think about it."

"We share a hotel suite with three bedrooms with separate baths, so you two won't necessarily have to bump into each other.

"The museum that you'll go to doesn't open until ten tomorrow, so you can sleep late. Tom and I plan to leave by six. By the time we rendezvous for lunch, he'll be over the shock."

"All right, Thor. I hope you're right."

Her secure cell phone chirped and she said the obvious, "It's Tom."

Tom said, "Julia, would you meet me in the hotel ballroom on the mezzanine level?"

"Sure. I'll be right there."

"Tom wants to meet me in the hotel ballroom. Do you mind if I leave you here, Thor?"

"Of course, you run along. I think I will take in the sights right here." He smiled and glanced at an attractive brunette dining alone.

"Thor, you enjoy yourself and thank you for dinner. I'll see you tomorrow."

"Good night, sweetie."

Thor watched as she walked away. He hoped that Tom was not going to give her a hard time about marrying Seth.

Julia followed the signs to the ballroom. Tom was sitting at a table for two lit by a single candle. The room was dark and no one was around. She took a deep breath and walked to where he sat.

He got up and pulled a chair out for her. "Please sit down, Julia. Thank you for coming."

Her mind was in overdrive as she tried to figure out why he wanted to talk to her in private. She folded her hands on the table and waited for him to speak.

"Julia, I will get to the point." Then he paused and opened his closed fist. In his hand he held a diamond ring. It glistened in the light of the candle.

"This was my grandmother's ring. She wanted me to give it to the girl who I love as dearly as her husband loved her. *You* are that girl, Julia. I know you said yes to Seth, but I hope I can change your mind. I love you, Julia."

"Tom, I don't know what to say."

"Just tell me you'll think about it, Julia."

"I can't do that, Tom. I don't want you to think there's a chance for us, there simply isn't. A few months ago, I would have said yes without hesitation. But now, I've found that not only do I love Seth, I *like* him. We enjoy each other. Our relationship works perfectly and we are both very happy."

Tom put the ring in his pocket. "I understand what you're saying and I should have seen this coming. The way Seth looks at you tells the whole story—at least on his part.

"I will be a gentleman and wish you happiness, Julia. However, you should know that I believe that we are meant to be together and I intend to wait until you come back to me."

He left her sitting alone.

She thought, *Well, it's not very gentlemanly to leave a lady sitting in the dark!*

She sighed deeply and walked to the lobby where she found Thor sitting on a sofa with the brunette he'd eyed at the restaurant.

He stood when he saw her. "Ah, Julia, let me introduce you to Claudette Pulaski. Claudette, this is Julia Hamilton who I was just telling you about."

Claudette spoke with an elegant French accent, "Oh, yes, Julia, it's so nice to meet you."

Julia said, "It's very nice to meet you too, Claudette. Are you from Quebec?"

"No, no. I'm originally from France. I came here with my parents in 1940 to get away from the war."

"That's interesting. What part of France are you from?"

"I am from the Alsace region—a little town not far from the Swiss border."

Wide-eyed, Julia looked at Thor. He was all smiles. She looked back at Claudette and asked, "By any chance would your parents be Marie and Franz from Alsace?"

Claudette's mouth dropped open. She said, "Sacre bleu! How did you know?"

"Well, I just read my uncle's journal. He wrote about his team rescuing some people from a town in the Alsace region in 1940…and so I thought to ask about your parents."

"Ah, then your uncle is Per Lundgren—our savior! He told us he would take us to safety. We were all so scared, Julia. Oh, and then I remember there was a little boy whom the team rescued before they found us. I think his name was…wait, I'll remember…Javier, yes, that was his name. My mother cared for him throughout the journey. His parents had been taken by the Nazis and he hid in an attic space for two days! Can you just imagine how terrified he must have been, Julia?"

"Oh, I have to sit down," Julia said. She took a tissue from her purse and dried her eyes.

Claudette said, "I'm sorry, I didn't mean to upset you, Julia."

"I think she's crying from happiness, Claudette. You see, Julia knows Javier. He lives in New York City."

"He does? I would love to see him again! Oh, my parents would be so happy. I wish they were alive to hear this news! We lost track of Javier as soon as we got to Canada. An American couple took him in. They lived on a farm in New York State, I think."

Julia recovered herself. "Claudette, you look so young, are you and Javier the same age?"

"Yes, we were both three years of age in 1940. If I look young, it's because I've had a good life. My husband, God rest his soul, took very good care of me. Henrique died ten years ago. I miss him terribly."

Thor said, "Please tell us about Henrique, Claudette."

"I met him at a museum here in Montreal when I was seventeen. He was tall and handsome and oh, so charming. He was fifteen years older than me and my parents wouldn't allow me to date until I was eighteen, so he would come for dinner every Sunday for a whole year.

"He loved my Mama's cooking. He said it reminded him of his Mama's cooking. He was Polish and rescued from the Nazis, too."

Julia looked at Thor. Tears were dripping down his face.

Julia said, "Claudette, tell us how your husband was saved from the Nazis."

"Well, it's quite a miracle that he and the other children survived. They'd been captured by the Nazis and taken to a facility in Germany where the Nazis separated those with Aryan traits and rejected those without those traits.

"Henrique was in the group that was rejected; his hair was too dark. He and some others who'd been rejected were put into a truck to be taken to a labor camp. However, a couple of guys dressed as Nazis saved them, put them on a ship and they were taken to Sweden. From there, a steamship took them to Nova Scotia, where they met other refugees from Europe."

Claudette hesitated, then looked at Thor. "Do you know of this Swedish ship captain? I think my husband called him Thor, just like you, Thor!"

"Yes, Claudette, my father was the Swedish captain. I am Thor Bjorn, Jr. My father worked with Per and the Blue Tango team to save the children who were being taken to camps. Your husband's name is in the ship's log my father kept. Please, continue telling us about Henrique."

"All right. The children were old enough to work and they earned their keep by fishing or farming in Nova Scotia. Henrique was very resourceful, and he knew how to speak French. After a year, he'd saved enough from his monthly wages to travel to Montreal and get a job in the university cafeteria. A benefit of that job was free tuition, so he studied finance. Four years later, he went into banking.

"He became very successful and soon opened a commercial mortgage company. Many of the buildings you see in Montreal were financed by Henrique's company.

"He never forgot those who were rescued with him. He hired two of the girls and three of the boys to work in his company.

"We had no children, and they became our family. We celebrated birthdays and holidays in the fine home Henrique had built for us in the 1970s."

She paused, "Oh, I've talked too long. It's late and I must be going. Perhaps you two would like to join me for dinner at my home the day after tomorrow?"

Thor said, "We'd love to, Claudette. Do you mind if our associate, Tom, joins us?"

He looked at Julia and said, "Wouldn't that be wonderful?"

She nodded.

Claudette said, "Of course, I'm accustomed to entertaining. Please do bring Tom with you. And maybe some of Henrique's friends will join us too. Oh, this will be such fun!"

Julia said, "It will be delightful, Claudette. It has been a pleasure to meet you."

"The pleasure has been all mine, my dear. Thor tells me you are engaged to be married. Where is your fiancé? It wouldn't be this Tom fellow, would it?"

"He wishes it were so!" Thor said.

Julia ignored the comment. "No, Claudette, my fiancé is at home in Manhattan."

Thor got up and said, "I'll hail a cab for you, Claudette."

"No need, my driver is around the corner. He will take me home."

She hugged Julia, offered her hand to Thor and said, "Until we meet again."

Thor sat on the sofa in the lobby with Julia. "Well, now, it looks as if meeting Claudette has made our job a little easier, Julia. Can you believe our good luck—discovering that Claudette was part of the group rescued from France was amazing enough. But *then* to find that she ended up marrying a Polish boy, the same team rescued from Germany!"

"No kidding, Thor! I cannot wait to tell Javier we found the family he was rescued with! This is simply mind-blowing! By the way, what drew you to introduce yourself to Claudette, Thor?"

He grinned. "Julia, I'm surprised that you, of all people, would ask me such a question. I heard my father's voice, of course. He told me she was someone special and that I should meet her."

Thor winked at Julia. "And so, you are not the only one who hears the voice of a dead relative."

"Oh, Thor, you knew that the journal was written by me, didn't you?"

"It wasn't difficult to figure. Besides, I've come to know you, as well as my father knew your Uncle Per. They were in sync with each other."

He switched the topic. "Oh, what did Tom want to talk to you about?"

"I asked her to marry me. She said 'No.'" Tom was behind them. He had seen them in the lobby as he came from the lounge.

Thor's response was simply, "Oh."

Then he said, "Tom, let me tell you who I just introduced Julia to."

Thor related Claudette's story to Tom, then Henrique's story. When he finished, Tom said, "What a stroke of luck, Thor. How did you know to introduce yourself to Claudette?"

"Oh, just a hunch," Thor said.

Thor and Julia exchanged glances.

Tom smiled. "Maybe you'll have a hunch as to how we might connect with the family that adopted Thora."

Thor stretched and yawned like a cat. "Maybe I will, but right now I have a hunch it's time for all of us to get some sleep."

"I'm for that!" Julia chimed in.

No one spoke as the elevator took them to the twelfth floor. Thor led the way to their suite, opened the door, and said, "Julia, you take the first bedroom on the left. Sleep well."

"Thanks, you sleep well too, Thor."

Thor said, "Tom, I'll see you at six for breakfast. Good night."

Tom said, "Right, Thor. See you in the morning."

Tom looked at her expectantly. When he realized she had nothing to say to him, he said, "Sleep well, Julia. I had your luggage put in your room."

She didn't look at him. "Thank you, Tom. Good night."

Before Julia went to sleep, she called Seth. He answered immediately, "Jules! I miss you. When are you coming home?"

She laughed. "Sweetheart, I just got here. However, I can tell you that I don't expect to be here long. We've had a very fortuitous meeting this evening!"

"That's great news! I read your journal, and now I can't wait to hear all about your investigation.

"How are Thor and Tom?"

"Thor's fine." She hesitated.

"What's wrong, Jules?"

They did not keep secrets from each other. Julia said, "Tom proposed to me tonight."

He didn't give her a chance to continue. "What the hell! Didn't you tell him we're engaged? What *did* you tell him, Julia?"

"He proposed after I told him I accepted your marriage proposal."

"I'm sorry, Jules. I got a little hot under the collar for a minute. I'm glad you told me. I'm sure you can handle Tom."

"Yes, I can handle him, sweetheart. I'm tired and I'm going to sleep. It's your bedtime too. Good night, Seth."

"Good night, Jules. I love you."

"I love you, too, Seth."

Tom's room was next to Julia's. He heard her conversation with Seth.

Chapter Twenty-Three

THE INVESTIGATION CONTINUES

Tom was already in the hotel café when Thor got there. "Good morning, Thor. Did you sleep well?"

"I certainly did, despite the excitement of meeting Claudette last night. How did you sleep, Tom?"

"I didn't sleep a wink...too much on my mind. There will be plenty of time to sleep when I'm dead." He laughed a vacant laugh.

Thor didn't respond. He knew what was on Tom's mind.

Thor looked up just as the Nazi who'd followed Julia walked into the café. He was wearing golf clothes. Apparently, it was his warped way of not calling attention to his true purpose.

Tom saw him at the same time and said, "Looks like we will have company on our travels today."

"Yeah, I thought for sure he'd wait to follow Julia to the museum. That's bad luck for us."

Tom chuckled as he remembered reading Julia's journal. "Too bad we don't have Wilhelm with us to cast an astrology chart so we'd know what the Nazi is likely to do."

"You're right, Tom. I'm sure the bastards are still using occult means. We may not understand the occult, but I know someone who has an abundance of intuitive ability. Why don't you give her a call, Tom?"

"Good idea, Thor." Tom pressed speed dial for Julia. She answered right away.

"How are you today, Tom?"

He answered flatly, "Fine. Thor and I think you should come along with us today, Julia."

She stood beside their table and said, "I agree. I'd like a cup of coffee, please."

Thor laughed when Tom's mouth dropped open. "See what I mean, Tom?"

Thor pulled a chair out for her.

Julia said, "Thank you, Thor. Did you two think I would sleep late and not help you find Thora?"

Tom scratched his head absentmindedly. "You certainly *are* full of surprises, Julia."

Thor said, "We realized the error of our ways, Julia. We're glad you're here to help."

Tom gazed into his coffee cup, perplexed by her perfectly timed entrance.

He really doesn't understand me, she thought.

She said, "I figured that our Nazi friend would follow you two today, so I didn't want to waste my time at the museum. Like you said, Thor, it will take the three of us to break through the invisible walls of the long-standing, Nazi kidnapping-adoption operation."

"Right you are, Julia. Tom, tell us your plan for our investigation, please."

For the next half hour, Julia and Thor listened intently to Tom's plan. When he finished, Thor said, "Tom, that's a great plan. This is exactly why I hired you to complete the work of my father and Julia's uncle. Julia, what do you think?"

She smiled at Tom. "I'm sure Tom knows precisely where to focus the search. My concern is that the Nazi seated over there will cause us a problem. Each of us must remain vigilant for ourselves *and* each other."

Tom said, "You're too sensitive, Julia. There are three of us and only one of them. Everything will be fine. No need to worry."

Thor said, "Wait a minute, Tom. I agree with Julia. The war still rages under the surface here because of people like that Nazi. Don't become over-confident, Tom. I'm warning you."

"All right, Thor. I'll be cautious."

Neither of them believed him.

They didn't figure they would be able to lose the Nazi, so they focused on the map that Tom had created during his sleepless night.

Tom was confident that the best way to find out the names of couples who had adopted kidnapped children in the 1940s, was to start with the present-day adoptions and work backwards.

He had learned of an underground adoption agency outside of Montreal that was financed by funds from an offshore account. It was a sure bet that it was Nazi-funded.

Tom's confidential informant told him that his brother recently adopted a Swedish baby from a secret adoption agency. After some investigation, Tom came up with the name and address of the agency.

The agency was only open by appointment. They hoped they would arrive early enough so no one would be in the office and they'd have uninterrupted access to the files.

Tom drove Julia's rental car and they managed to slip away before the Nazi got to his car. Even so, Tom took a circuitous route to their destination.

They spotted the agency entrance, which was in the basement, down a short flight of stairs from the sidewalk. As they looked for a parking space nearby, they saw a woman coming out of the adoption agency. She was dressed in a nun's habit.

Thor said, "Isn't it just like the Nazis to use the church to do their dirty deeds. I would hope that those who work there are not aware of who's behind the adoptions."

"I would hope so," Tom said.

Julia said, "Tom, stop and let me out while you park. I want to talk to the nun."

Tom said, "No. Bad idea, Julia. You're staying with us."

Thor's voice boomed, "Stop the car and let Julia out, Tom! She knows what she's doing!"

"All right! All right!" He stopped the car a few doors away from the agency.

Julia jumped out and approached the nun. "Excuse me, Sister, do you work at the adoption agency?"

She was abrupt and not very friendly. "Read the sign on the door."

Julia looked at the sign. It read "BY APPOINTMENT ONLY." She looked back at the nun. "Oh, dear, I need an appointment. What is the telephone number to call?"

The nun had a sour look on her face. She replied, "It's unlisted. Good day."

"Oh. Okay then. Thank you, Sister."

Julia walked in the opposite direction from where Tom was parked. The nun waited at the bus stop on the corner next to the car. As soon as the nun got on the bus, Julia walked back to the car. Thor rolled down the passenger window.

Julia said, "All right, the agency is empty, and I *sort of* made us an appointment." She grinned. "Let's go look at some files, shall we?"

Tom and Thor met Julia at the front door of the agency. Tom produced a lock pick and made short work of the lock. With much fanfare, he held the door open for them and said, "Please *do* come in!"

Tom locked the door behind them and handed both of them a flashlight. He said, "No lights. Use flashlights to read files."

Julia looked around. "There are no computers. That must be so that files cannot be hacked. Do you think this could be the agency that handled Thora's adoption?"

"We'll soon find out," Thor said. "There are a lot of file cabinets here. Where should we start?"

Julia walked to the first cabinet. "Give me a minute to check some cabinets. Maybe I will be able to see how cases are filed."

She checked the first six cabinets and said, "Wow, we are in luck! The cases are filed first by year, then by country of origin. Let's see if we can find 1941, Sweden."

Tom said, "Great. You two check the files, and I'll keep a lookout at the front door. Try to hurry!"

Julia noticed that Tom guarded the front door with his handgun drawn. That encouraged her to pick up the pace.

She whispered loudly to Thor on the other side of the room, "Any luck, Thor?"

He sounded disappointed, "No, these files only go back as far as 1950. Maybe this is not the agency that had Thora adopted."

Julia felt desperate. She had not found any files earlier than 1950 either. She was about to give up when she saw a credenza at the back wall. She could see there were file drawers on both ends of it.

She whispered, "Thor...over there...let's look in this credenza!"

Julia ran to the credenza and shined her light on the file drawers. "This looks promising; and *look*, this drawer is marked '1949-1945' and the other drawer is marked '1944-1939.'"

She got Tom's attention. "Tom, we need you to unlock these file drawers!"

He checked the front door and ran to where Julia and Thor stood.

Thor was getting nervous, "Hurry, Tom!"

"I'm going as fast as I can." Tom worked feverishly. "There's one drawer unlocked. Julia, you look in that one. And there's the other drawer unlocked. You look in that one, Thor. We've been here long enough. Let's hurry it up!"

He went back to the front door while Julia and Thor scanned the files as quickly as they possibly could.

Julia said, "This drawer only goes back as far as 1945. You must have the 1941 files, Thor. Do you see files from Sweden?"

"Just a minute, I can't tell. Someone has misfiled a lot of these files. The 1941 files are mixed in with all the other years. Damn, this is maddening!"

Then Thor shouted, "Oh my God, here's a subsection labeled 'Stockholm!' Maybe Thora's file is here!"

Tom heard Thor shout. "No more time! Take all the Stockholm files and let's get out!"

Thor was breathless. "Julia, help me carry these files!"

Julia looked around frantically and said, "Wait, there's a box to put them in. I'll get it!"

Thor and Julia tossed about thirty files into the box. Thor said, "Go, Julia! I'm right behind you!"

She didn't hesitate. She ran to the door and opened it slowly to double-check that no one was nearby. The coast was clear. She looked at Tom. He still had his gun trained on the door.

Tom tossed her the car keys and said, "Start the car! I'll be right behind Thor!"

She snatched the keys out of midair and said, "You got it!"

Julia walked to the car as nonchalantly as she could bear to. She wanted to run, but she could not afford to attract attention.

As she unlocked the car door, she turned and looked back at Thor. He was struggling to carry the heavy file box.

Suddenly, gunshots rang out. Julia was confused about what had happened. She turned around and saw the Nazi lying dead right next to her. His gun was beside him.

As if in a dream, she turned to look at Tom. He was down on the sidewalk. Thor was bent over him.

She ran to them. Thor said, "He's shot…the Nazi shot him! Son of a bitch, the Nazi shot him! Julia, carry the box and open the car door so I can put Tom on the back seat!"

It took them only a matter of seconds to get Tom into the car. Julia put the box of files on the front seat beside her.

Thor knelt on the floor next to Tom while Julia drove. He tore off a piece of his own shirt and pressed it on Tom's chest to stop the bleeding.

Tom was in and out of consciousness. At one point, he yelled, "Julia! Behind you!"

Thor said, "Tom, Julia is safe. You shot the Nazi and saved her."

He moaned, "Julia, where are you?"

Julia sobbed as she drove. "I'm right here, Tom. I'm all right. You saved me."

He slipped into unconsciousness again.

Julia drove to the hotel parking garage. Thor had his hands full trying to keep Tom alive. That left Julia to figure out how to get into the suite without being noticed.

She heard her Uncle Per's voice, "Use the service elevator."

Just then, she saw an empty parking space next to the service elevator. She'd previously noticed that it opened next to their suite.

She parked and said, "Thor, can you manage Tom by yourself?"

"Yes, you can open the doors for me and I'll carry him. Anyone around?"

"No one's around. Are you ready?"

"Yes, let's go. I stopped the bleeding but when I move him, it will probably start again."

Julia remembered that there was a blanket in the trunk. She grabbed it. "Here, wrap him in this to contain the blood."

She helped wrap Tom in the blanket. Tom gained consciousness just long enough to say, "I love you, Julia."

Tom died that day. Thor arranged for his body to be airlifted to a private mortuary in New York, where he was cremated and laid to rest.

Julia asked Thor, "Aren't we going to have some sort of services for Tom?"

Thor put his arms around Julia and hugged her close. He said, "Sweetie, I promise you that we will honor Tom with a memorial service as soon as we possibly can."

He held her at arm's length and looked her squarely in the eyes. He said, "I promise."

Julia whispered, "Okay, Thor."

Thor and Julia stayed in Montreal. They still had a job to do...to find out if Thora was adopted and if so, who her parents were. Tom would expect nothing less of them. It was the best way to honor him, and it kept them from thinking about his death.

They worked quickly, knowing that word of the death of the second-in-command Nazi would soon get out. When that happened, other Nazis would be sent to protect the nefarious adoption agency.

With any luck, there would already be private investigators looking for the team of Nazis and they'd make the connection between the dead Nazi in the street and the adoption agency just doors away and their activities would be exposed at long last.

Thor opened the box of files and gave Julia half of them. "Let's find our girl," he said.

He paused and said, "My father loved little Thora as much as your uncle did, Julia. I think we'll find her. I can feel it."

Julia felt hot tears on her cheeks. "I *know* we'll find her, Thor."

By dinnertime, they were both bleary-eyed from reading the faded documents.

Julia was tired and hungry. She said, "I'll go to the café and order some takeout. What do you want, Thor?"

He jumped up and shouted, "What do I *want*? I want you to look at the file of Thora Lundgren right *here*!"

She hugged him and they danced around the room, now strewn with files.

Suddenly, Julia stopped. "Did you hear that?"

"Hear what?" he said.

"I heard a woman singing. You didn't hear it?"

Thor paused to listen. He said, "Oh, yes, I do. I've heard that woman singing since we opened the box of files today."

Uncle Per chuckled. Thor said, "Did you hear *that*?"

Julia laughed. She was very happy indeed. She kissed Thor on the cheek and said, "Yes, I've heard that chuckle on many occasions."

Chapter Twenty-Four

THE ADOPTION FILES

Thor sat at the breakfast bar in their suite with Thora's file spread out in front of him.

He said, "What do you think we should do with the other files that we took, Julia?"

She had reorganized the files that were in the box. "Well, I thought about that and here's what I think. We should have all the files scanned and sent to the National Police Commissioner in Sweden. All of them except Thora's file, of course."

"Julia, you're a genius! There are so many families in and around Stockholm who lost children to the Nazi kidnappers. Now the police can reopen cold cases. Plus, the Nazi organization that has operated here, and in other places, will be exposed."

She said, "After we find Thora, and I pray she's still alive, we should inform the Canadian authorities so they can secure the files we saw at the agency. It could even lead to kidnapping operations in other countries being exposed."

She suddenly had a flashback of Tom lying on the sidewalk in a pool of blood.

Thor saw the look on her face. "What's wrong, sweetie?"

He sat beside her on the sofa and gathered her in his arms.

She stopped crying. "It's still sinking in. Tom is dead. He should be here to celebrate what we have found so far. If we find Thora, he should be with us when we tell her about her parents. It's so unfair!"

"Yes, it is unfair, Julia. But I know Tom would do it all again even if he knew the sacrifice he would make. We will never forget that his investigation skills led us to find Thora's file."

Julia replied, "Yes, I'd like to think Tom will somehow be aware of what we find next."

The two of them sat quietly on the sofa, lost in their thoughts. They heard rustling on the counter where Thor had sat moments before. A paper fell on the floor. He got up and retrieved it.

She watched as he read it.

"Julia, did you put a paper in Thora's file?"

"No. Why?" She got up to look at the document with him.

She gasped, "It's Thora's actual birth certificate! Where did it come from?"

He said, "I have no idea. It was not with the file before now! This will help the authorities prove the case against the Nazis!"

Julia jumped with joy. "Yes, and look, it even has her blood type noted. It's AB negative, a rare type, just like me! Who cares how it got here. We have it and that's all that matters, Thor!"

Thor grabbed Julia's arm. "I don't know how this birth certificate got here either, but I think we'd better stash it somewhere right now, along with the rest of Thora's file. Did you notice a safe in the suite?"

"No, but let's look. Maybe it's hidden," Julia said. "I'll check the bedrooms."

"All right, I'll check the other rooms." Thor started his search in the kitchenette.

Soon Julia yelled, "I found the safe! It's in my room!"

He ran to her bedroom and found Julia had cleared the bookshelf. There, behind where the books had been, was a wall safe.

He tried the handle. "Damn, we don't have the combination. How do we open it?"

Julia said, "I bet Tom would have known about the safe and set the four-digit code. I'll try some numbers."

It opened on the first try—her birth date. She flung the safe open and inside was the diamond ring Tom had offered her with his proposal.

Julia cried as she held the beautiful ring. She could feel Tom's love for her.

She looked at Thor and said, "I don't know what to do with Tom's ring."

"You'll figure it out, Julia. I'm sure of it."

She held the ring against her heart for a moment and then put it back into the safe.

Thor put Thora's file into the safe, locked it and breathed a sigh of relief. "Now, let's go back into the living room and I'll tell you where I think we will find Thora. I mapped out the clues I found in her file and put them together with notes that Tom had made."

"You see, Tom is still with us." She smiled wistfully.

Thor sighed. "Indeed he is."

Thor told Julia about his plan. She said, "Isn't it wonderful that our search for Thora leads us right back to New York State. I will be so glad to get out of Canada and back on home turf."

"Me too, Julia. Let's pack up, but before we leave, I must call Claudette and tell her what has happened, and we will not be able to attend her dinner party tonight."

"Yes, please give Claudette my regards and tell her we'd like her to come to Manhattan to visit soon.

"Oh, Thor! Mrs. Wellington would love to meet her, especially since Claudette's husband, Henrique, was from Poland!"

"That's a great idea, Julia. I'll send a car for her and for whoever wants to come along. I'll call Claudette now."

"While you make that call, I need to call Seth. I'll be in my room."

Julia knew Seth would be upset that she hadn't returned his calls. She couldn't bear to talk about Tom's death. He'd left numerous messages, each more desperate than the last.

She took a deep breath and dialed his cell number. He didn't answer right away, and when he did, his voice was tense.

"Julia, are you all right? I've been trying to reach you."

"Yes, I'm all right, but something terrible has happened." She sobbed into the phone, and he could not make out what she said.

"Sweetheart, don't cry. You can tell me everything as soon as I get there. I just crossed the border and should be at your hotel soon. I'll call you when I get there."

All she could manage to say was, "Okay." She hadn't realized how much she needed Seth.

Thor knocked on her door. She wiped her eyes and said, "Come in, Thor."

He was not surprised to see that she was crying again. Tom's death was hard on both of them.

He said, "I arranged for the rental car to be picked up. I told them I delivered a baby in the back seat, and I would pay the costs of cleaning."

If the real reason for the blood wasn't so awful, she might have laughed.

He continued, "I spoke with Claudette and she sent her condolences. She also said she would be delighted to come to Manhattan for a visit. She loves to stay at the Plaza.

"When I suggested she bring along some of the friends who were rescued with Henrique, she was thrilled.

"I also filled her in about our search for Thora. She wants us to keep her updated on our progress. Claudette is a dear woman. I'm glad she had a happy life with Henrique."

"Yes, I'm happy for her too. I'm also glad Tom got to meet her and to know she connected us with the Polish children your father helped to rescue.

"I just called Seth. He'd been trying to call me and I didn't answer, so he's on his way here. He should arrive any minute."

There was a knock on the door. "And that should be him now. I need to wash my face. Would you please let Seth in, Thor?"

"Of course. Take your time."

Fifteen minutes later, she walked into the living room where Seth and Thor talked in hushed tones.

Seth stood.

She walked to him and he wrapped her in his arms. A wave of relief washed over her and she knew with him, everything would be all right.

He let her go and they both said, "I'm so glad to see you!"

Thor laughed with them and said, "Okay, you lovebirds, let's get our luggage and get back to the good old USA!"

"Julia, Seth has offered to take the files to my office in Manhattan and give them to Nash, my secretary. You ride with Seth and I'll meet you at your apartment tomorrow morning."

Julia said, "All right."

Then she added, "By the way, Thor, is Nash someone special to you? I was just wondering because he seems very protective of you."

He stopped packing his briefcase and looked at her. "Yes, he is special to me. His name is Nash Bjorn and he's my half-brother. After my mother died, my father vowed not to marry again. However, he did have a girlfriend for many years. Her name was Inga - she is Nash's mother."

Thor winked at Julia and she screeched, "Inga? Her name was Inga? Was that Uncle Per's Inga? Nooo, it couldn't be!"

"Yes, my dear, it *could* be and she was the same Inga who worked for your Uncle Per. My father and Inga became very close when Per and Raya lived with Sven. They went through a lot together."

Julia was speechless.

Seth grinned. "Small world, eh, Jules?"

She nodded. "Thor, you and Nash come from good Swedish stock. I fell in love with both your father and Inga as I wrote the journal."

Thor said, "Okay, I have *everything* that was in the safe, Julia." He looked at her meaningfully.

She realized he wanted her to know that he had Tom's diamond ring. "All right, Seth and I are ready to go. We'll see you in Manhattan. Have a safe trip, Thor."

She hugged him and he said, "You two do the same. Call if you need me."

Seth shook Thor's hand. "Goodbye, Thor and thanks for taking care of Julia."

Thor sighed, "Oh, it wasn't me."

Seth listened as Julia told him all about the investigation in Canada. He smiled and held her hand as she spoke. Her enthusiasm was contagious.

Finally, she said, "What do you think about all of that, Seth?"

"I think my life with you will be *very* interesting, Jules. And I wouldn't have it any other way."

"Oh, I forgot to call Javier and ask him to open the apartment for us!"

Julia dialed Javier's number. When he answered, he said, "Julia! When are you coming home?"

"It's good to hear your voice. I've missed you, Javier. I'm coming home later tonight. Would you please have my apartment opened? Seth and I will be coming in."

"Tonight? Why, that's wonderful! I will ask maintenance to open your apartment and I will check on it myself later.

"Julia, I can't wait to see you. Is your work in Canada finished?"

"Not exactly, Javier. My work has moved to New York State, so I can use Manhattan as home base."

"Wonderful, it will be good to have you home. I will be gone when you get here, but I will see you tomorrow. Goodbye, Julia."

"Goodbye, Javier and thanks!"

She put her phone into her purse.

Seth thought she looked glum. "Jules, if you want me to, I'll tell Javier about Tom. I know it will be hard for you to tell him."

"How did you know what I was thinking?"

"Because I know you, Jules. I will do anything I can to make your life easier."

"Thank you, sweetheart." She thought for a minute and said, "You know, Seth, we would not be together if Tom had not saved me."

"I'm acutely aware of that. I will be forever grateful to him for giving his life for yours."

"I will too, Seth. I must admit I feel guilty—he was sad at the end of his life because of me. He was sure I was meant to be with him."

"You're sensitive and you don't want to hurt anyone. I understand that. Can we talk about something else for a minute, Jules?"

"Sure, what would you like to talk about?"

He looked at her hopefully. "Jules, I know you will be busy working with Thor for a few weeks. But how about we get married next month?"

She surprised him. "How about one month from today?"

"Great. The sooner the better. One month from today it is!"

"Okay, I will start working on the details. Where do you think we should live, Seth?"

"I'm glad you asked. I love your apartment, but it's too small for both of us and all our accoutrements, and so…"

He glanced at her to see if she would guess his idea.

She smiled and pursed her lips to indicate she knew but wouldn't say. "Surprise me, Seth."

"Last week, I bought the co-op next to yours and presented my builder with plans to combine them."

"You did? What a great idea. I never would have guessed."

"Yes, and we'll need your interior design plan as soon as you have time. I'm anxious to show you my architectural drawings!"

"Seth, you *do* make me very happy!"

"That's my plan, Jules!"

It was dark when Seth parked the car in her apartment garage. He said, "Jules, leave your luggage. I'll come back for it. Let's unlock the apartment and I'll take the box of files up first."

"Okay." She hopped out of the car, happy to be home.

Seth put the box of files in the back of Julia's walk-in closet and went to the car to get her luggage.

When he came back to the apartment, he detected some good smells wafting from the kitchen and followed his nose.

Julia had put on an apron, perked coffee, set the table and heated something for them to eat.

"That smells suspiciously like our favorite chicken soup from the corner deli…could it be?"

"Javier left it in the fridge for us. Isn't he thoughtful?"

"He sure *is,* and I'm starving!"

They gobbled up the soup along with butter crackers and then Julia served coffee.

"That was good, now the only thing that's missing is one of your cupcakes."

She got up and opened the oven. "Oh, do you mean one of *these?*"

"How did you do that, Jules?"

"My secret." She smiled as she put a cupcake on a dessert plate and gave it to him, along with a kiss.

He picked up the cupcake, took a giant bite. "Yum!"

Early the next morning, Julia unpacked her luggage and perked a pot of coffee.

She turned on the SiriusXM in the corner and enjoyed the feel of the warm tiles on her bare feet as she sipped her coffee. She hummed along with a Mills Brothers tune, "Till Then." It was one of her favorites.

Seth stood in the kitchen doorway enjoying her happiness, until the song ended. "Good morning, Jules."

"Good morning, sweetheart. Come and sit with me, there's a cup of coffee here with your name on it."

He laughed. "You come *here* so I can kiss you goodbye."

"Goodbye? Where are you going?"

"I want to get the files to Thor's office to be scanned. I don't want them here with us."

"I agree. But no coffee first?"

"No thanks. I'll get a cup on my way. See you later."

She kissed him. "All right, see you later too."

Alone, Julia suddenly felt the emotions of all that had happened since she started writing the journal. Her tears began to fall just as there was a knock on the door.

She jumped up and looked through the peephole. It was Javier. She opened the door and greeted him with a hug. "Thank you for leaving the soup for us, Javier. It was wonderful. When we got home, we were famished!"

"You're welcome, Julia. I'm glad you're back safe and sound."

A strange look came over her face. She wondered if Seth had seen Javier and told him about Tom.

"Yes, I know about Tom. Seth told me. I'm so sorry, Julia. It must have been terrible. I'm glad that Seth went to get you."

"Seth has been wonderful. I'm lucky to have him."

Javier's cell phone buzzed. He looked at the text message and said, "Duty calls. I'll see you later, Julia."

"Thanks again, Javier."

Julia was glad Javier was interrupted by work. She wanted to tell him about Claudette when they had more time. Besides, maybe she'd find out when Claudette would visit. Then she could tell Javier when he would be reunited with her.

She was jolted when the secure cell phone that she and Tom shared chirped and vibrated.

She answered and out of habit said, "Tom!"

"No, sweetie, it's Thor. I'm sorry. I didn't think not to call you on this line. I'll have Nash terminate the service right away."

She sniffled. "It's okay, Thor. I just thought for a minute…"

"I know, I know. Do you want me to call you later?"

She took a deep breath and her heartbeat slowed slightly. "No, I can talk now."

"Okay, Seth is here. He and Nash are scanning the files. Today, I want to follow the clues Tom and I put together to find Thora. I intend to drive to Tarrytown and talk to the town historian there. Do you want to come with me?"

"I sure do! My car is still in storage, otherwise, I would drive."

"I don't want to attract attention, so I asked Nash if I could borrow his Prius. I'll pick you up in, say, forty-five minutes?"

Julia replied, "Okay, I'll meet you out front. See you soon."

On the trip to Tarrytown, Thor explained what he hoped to discover from speaking with the town historian.

Julia said, "Maybe she will have the key to help us find Thora. As we know, stranger coincidences have happened."

"I don't believe in coincidence, Julia. I think if we're meant to meet someone, it will fall into place. Some people call it fate; I call it kismet."

"Now you sound like my Uncle Per, Thor. That's just what he said when he met Raya."

"I would have liked that old boy! And here we are at the historical society. Looks like parking is on the side of the building."

He parked the car and they walked to the main entrance. Thor held the door for her, "After *you*, sweetie."

"Thank you, Thor."

They stood in the foyer and looked up into the dome.

Julia said, "This reminds me of the dome at the planetarium where Seth proposed to me."

Thor said, "It's magnificent!"

A young lady approached them and said, "We're very proud of our building. How may I help you today?"

Thor answered, "I have an appointment with the historian at one o'clock."

"You must be Thor Bjorn. Miss Lorenzo said to send you to her office when you arrive. Walk up that staircase to your right. Her office is the last on the left."

Thor said, "Thank you."

Julia and Thor walked up the winding, marble staircase and the young lady who'd directed them walked alongside. She said, "I see that you admire our staircase. It's inspired by the grand staircase at the Lyndhurst Mansion. Maybe you know of it?"

Julia said, "Yes, I've heard of the Lyndhurst. My fiancé is an architect and I would love to tour the mansion with him."

"I know the curator there. I would be happy to set it up for you. Give me your card before you leave. Well, here's Miss Lorenzo's office. Go on in."

The door was open. They heard her melodious voice before they saw her. "Please, come in, Mr. Bjorn."

Thor mumbled to Julia, "She's gorgeous!"

She offered her hand first to Julia, then to Thor and said, "It's a pleasure to meet you, Mr. Bjorn. Who is this lovely lady with you?"

Julia said, "I am Julia Hamilton, a friend of Thor's. Thank you for seeing us, Mrs. Lorenzo."

Thor seemed to be tongue-tied.

"Please call me Dora, it's short for Theodora, and it's *Miss* Lorenzo."

She motioned to a table. "Please have a seat over there, won't you?"

She looked at Thor and said, "May I call you Thor?"

He didn't seem to hear her.

Julia touched his arm and said, "Dora asked if she could call you Thor."

"Yes, yes, call me Thor. I was distracted for a moment, please excuse me."

"Of course, Thor. You said you wanted to ask me some questions?"

Thor heard his father's voice crackle in his ear, "Snap out of it, boy!"

That was all he needed to focus. He said, "Yes, we have reason to believe that a family here in Tarrytown adopted a baby girl from Sweden in 1941, and we were hoping your records might be able to confirm it."

"Possibly. Do you have the name of the adoptive family?"

He opened his folder, "Yes, it's right here. The name is…wait, it's Lorenzo. Isn't that *your* name, Dora?"

Julia said, "Do you mind if I ask if you were adopted, Dora?"

Dora stood. "I was *not* adopted! If that was the case, my parents would have told me!"

Thor said, "I apologize, Dora. We obviously have the wrong information. Thank you for your time."

He touched Julia's shoulder. "Let's go."

Julia got up. "I'm very sorry to upset you."

Dora did not reply. She stiffly walked them to the office door and closed herself inside when they left.

She thought, *how dare those people come into my life and ask if I'm adopted!*

Downstairs, the young lady who'd directed them to Dora's office said, "Leaving so soon?"

"Yes, thank you," Julia said. "Oh, here's my business card so you can call me about a tour of the Lyndhurst Mansion. I'd appreciate it if you could connect me with the curator."

The girl took Julia's card and read it. "You're an Interior Designer. That must be very interesting work."

"Yes, it is. Goodbye and thank you again."

"Goodbye, Miss Hamilton. I'll call you soon."

Thor winked at her. "Thanks, young lady."

She smiled, "You're welcome, Sir."

They walked outside and stopped on the sidewalk. Thor said, "I hate it when people call me 'Sir.' It makes me feel old!"

Julia giggled. "Well, you *are* sixty-eight years old, Thor."

She hastened to add, "But you sure don't look like it!"

"Seriously, Julia, do you think Miss Lorenzo is our Thora?"

"She certainly doesn't look Italian, as her name would suggest, Thor. With that blonde hair and blue eyes, she looks like a member of my family. Thora would be my cousin, you know."

He said, "I'm sure she's Thora. However, I don't know how to convince her that she was born Thora Lundgren. Her adoptive parents would be long dead by this time, so they can't help us."

Julia put a hand on her stomach. "Let's find someplace to eat. I can think better when I'm not starving."

"All right, sweetie. I noticed an Italian café as we drove into town. How does that sound?"

"Fine by me. Pasta is one of my best friends. Let's go!"

Thor commented as he drove into the parking lot, "Looks like a popular lunch spot. There are no parking spaces. Let's go to the diner across the street."

Julia said, "Wait, there's a space next to the entrance."

He drove into the empty space. The Prius only took up half of it. He said, "I saw the space but thought I was driving the Bentley and it wouldn't fit."

They enjoyed a laugh at the expense of Nash's little car. Then they walked arm-in-arm into the café.

All heads turned in their direction as they were escorted by a waitress to the only booth available.

Julia said, "Apparently, strangers don't come around here too often. Everyone is looking at us."

"The good news is that if all of these people are locals, someone may be able to help us," he said.

"That's a smart idea, Thor."

The waitress took their order and scurried off to the kitchen to place it.

Thor said, "Julia, you're perceptive. Look at the people here and see if you pick up any vibes related to the Lorenzo family."

"I'll give it a go."

She looked around and said, "No, nothing, Thor. Don't worry, we'll figure out what to do next. As Inga would say, everything works out perfectly as long as you stay calm."

Just then the waitress placed a beautiful platter of antipasti on their table. She said, "Lorenzo would like you to have his special appetizers, especially for the young lady."

"Thank you, but who is Lorenzo?" Julia asked.

"Oh, he's the owner-chef. Vicente is his first name and Lorenzo is his last name. He said you remind him of his sister, Miss."

The waitress walked away.

Thor sat back and smiled. "Well now, isn't that interesting?"

Julia said, "Indeed, I think we may have stumbled upon Thora's adoptive family, Thor! You found the clues that led us here, you made the appointment with Dora and you chose the café that we are sitting in right now. You are amazing!"

Happy tears sparkled in his eyes. "My father would be thrilled that we found Thora. Now we must convince her of who she is."

Julia saw Dora walk into the café…right to their table. "Do you mind if I join you?"

Thor choked on an olive.

Julia said, "Yes, Dora. Please sit next to me."

Dora looked at Thor who still struggled with the olive. She said, "First, please accept my apology for my rudeness earlier."

Thor said, "We understand. Perhaps we were indelicate."

She continued, "My mother passed more than twenty years ago. She left me a letter in our family safe that I never read until after her death.

"In the letter, she explained that she and my father had learned that I had been kidnapped before my adoption and I was born in Sweden. Now mind you, this did not come as a complete shock to me because I had overheard their disagreement years earlier about trying to locate my birth parents. My mother was not in favor of telling me I was adopted and my father told her I deserved the truth.

"I remember they fought for days before my father left for a trip. I didn't know it then, but the letter from my mother said my father went to the adoption agency outside of Montreal for information on my birth. When he got there, they would not even acknowledge that it was the agency he'd paid thousands of dollars to when they adopted me. Well, my father was not one to take 'no' for an answer. He was shot while breaking into the agency after hours. He wanted to find my birth certificate."

Thor reached into the breast pocket of his sports jacket and put a piece of paper in front of her. "Miss Lorenzo, may I introduce you to Thora Lundgren."

She covered her mouth to muffle her cry of joy as she looked at her birth certificate. "You found it! I can't believe it!"

Then her tears began to flow. "My father would want me to have this. He died trying to get it to me."

"Yes, Thora. Julia and I came into possession of your adoption file and voilà, there was your birth certificate!"

She smiled, "That's interesting. How is it you have my adoption file, or shouldn't I ask?"

"That is a story for another day, Thora. Allow me to introduce you to Julia Hamilton. She is the great-niece of your birth father, Per Lundgren."

Thora looked shocked.

Julia put her arm around Thora's shoulders. "We have a lot to talk about. I think you would be interested to read the journal that your father wrote."

At that moment, Lorenzo came to their table and kissed Thora on the cheek.

She said, "Vinnie, I would like you to meet my cousin, Julia, and this is her friend, Thor. They found my birth certificate, Vin!"

"That is the most wonderful thing I've ever heard, my darling Dora!"

Everyone laughed and she said, "Please, call me Thora."

Then she paused. "Did anyone else hear that chuckle?"

Chapter Twenty-Five

CELEBRATIONS

"I want to call Seth right away," Julia said as they left the café.

"I'll use the speaker so you can talk too, Thor."

Seth answered right away, "Hi, Jules, how are you?"

"I'm better than ever, Seth. I'm in the car with Thor and we're on the speaker phone with you."

Seth said, "Hi, Thor. What are you two up to? But, before you say anything else, let me first tell you that all the Stockholm files have been scanned and transmitted to the National Police Commissioner in Sweden along with a cover letter explaining the source of the files and your contact number, Thor."

"That's great, Seth! Did Nash put the original files in the vault?"

"Yes, they're safe and sound. Okay, Jules, I interrupted you... go ahead. What good news do you have?"

Suddenly, Julia got a lump in her throat. She motioned for Thor to talk to Seth.

"Seth, Julia is a little bit emotional at the moment. You see, we came to Tarrytown today to speak with the town historian about Thora's adoptive family and to make a long story short, it turns out that the historian is our Thora!"

Seth shouted, "That's wonderful!" He startled Julia so much that she laughed the lump right out of her throat.

"You two make a great team," Seth said. "I could not be happier for all of us!"

"Thor made the appointment here in Tarrytown based on clues Tom left in his notes. Tom is part of our team," she responded.

"That's right," Thor said. He reached over and patted Julia's hand.

She smiled.

Seth asked, "So when do I get to meet Thora?"

"Well, Seth, she promised to visit very soon."

"That's great, Jules. We will invite her to our wedding."

"Of course we will. I think I will ask her to be my one bridesmaid, just like in an old-fashioned Swedish wedding."

Thor gave her a surprised look, followed by a big grin.

Julia asked, "What do you think, Seth?"

"I like the idea of Thora being your bridesmaid and I like the idea of an old-fashioned Swedish wedding even more."

Knowing that Thor was listening, Seth said, "I thought I might ask Thor to be my best man. Do you think he will accept, Jules?"

She laughed. "I think he just *might* accept!"

Thor laughed loudly. "Seth, I would be most honored to stand up for you as you marry my best girl!"

Julia leaned over and kissed his cheek. "I love you, Thor."

Thor's eyes glistened with fresh tears.

"All right, you two…get back to Manhattan so we can celebrate!"

They both responded, "We'll see you soon, Seth!"

Their conversation was full of plans for Seth and Julia's wedding, and for introducing Thora into their lives in a big way.

Thor dropped Julia off at her apartment building. Javier opened the door. "My, but don't you look happy, Julia!"

"I *am* happy! I haven't had a chance to catch you up on what's happened since I left for Canada. However, you read my journal, so you know about the kidnapping of Uncle Per's baby, Thora."

"Yes, of course. My heart broke for Per and Raya."

"Thor and I found her today in Tarrytown, just forty minutes from here!"

"Julia, that's fantastic!"

"Yes, it is…and Javier, when you have time, I will tell you about our investigation in Canada. I'll see you soon!"

"That sounds intriguing, Julia. How about if I come up to your apartment when my shift ends today?"

"Okay, that will be great. Thor and Seth will be there too. Goodbye, Javier."

At six PM, Javier rang Julia's doorbell. Seth said, "Open the door, Jules. I can't wait to see the look on Javier's face when he hears the news you and Thor have. He'll be very happy."

Julia ran to the door and flung it open. She tried to be subtle but could not manage it. She grabbed Javier by the hand and pulled him toward the kitchen.

He laughed and said, "Hey, what's this about?"

Julia and Javier appeared in the kitchen doorway. "Gentlemen, I give you Javier. Thor, would you please do the honors?"

"Yes, it would be my pleasure, Julia. Please, Javier, have a seat next to me. You should be close to me just in case I have to catch you when you faint."

Thor smiled and Javier said, "I cannot imagine you could surprise me. At my age, I've heard it all!"

Javier sat between Thor and Julia.

She said, "Javier, would you like some iced tea with lavender honey?" She knew he loved the lavender honey from the Alsace region of France.

"Yes, I would, thank you."

"All right, while I get the tea, go ahead and start, Thor."

Thor leaned forward and put his hand on Javier's forearm. "I know you think you've heard it all, Javier. What I am about to tell you will knock your socks off!"

Javier looked a bit uncomfortable. He leaned back and folded his arms across his middle to brace himself emotionally. "I'm listening."

Thor drilled his eyes into Javier and said, "What you already know is that Tom, Julia and I went to Montreal for two reasons: to find Thora's adoptive family and to try to find people my father and Julia's uncle saved from the Nazis.

"You also know that in the process of investigating an adoption agency, Tom was shot and killed, but not before he left clues as to where Thora's adoptive family may be located. It was due to Tom's notes that Julia and I went to Tarrytown today and found Thora herself. She is beautiful and delightful. You'll meet her when she visits in a few weeks."

Javier said, "That's wonderful. Does she sing like her Mama?"

Julia answered, "We'll find out. We have so many questions for her and so much to tell her about her birth family."

She smiled at Seth and said, "Maybe we will ask her if she would like to sing at our wedding. It doesn't matter to me if she has Raya's singing ability or not."

Javier said, "Whoa…you two are getting married? When was this decided?"

She flashed her diamond ring for Javier to see. "Seth proposed before I went to Canada. Just yesterday, we set the date for a month from now."

He said, "That ring is quite beautiful, Julia. And Seth, you are a very lucky man!"

Seth beamed with happiness, "Don't I know it! I can also tell you that I recently purchased the co-op next to Julia's and we intend to combine the two and live right here."

"Oh, I saw the paperwork with your name on it but I assumed you were just the architect on the project. Now that *is* a wonderful surprise. I'm very happy for you two!"

Javier looked at Thor, "So that's what you wanted to tell me?"

"Not even close, my man…I'll cut to the chase. We found the daughter of Franz and Marie, who was rescued with you. Her name is Claudette. You were both three years old when the Blue Tango team found you. Do you remember her?"

"Of course I remember her! She and I were the best of friends. She told me she would share her Mama and Papa with me until I found mine. How we cried when we were separated."

He got a faraway look in his eyes. "I never forgot my best friend, Claudy."

Javier's checks were wet. "Excuse me for the tears. It's just that I never dreamed I would see her again."

"You're not alone, Javier. Claudette also cried when we told her that we knew you. She is very anxious to see you," Julia said.

"And I am very excited to think that I will see her! I can barely contain myself. Julia, please pinch me so I know I am not dreaming!"

She got up and put her arms around his neck. "Dear Javier, I assure you, this is not a dream."

"I will never be able to thank you and Thor enough." He grabbed Julia's hand and kissed its back, just as he had kissed Per's hand when they parted so many years before.

"Julia, tell Javier about the other surprise we found in Montreal."

"Okay, Thor." She sat back down and grinned at her dear friend. "Javier, Claudette got married…"

His shoulders slumped. "Oh."

"However, she is widowed. Her husband's name was Henrique Pulaski and he was quite a successful banker in Montreal.

"Believe it or not, Henrique was one of the children rescued by the Blue Tango team with the help of Thor's father, as they were being taken to camps by the Nazis."

"That is just fantastic! I read in your journal about the eight Polish children your father managed to get to Sweden on his ship. He was quite a man, Thor!"

"Indeed, he was, and he and Julia's Uncle Per were great friends."

Seth broke the silence. "Julia has Claudette's telephone number if you would like to call her, Javier."

"Yes, I would love to talk to her!"

"I will get her number and be right back." Julia jumped up from the table and went to get her cell phone.

When she returned to the kitchen, the men went silent. She said, "Okay, you guys. What were you talking about?"

"We were talking about our wedding, Jules. That's all."

She assumed they were discussing Tom's death. She decided to leave it alone.

"Here is Claudette's number, Javier. She will be happy to hear from you."

He got up and said, "If you will excuse me, I have a lady to call."

"Go ahead, Javier, I'll see you tomorrow. Please give Claudette our regards."

"You bet I will." He hugged her, then Thor and then Seth.

"I'll see myself to the door. Thank you for everything…all of you."

Seth, Thor and Julia burst out laughing. To see Javier so joyous and youthful was wonderful.

Seth said, "The only happier man I know of is *me*!"

"That's obvious, Seth. I'm happy for you and Julia."

Julia said, "Enough emotional talk. Who's for Chinese take-out?"

"Sorry, Jules, I had Chinese for lunch. How about pizza?"

"Julia and I had Italian for lunch. How about we walk to the Swedish deli for dinner?"

Seth jumped up, "Let's go. I'm always in the mood for Swedish anything." He gave Julia a sly grin.

"Then you're in good company with Thor and me. Let's go!"

"Dinner is on *me* tonight," Thor announced.

"Even better," Seth said.

They walked three abreast down the street and around the corner to enjoy the smorgasbord of the day.

The manager greeted them in Swedish and Thor replied in kind.

Julia looked at Thor in surprise. "Have you been here before?"

"Have I been here before? I should think so—I own this deli."

He smiled proudly as he shook hands with the manager. "Isn't that right, Sven?"

Seth and Julia exchanged glances.

Seth said, "Stranger things have happened, Jules."

Seth looked at Sven. "Would you by chance be related to the man who worked for Per Lundgren in Sweden in the 1940s?"

"Yah, he vas my uncle."

Julia shot a look at Thor.

She said to Sven, "Did you know he kept my uncle in hiding during the war?"

"Yah, Uncle Sven told me about him and about his lovely vife, Raya."

He looked sad and continued. "The loss of their baby destroyed them."

Thor piped up, "Well, young Sven, we have some wonderful news. That baby, Thora, is now seventy-eight years old and living in Tarrytown, New York."

Sven yelled and grabbed Julia by the shoulders, "Tack och lov; du hittat henne!"

They looked to Thor for interpretation. "Sven said, - 'thank God, you found her!'"

They laughed and hugged as tears of joy flowed.

"I shall have the cook prepare *everything* ve have fer yer smorgasbord this night!"

Sven went off to the kitchen and soon reappeared with a huge tray of food balanced on his shoulder. "Please, friends, eat as much as you like, but save room for the almond cake I made fresh this morning. It was the favorite of Uncle Sven's household. Ve vill all have a piece in celebration of Thora Lundgren. Yah?"

As they sat at a table with a blue and yellow tablecloth, Julia glanced at Thor's plate. He'd piled it high with meatballs and noodles and she was reminded of his father. Although she'd never met him, she felt as if she knew him from writing the journal. And here was the nephew of Sven, the son of Thor Sr., and the niece of Per all sharing a smorgasbord much like the wedding feast Sven's uncle had prepared for Per and Raya. She thought how appropriate it was.

Seth squeezed her hand and whispered, "It's bittersweet, isn't it, Jules?"

She nodded.

The next weeks were extremely busy for all of them. Julia was planning her wedding, Seth was working with his builder to combine the co-ops, and Thor was communicating with the Swedish authorities daily about the adoption files he'd transmitted to them.

The day after their dinner at Sven's deli, Mrs. Wellington called Julia to invite her to the annual ball.

"I heard you were back from your trip, dear, and I thought how wonderful it would be if you could attend my ball. It's next Saturday. Please say that you will come!"

"Yes, Mrs. Wellington, I'd be delighted to attend. Thank you."

"You're welcome, Julia. Now, let me ask, are you back at work yet? I have a friend who wants to hire you as soon as possible to design her guest suite."

"Oh, I'm sorry. I won't be back at work until after my honeymoon."

"Your honeymoon! When are you getting married and who's the lucky man?"

"You've met my fiancé, Mrs. Wellington. His name is Seth Schmidt, the architect who helped design your fountain. Do you remember him?"

"I do recall meeting him. He is delightful and so handsome. I'm thrilled for both of you. When is the happy event?"

Julia smiled, "It's just about three weeks from now."

"Wonderful, dear…that's wonderful!"

"Before we hang up, Mrs. Wellington, I have something to tell you."

"Go ahead, dear."

Julia spoke carefully. She didn't want to divulge the details of Thor's investigation company. She took a deep breath and began to tell the story. "I visited Montreal and met a woman who had escaped from the Nazis with her family in 1940. She told me her late husband was Polish and he too was rescued from the Nazis that same year. I know your annual ball is for those who survived the war, so I thought you might extend an invitation to her."

"Of course, dear. Do you happen to recall the name of her husband?"

"Yes. His name was Henrique Pulaski."

Julia paused. "Mrs. Wellington, isn't Pulaski your maiden name?"

There was complete silence, then Julia heard her sobs.

"Mrs. Wellington, what's wrong?"

"Henrique was the son of my brother and his wife who were carted off to a prison camp when the Nazis attacked Poland. I never knew what happened to Henrique, their only child.

"Oh, I do hope he had a happy life. What did his wife tell you? What is her name?"

Julia breathed a sigh, now that she knew the cause of Mrs. Wellington's sobs. She said, "Her name is Claudette. She told me that Henrique was intelligent and industrious and he became a successful banker. He hired many of the others he was rescued with, to work in his bank. Claudette plans to visit. We will have lunch and she can tell you about your nephew."

"I would love that, Julia. Please invite her to my ball and ask her to bring her friends who were rescued with Henrique.

"Oh, this will be the most wonderful gathering of those who escaped Europe! Julia, you cannot begin to imagine how happy you have made me once again!

"And will you bring your fiancé to the ball with you?"

"I'm sure Seth would love to attend, Mrs. Wellington, and I will call Claudette right away. Goodbye for now, Mrs. Wellington."

"Goodbye, dear."

Claudette graciously accepted Mrs. Wellington's invitation. She arrived in Manhattan the day before the big event. She brought with her letters from Henrique's friends, addressed to Mrs. Wellington.

Claudette booked an apartment at the Plaza, and the moment she arrived, she dialed Julia's number. "Julia, can you join me for lunch at the Plaza at one o'clock today?"

Julia looked at the stack of papers on her desk and decided to ignore them. "Of course, Claudette, I would love to have lunch with you. I will be there at one o'clock."

"Wonderful, I will see you then. Goodbye, Julia."

Julia found Claudette seated in the garden room across from a gray-haired gentleman who had his back to Julia. They seemed engrossed in animated conversation.

Claudette waved her over to their table. The gentleman rose and said, "Hello, Julia."

"Javier, what a pleasant surprise! Claudette, you didn't tell me that my friend would be here. I'm delighted!"

She laughed, "I thought it would be nice for the three of us to enjoy lunch. I'm so glad to see you. Please have a seat, won't you, Julia?

"Now, since Javier and I are from France, I've taken the liberty of ordering for us from the French menu today. Will that be all right with you, Julia?"

"It's *very* all right with me."

Julia smiled. Javier held Claudette's hand as they reminisced about early life in the Alsace, their rescue and the journey to North America.

Julia thought how interesting it was that their lives had come full circle after so many years…all because of Uncle Per, Thor Sr. and the Blue Tango team…plus the journal, of course.

Her thoughts were interrupted by Javier. He said, "Julia, I called Claudette on the day you gave me her number. Since then, we have talked every day."

Claudette squeezed his hand. "Go ahead, dearest."

He looked at Julia. "We've decided that we want to spend our remaining years together. We're getting married, Julia."

Julia believed that after writing the journal, nothing could surprise her. She looked from Javier to Claudette and back again.

Claudette reached for Julia's hand and said, "My dear, are you all right?"

"Yes, of course, and I am very happy for the two of you. It's just that there have been so many changes lately, and I did not see this one coming."

Julia reined in her emotions. "It's wonderful! When are you getting married, and how can I help?"

Claudette, however, did not try to contain her emotions. She glowed with enthusiasm. "Julia, we're going to City Hall Monday morning, and we hope you and Thor will be our witnesses!"

Julia closed her eyes for a moment and with a hand on her heart, said, "It would be my honor to witness your marriage."

She looked sadly at Javier and said, "I suppose you will move to Montreal."

Claudette replied for him, "Oh, no! I've taken an apartment at the Plaza and Manhattan will be our oyster! I've already found a buyer for my estate in Canada and Javier will sell his co-op. We will live happily ever after. Isn't that right, dearest?"

"One hundred percent correct, Claudette."

He looked at Julia. "It's time for me to retire but I promise you we will invite you and Seth to our apartment so often that you will tire of us!"

"Well, I doubt we will ever tire of you two! You will have an open invitation to our apartment too. As soon as Seth finishes the renovations, that is."

Javier looked happier than Julia had ever seen him. "I'm truly happy you and Claudette have found each other again."

Claudette said, "We have your Uncle Per to thank for our lives, and now that you are in our lives…well, it doesn't get any better than that."

They were quiet as they remembered what they'd endured to get to this time and place.

Julia felt a feather-touch against her cheek and smiled.

On Saturday evening, after the guests were assembled around Mrs. Wellington's fountain, she interrupted the merriment.

"Ladies and gentlemen, thank you all for coming to our annual ball to celebrate those of us who survived the war.

"This year, we have more cause for celebration than ever. Before I tell you about that, I would like to introduce you to the interior designer who renovated my solarium, complete with this amazing fountain."

She pointed to the fountain at the exact moment when the lights began to twinkle. Everyone clapped with delight.

"Julia, you and Seth, please come next to me."

Julia stepped forward and took Seth by the hand.

"Here is Julia Hamilton of Hamilton Interiors and this handsome gentleman with her is her fiancé *and* the architect who helped with the fountain design, Seth Schmidt."

The guests clapped again. Julia said, "Thank you. I must say that Mrs. Wellington's story of her shop in Germany was the inspiration for this lovely solarium. I am glad I could bring her some happiness from the past."

Seth said, "Thank you, everyone."

They stepped back from the central focus.

Mrs. Wellington caught Claudette's attention and motioned for her to come forward.

She said, "My dear friends, we all have stories to tell of broken lives."

She took Claudette's arm. "This lady is a happy ending to my story."

When Mrs. Wellington finished telling her guests who Claudette was to her, there was not a dry eye.

Seth put his arm around Julia's shoulders and she gladly leaned on him. A single teardrop fell on her shoulder. It was from Seth. He too understood what these people had gone through.

The balance of the evening was full of introductions to Claudette, as well as music, dancing and fabulous food.

Precisely at ten PM, Claudette's driver rang the doorbell to let her know he was there to drive her to the hotel.

Before she left, she gave Mrs. Wellington an envelope of letters from Henrique's friends. She'd also included pictures of herself with Henrique.

Mrs. Wellington accepted the envelope and hugged Claudette. "I so wish you lived closer, Claudette."

She laughed, "Then you will be happy to know that your wish has already come true. I've taken an apartment at the Plaza." Claudette didn't think it was the best time to tell her that she and Javier were getting married.

"Isn't that marvelous! Then we will have time to get to know each other!"

She turned to Julia, "And you, my dear, are responsible for bringing my nephew's wife to me. Thank you, Julia!"

Mrs. Wellington took Seth's hand. "You'll take care of our girl, won't you?"

"You bet I will, Mrs. Wellington. Thank you for a wonderful evening. We'll say good night now."

Julia said, "Yes, thank you so much, Mrs. Wellington. I hope to see you soon. Good night."

Mrs. Wellington beamed with delight. She said, "Good night, my children!"

The wedding ceremony of Claudette and Javier was short and sweet.

When the Justice of the Peace pronounced them "Husband and Wife," Thor shook Javier's hand and said, "I want you to know how lucky you are to have married this lovely lady before I had the chance to!"

They both laughed and Julia thought back to when Thor had his eye on the beautiful Claudette in the Montreal restaurant. There was probably a great deal of truth in Thor's statement.

Claudette hugged Julia. "I am so happy with Javier and we owe you a debt of gratitude that can never be repaid. Thank you!"

"No thanks necessary, Claudette. As Uncle Per would say, it's kismet!"

Claudette was wistful for a moment. "Even though I was only three years old, I loved your Uncle Per, Julia. Javier let me read your journal and I realized what Per sacrificed to save us. He was a wonderful human being."

"Thank you for saying that, Claudette. I wish I had met him."

Thor said, "All right, ladies, time to celebrate. No more serious talk today!"

Chapter Twenty-Six

New Beginnings

The crew reported for work at Seth's co-op at eight AM every day of the week except Sunday. Because the contractor was Seth's personal friend, the crew worked overtime until six PM to get the job done as quickly as possible.

It was nearly impossible for Julia to work on her wedding plans, given the commotion next door, so she called Thora and asked if there was a desk in her offices she could work at.

Thora offered the library next to her office. She said it would be quiet and Julia would not be disturbed.

Later that day, she walked into Thora's office building and was greeted by the same young lady whom she and Thor had met on their first visit.

She said, "Welcome, Miss Hamilton. Miss Lorenzo is expecting you. Go right on up."

"Thank you. I must apologize. I did not get your name when I was here last."

She offered her hand to Julia, "My name is Kimberly MacGregor, Miss Hamilton."

"Well, it's a pleasure to make your acquaintance, Kimberly."

"Same here, Miss Hamilton. I called my friend at the Lyndhurst Mansion. He said you can tour the mansion any day between noon and five o'clock.

"He's heard of you, Miss Hamilton. He said you're the designer of choice in Manhattan!"

Kimberly giggled, and Julia smiled. "Well, I'm not sure about that, but it's kind of him to say. Maybe I'll tour the mansion this afternoon. Thanks, Kimberly."

"Oh, you're welcome, Miss Hamilton."

Julia walked up the marble staircase to Thora's office.

She was on the telephone and motioned for Julia to sit down. Thora finished her call and got up to hug her. "I am so glad to see you again, Julia."

She let go of Julia and held her at arm's length so she could look at her. "My brother, Vinnie, says we look alike. I believe he is right, but you're much prettier than I am, Julia."

"Thank you, but I think it's the other way around. In any event, we *are* closely related. Speaking of that, I have your birth father's journal for you to read."

Julia handed her the copy that she'd wrapped with pink ribbons. She knew that Thora would read about the gift given to her by Thor Sr. also wrapped in pink ribbons.

"Oh, this is lovely, Julia. I want to read it right away. Thankfully, I have no more work to do this afternoon.

"Come along, I will show you where you can work in peace."

She led her to the mahogany-paneled library adorned with paintings by the great artists. It was strikingly like Thor's library.

"This is beautiful, Thora, and the writing desk is exquisite!"

"Yes, it was my mother's desk that she had shipped here from Tuscany. She and my father traveled there before the war broke out. Whatever my mother admired, my father bought for her, and the same went for me. I had everything a girl could ask for."

She paused, "And yet, I always felt a deep longing for something or someone. I never understood it…until you and Thor came into my life. Now the pieces of my life fit perfectly. I know who I am and I feel complete!"

"I'm glad, Thora. You'll understand more when you've read the journal."

"Wonderful, I'll get started right away and leave you to your work. You're planning your wedding, right?"

"Yes, I *am*. Seth has asked Thor to be his best man. Would you consider being my maid of honor, Thora?"

"Yes! I will, Julia! Believe it or not, I've been studying Swedish wedding customs, thinking you might ask. You *are* planning a Swedish wedding, aren't you?"

"Yes, I certainly am!" Julia decided not to say how her birth mother Thora seemed to be. She would read about her in the journal.

"I'll close the door so you will have privacy, Julia. Let me know if you need anything."

"Okay. Thank you, Thora."

Four hours later, Julia got up from the desk and stretched. She surveyed her accomplishments and was very pleased. Her wedding was completely planned. The only item to be completed on her "to do" list was to tour the Lyndhurst Mansion. She was almost certain the castle on the grounds was the perfect venue for her wedding. She just wanted to confirm that she was correct.

Julia opened the library door and saw Thora at her desk. She went closer and saw Thora's tear-stained face.

Thora looked at Julia. She sat up and smoothed her skirt.

Softly, she said, "I finished the journal, Julia. It must have been difficult for you to write."

"No more difficult than it was for you to read, Thora. I shed more than a few tears, just like you."

Suddenly, Julia saw the spirit of her Uncle Per behind Thora. He had a smile on his face. Julia had seen only one photo of her uncle. It had been taken just after Thora was born and he looked just like he did as he smiled down on his daughter at that moment.

Another full circle, Julia thought.

Thora said, "As early as I can remember, I had nightmares of a woman crying over my cradle. I felt as if I had a hole in my heart, Julia. Now I know how real my dreams were. It's so very sad, and unfair."

"I agree, Thora. Are you all right? Would you like me to drive you home?"

"Thank you, but no. I've had the love of two sets of parents and it has given me great fortitude.

"My father's journal has filled the hole in my heart with more love than I knew existed. I feel as if I can do anything, just like my father, Per Lundgren. And…I can sing like my mother. Does that surprise you, Julia?"

"Not at all, Thora. I'm thrilled the journal has given you knowledge of your heritage and I'm sure your birth parents *and* your adoptive parents would be happy."

Julia was misty-eyed. "My parents were killed in an auto accident when I was only five years old. My Uncle Charles raised me. At the funeral services for my parents, my uncle told me that my parents loved me enough to last my whole life. I never forgot what he said. Those words sustained me through some very dark days."

"Julia, I'm very sorry you lost your parents. What your uncle said to you, I felt for myself on a subconscious level. It's as if my birth father said those words to me as I slept. So, I do know what you mean when you tell me those words sustained you. I thought I imagined my father talking to me to make myself feel better. The confirmation that you've just given me is what I needed."

Thora opened her desk drawer, took out a tiny box and handed it to Julia. She said, "This was in my family safe along with my parents' wills."

Julia's hand automatically went to her heart before she opened the box. She intuitively knew what it contained, but when she actually saw it, she was overcome with emotion. It was the locket that Thor Sr. had given to his beloved goddaughter on the day of her baptism.

She looked at Thora. She was also crying.

Finally, Thora said, "There was a note from my mother inside the box that said, 'Dora, this locket was pinned on your little blue and yellow pinafore when we adopted you. The angels have protected you as 'TB' intended. I hope one day you will know who gave this locket to you. Love, Mom.'

"Julia, I can feel the love of my godfather when I touch the locket."

"I know what you mean, Thora. It represents how precious you were to him. I visualized the locket when I wrote about it in the journal and never dreamed I would someday have it in my hands."

"It *is* a symbol of never-ending love, isn't it, Julia." It was more a statement than a question.

"Yes, and just wait until Thor hears about *this*! He'll be over the moon!"

She handed the box with the locket back to Thora. "Do you mind if Thor sees your locket?"

"No, I feel he is part of our family. I'll wear it for your wedding."

"Oh, speaking of my wedding, the last thing I need to do is tour the Lyndhurst Mansion. Care to come along?"

Thora hopped up from her chair. "Yes, I know the mansion well. I'll be your tour guide! Do you really want to have your wedding there?"

"I think so. I just want to check it out."

"I've always wanted to go to a wedding at the Lyndhurst. You'll love the old-world charm, Julia!"

Thora led Julia on a walking tour of the grounds surrounding the mansion. She pointed out the beautiful weeping beech trees with their branches that touched the ground in spring and summer, the gazebo in the rose garden and the great lawn outside the veranda that offered fabulous views of the Hudson.

"The grounds are so peaceful and beautiful. Let's go inside the main building and see what we think," Julia said.

Both Julia and Thora liked the picture gallery room the best. It was the replica of a scene from the movie "Winter's Tale."

After they'd walked through the entire mansion, Julia said, "This is too big for my small wedding. Maybe I should have a tent outside. What do you think, Thora?"

"You *could* do that. However, you have not seen the carriage house yet. I think you'll like it."

Julia was ecstatic when she saw the quaint carriage house. "This is picture-perfect for our small group. Sven can set up the smorgasbord on the far wall, and the band can use the alcove beside the dance floor."

Thora hugged Julia and said, "Thank you for including me in your wedding, Julia. It means a great deal to me. Would you mind if I sang at your wedding?"

"Absolutely. I intended to ask you to sing. *You* will make our wedding special! I'll put you in touch with the band leader. After I find the band, that is, and you can tell him what your choice of songs is. I'll leave it totally up to you!"

"All right. I promise I will not disappoint you, Julia."

"I *know* that I can always count on you, Thora."

Julia told Seth about their wedding plans over dinner that night.

He said, "You've been busy, Jules. I'm sure everything will be perfect with you at the helm. By the way, when are you going to tell me where the reception will be?"

"That's on a need-to-know basis, and you don't need to know," Julia said with a self-satisfied grin.

"Won't you at least give me a hint?"

"Sure. The ceremony and the reception will be in the same place. And here's one more clue—you will be dazzled!"

"Can I have three guesses, Jules?"

"You may have as many guesses as you like, but I don't intend to tell you where our wedding will be."

He smiled and thought, *I'll let her keep her secret.*

Then he said, "You're fun, Jules. It's hard to imagine life without you."

She laughed, "Good, because I'm with you through thick and thin, sweetheart!"

"Speaking of thick and thin, Jules, let me update you on the progress of the joining of our co-ops."

She didn't see the "thick and thin" segue but didn't interrupt him.

He continued, "Frank, the contractor, told me the crew is ready to break through from my co-op to your co-op."

She looked concerned.

Seth said, "Don't worry, they will only break through the walls in two places—the kitchen and the hallway leading to the bedrooms. And Frank promised me that everything will be covered with plastic so the dust will be contained."

"Good. We don't need extra work before the wedding. Do you think the project will be finished by the time we get back from our honeymoon, Seth?"

"Hmm…about our honeymoon. As you know, I've neglected my work during our renovations." He waited for her reaction.

"Would you be very upset if we put off our honeymoon for a few months—just until I can catch up on some work projects?"

She got up from her chair, put her arms around his neck and said, "It's fine with me. I feel like we're on a honeymoon right here in the kitchen."

She kissed his cheek.

"I knew you'd understand. Thanks, Jules."

"Say, what about the kitchen in the co-op you bought. Will we have two kitchens, Seth?"

"Ha-hah! *You* will have to wait and see, and I assure you that you will be dazzled!"

She grinned. "Touché!"

It was warm and sunny on their wedding day. Seth had stayed at Thor's apartment to be out of the bride's way.

He tried and tried to pry out of Thor where the wedding would be, to no avail.

Thor said he feared the wrath of Julia if he gave it away. "Relax and enjoy the show, Seth. I don't know much more than you do, buddy. I only know what time the limo will pick us up. Julia has ordered that we be dressed in our tuxedos and ready to roll by eleven o'clock for the noon ceremony."

Seth relented. "Then that's just what we'll do. It certainly is a beautiful day to get married."

Thor clapped Seth on the back, "That it *tis*, me boy!"

The limousine driver was also sworn to secrecy under Julia's threat of death.

As the stretch limo headed north out of Manhattan, Seth said, "I feel like royalty—just the two of us in this limo."

"Today you *are* royalty. You're marrying into the Swedish royal family, although at this point, it doesn't make much difference to anyone other than us."

Seth looked to his left. "There's the Tappan Zee Bridge. I can't imagine where we're going.

"Driver, how much longer before we get there?"

The driver simply shrugged as if he didn't speak English. He had his orders.

Just before the bridge, the driver veered off to the left and headed south along the Hudson.

Neither Seth nor Thor guessed where they were headed until the car turned left again and drove onto the palatial grounds of the Lyndhurst Mansion.

"I *know* this place!" Seth exclaimed. "The architecture is classic Gothic. The president of my company has black and white photos of the castle hanging on his office walls. This is fabulous!"

Seth paused. His mouth dropped open.

Thor looked at him and said, "What is it, Seth?"

Seth had tears in his eyes, and he could not speak. He pointed toward the rose garden on their left.

Thor gasped. There under the gazebo stood Julia dressed in a long white wedding gown, its skirt billowing in the breeze. He laughed, "Looks like this is the place, Seth!"

Seth said, "Wow, I mean *wow!*"

Thor nodded as he caught a glimpse of the other beauty dressed in a sky-blue gown, walking toward Julia. He remembered reading in the journal that Raya was dressed in a sky-blue gown on the night she met Per.

"She looks like a goddess," Thor said.

"Indeed she does, Thor!"

Seth turned to Thor and saw that he was referring to Thora. "Hey, you're supposed to have your attention on my bride, not the maid of honor!"

"Sorry. It's just that…did you *see* Thora?"

Thora now stood next to Julia.

Seth said, "Yes, those two are quite a pair of beauties!"

The limousine stopped next to the path leading to the gazebo. Seth was out of the car and next to Julia, almost before Thor saw the car door open.

The driver smiled.

Thor said, "He's the groom! Thanks for the ride!"

Thor kept his eyes on Thora as he walked the path to take his place beside Seth. She watched as he approached.

The minister joined the wedding party, and a photographer popped out from behind a nearby tree to capture the event. It was perfectly timed.

The minister asked, "Shall we begin?"

Seth smiled at Julia and said, "Yes, let's begin."

Julia handed her bouquet to Thora and turned to Seth. He took both of her hands in his.

Seth felt Thor slip the rings into his right jacket pocket.

The minister said, "Seth, would you please read your vows to Julia?"

Seth searched his breast pocket for the scrap of paper with the notes he'd written. Finally, he found it and breathed a sigh of relief. He held the paper at arm's length to read and suddenly a strong wind blew the paper out of his hand.

Thor snorted. Julia gasped. Thora giggled and Seth said, "Aw, I didn't need it anyway. I remember every word."

From memory, he said, "Julia, you complete me, you make me laugh and you bake me cupcakes. That's all I ever want and you are more than I could have imagined would come my way. I want to grow old and grumpy with you. I love you, Julia."

With a sheepish grin, he added, "That wasn't exactly what I wrote."

Everyone laughed, except the photographer, who was busy capturing the comical expressions of the moment.

"Julia, you may read your vows to Seth," the minister said.

She looked into Seth's eyes and recited her vows. "Seth, I love that you encourage me to follow my heart and that you accept me exactly as I am. Together, we will discover each other's dreams. You make me happy. I love you, Seth."

All eyes went to the minister. He dabbed at his eyes with a tissue and asked, "Who has the rings?"

Seth felt in his pocket and found the smaller of the two rings. He took Julia's left hand in his and recited each phrase after the minister, with such reverence and joy that it seemed even the birds in their nests sang approval.

Then he handed Julia his wedding band. She took his left hand in hers and she recited after the minister…in Swedish.

Seth's face showed his delight. He looked at Thor who also seemed delighted about the Swedish wedding vows.

Thor glanced at Thora who was all smiles and obviously proud of her cousin.

Thora and Julia must have studied long and hard for this occasion, Thor mused.

That's when Thor saw it glistening in the sunlight...the locket that his father had given to her at her baptism. She'd fastened it into her hair so that he'd be sure to see it. He was awestruck.

He didn't hear the minister when he said, "And now you may kiss the bride."

He heard his father's voice in his head. "Snap out of it, boy!" It was just what he needed. He came back to the present.

Seth gathered Julia in his arms and kissed her with more passion than he'd ever felt. When he released her, Thor and Thora clapped.

Julia whispered in Seth's ear, "If that kiss is any indication of what it will be like to be married to you, I'll be a very happy wife."

"That's my plan, Jules!"

All morning, preparations had been underway at the carriage house. Sven's crew had set out the cold dishes on a smorgasbord to end all smorgasbords. The hot dishes waited in chafing dishes in the summer kitchen.

The stage for the band had been set up the night before. There would be four pieces: a miniature baby grand, a guitar, a flute and a violin. It was a unique combination that Julia had discovered in her internet search. She had been thrilled to find that the group had a concert at Lyndhurst and she and Thora had attended and been impressed.

The band did not normally have a singer, but the leader said he would be pleased if Thora wanted to sing for Julia's wedding.

Guests began to fill the carriage house at twelve-thirty. The wedding party was announced promptly at one o'clock.

Sven had asked for the honor of announcing the bride and groom. When they appeared in the doorway, he proudly said, "Ladies and gentlemen, for the first time anywhere, I am pleased to introduce *Mr. and Mrs.* Seth Schmidt!"

Before they presented themselves, Seth scooped Julia up in his arms and carried her to the center of the dance floor amid applause and whistles.

He put her down ever so gently and bowed before her.

Someone yelled, "Hold that pose!" and pictures were clicked by anyone with a camera or a smartphone.

Thora whispered to Thor, "The princess has married her prince."

He cleared his throat and replied, "Indeed, they are a perfect pair."

The bride and groom took their seats at the head table next to Thora and Thor.

Julia said, "Are you ready to sing, Thora?"

"Yes, I am." She walked to the stage and looked to the band leader for an indication that they were ready. He nodded.

She spoke into the microphone, "Ladies and gentlemen, my name is Thora Lundgren and I am Julia's cousin, originally from Sweden. I would like to sing for you a song dedicated to Julia and Seth. It's a special love song recorded by the Beatles."

Everyone was captivated by Thora's singing, especially Julia and Seth. When she had sung the last note, she received a standing ovation. She thanked them and motioned for the guests to sit.

She said, "Next, I will sing a tune chosen by Seth for his wife. This one was written by John Legend."

Seth got up, took Julia by the hand and led her to the dance floor. He twirled her in perfect time to Thora's song.

As she danced, Julia looked at each of their guests. They all seemed to be happy for her and Seth. It was a small group of the most important people in their lives.

Javier and Claudette sat with Mr. and Mrs. Wellington. Sven, his wife, Ingrid and their two daughters sat with two friends of Henrique Pulaski's and their dates. Mack and Sheila, who'd visited the Met with Seth and Julia, sat with their spouses.

The song ended and once again, the guests stood and clapped until Thora took her seat next to Julia.

Thor leaned close to Thora. "Not only are you a vision in blue, you sing like an angel."

"Thank you, Thor. I'm glad you enjoyed it. Do you sing?"

"Not a note! My talents lie in other areas." He gave her a sly glance.

She giggled despite being slightly embarrassed by his comment. She asked, "Why have you never married?"

"Why have I never married? Well, it's very likely for the same reason that you, my fair lady, have never married."

"What do you mean?"

Thor did not hesitate. "You and I have waited for each other. I knew it the moment I saw you, Thora."

She was flustered and for a moment, she said nothing.

Thor held his breath until he thought he might burst.

Finally...finally she said, "Yes, I believe you're right, Thor."

He didn't want to make a spectacle of them, so he simply squeezed her hand and looked deep into her blue eyes.

Sven announced the food was ready and the guests could eat to their heart's content. He added that a traditional Swedish wedding smorgasbord was served for three days, but this one would be served for three *hours*. That earned him a big laugh.

Over and over again, the wedding party and the guests complimented Sven on the smorgasbord.

"It was fabulous! Thank you so much for your hard work," Julia said to Sven.

He bowed and humbly said, "I am so happy to be able to prepare your wedding smorgasbord, just as my Uncle Sven did for your Uncle Per and his beautiful Raya."

After the meal, Thora went to the microphone. She said, "Let's give Sven a round of applause for this marvelous smorgasbord!"

She waited for the applause to die down and continued. "Now the happy couple would like to share a dance with all of you. I wrote this song especially for Julia and Seth."

Everyone drifted onto the dance floor.

Julia said to Seth, "They all seem to be having a wonderful time."

"Yes, sweetheart. You put together a fabulous wedding. By the way, did you notice Thor and Thora together? I think there may be a romance budding there."

"You're funny, Seth. Their romance is in full bloom."

"Oh, do you think so, Jules? That would be nice for all of us."

"Yes, it will be, Seth."

When the song ended, everyone clapped and Thor approached the microphone. "I am Thor Bjorn, Seth's best man. I did not have anything to do with this beautiful couple meeting, but I can tell you that if I was charged with choosing the perfect husband for my beloved Julia, I could only hope to find Seth for her!"

Thor raised his glass of champagne toward the bride and groom and said, "A *toast*! To Julia and Seth!"

Then there were shouts of "Hear-hear! To Julia and Seth!"

Julia nudged Seth and pointed toward the door of the carriage house. There stood an old gent dressed in a tweed suit and a top hat. He stayed only long enough to smile and tip his hat to the newlyweds.

Thor continued, "Ladies and gentlemen, I have asked one of our guests to sing a song for Thora."

He motioned for Sven's wife, Ingrid, to come and sing. Then Thor took Thora by the hand and asked, "May I have this dance?"

She smiled and said, "Yes, you may."

The guests stood around the dance floor to watch them dance while Ingrid sang a lovely tune about a nightingale.

Thor held her close and said, "This song is for you, my dear. You are my songbird."

She said, "And I am happy to be."

Most everyone was misty-eyed by the time the song ended. It was a sentimental song from wartime and apropos for Thor and Thora for many reasons.

Someone shouted, "It's cake time!" Sven brought out the seven-tiered almond cake and announced that it was a Swedish favorite.

After the cake and coffee, Thora sang one more song. She said, "Julia chose this song for Seth. It's from the Broadway musical Aladdin. I know you will recognize it."

Julia and Seth danced. Thor sat back in his chair and listened to *his* whole new world, singing…as if it was only to him.

Near the end of the song, Thor got up, gently took the microphone from Thora's hand and coaxed her onto the dance floor. The band played on, while the wedding party gracefully whirled around and around.

The reception ended at five PM. Julia and Seth thanked each guest as they left the carriage house.

When everyone had left, Thor said to Julia and Seth, "Come with me. Your wedding gift is beside the gazebo."

Julia said, "Oh, but Thor, you've already done so much for us."

"*And* I might add," Thor said, "that I could not have it delivered until I found out where your wedding was!"

The four of them walked to the parking area past the gazebo. Seth said, "All right, Thor...where is it?"

Thor laughed and walked between Julia and Seth. He put an arm around each of them. "Well, it's right in front of you...it's a 1927 Volvo just like Julia's Uncle Per used to drive or *try* to drive! I had her completely restored and she purrs like a kitten."

Thora heard the chuckle first. She looked at Julia, Seth and Thor. They all smiled.

Epilogue

ONE YEAR LATER

It was their first wedding anniversary and as usual, Seth said he had a surprise for Julia.

As he went off to work that morning, he'd kissed her and said, "You, my love, do nothing but relax today so that we can thoroughly enjoy our anniversary celebration tonight!"

"All right, I'll just do some reading," she said.

Aunt Margaret's chair rocked in agreement. Julia grinned.

"Have a nice day, Seth."

"Okay, call you later, Jules."

The moment the door closed behind him, Julia got up and once again walked through the rooms of their renovated apartment.

She went through the kitchen to the room that had been a kitchen in the co-op that Seth bought. It had been transformed into the most fabulous spa she'd ever seen. It had a giant shower with a waterfall shower head, a huge Roman bath and oodles of storage. But, the best feature as far as Julia was concerned, was the sauna, complete with a sound system.

The bedrooms of the second co-op had been converted into guest quarters, with two full bathrooms. She'd decorated them with fresh green and turquoise colors for spring and summer. For fall and winter, she changed the décor to bright, bold primary colors.

The living room had been converted into Julia's work room, which she painted white on white. She said she created her best work while surrounded by a blank canvas.

It was true, she'd begun to write historical novels and she was very happy.

She hoped Seth would surprise her with tickets to Europe for their long-awaited honeymoon so she could see the places she wrote about.

Just then her cell phone chirped. It was the delivery man calling. He said her furniture had arrived. She told him to use the service elevator and she would open the apartment door.

The anniversary gift that she'd ordered for Seth barely fit through the foyer doorway. Julia asked the delivery men to place it in the largest guest room.

After they'd left, she sat in an easy chair in the guest room. She marveled at the gift she'd chosen for her husband. It was an architect's desk that had been handcrafted by a Vermont artisan. She was sure Seth would love it.

Julia went to her bookshelf. She felt like a kid in a candy store as she looked at the many titles she'd put aside for when she had a day all to herself. This was the day she'd been waiting for.

A few hours later, while she was taking a coffee break, Seth called. He said he would be home by six o'clock and he'd pick up an order from Sven's deli.

She smiled. "That sounds great, Seth. I look forward to dinner with just the two of us."

"Me too, Jules. See you later!"

Promptly at six, Seth arrived laden with dinner, two dozen pink roses and a bottle of champagne. He had no free hands, so he rang the doorbell with his elbow.

Julia opened the door for him. She took the dinner basket and the champagne and Seth followed her to the kitchen. She put it all on the counter and turned to him.

He presented her with the roses and said, "Happy anniversary. I love you, Jules!"

"Thank you, they're beautiful! Why don't you put them in the empty vase that is waiting on the table?"

He laughed, "It's not easy to surprise you, Jules."

He placed the roses in the vase and then he said, "Shall I pop open the bubbly?"

"In a minute. First, I want to give you your anniversary gift."

"Oh, boy, I can't wait! Should I close my eyes?"

She grinned, "You're funny. Just follow me if you please."

She led him to the guest room. When he saw the desk, he said, "It's fabulous, Jules! Where did you find it?"

"It's made by a Vermont woodworker who made furniture for one of my designs just after I met you. He told me he used special woods that are hearty, yet beautiful."

"Yes, I see that. He is obviously a master craftsman. Thank you, I love it!"

He kissed her and said, "It would seem that you've guessed one of the surprises I had for you."

"Oh, really? What do you mean?"

"Well, I've given notice at work and I am starting my own architectural consulting firm."

Julia threw her arms around his neck and said, "That is superb! With your expertise and experience, you will be a surefire success!"

She thought for a minute and asked, "Where will you work?"

"I will work right here at my fancy new architect's desk!"

"Great! It will be fun to have you close by. You'll be working on your designs and I'll be writing in my studio in the next room!"

Seth put his arms around her waist and lifted her into the air. He said, "Jules, I'm so happy with you!"

"I'm very happy too, Seth. Now, please put me down so I can set the dinner table."

As they walked back to the kitchen, Julia said, "It's a wonderful surprise that you are opening your own firm, Seth."

"There are more surprises in store for you this night, Mrs. Schmidt!"

"Well then, let's eat. What has Sven put into our dinner basket?"

She unwrapped the packages in the basket and found Swedish meatballs, noodles, buttered carrots, baked wild-caught salmon filets and stewed tomatoes. She left the package marked "Open Me Last" in the basket.

They ate to their heart's content. Seth said, "Did you make us coffee to go with dessert, Jules?"

"Of course, I'll get it and you can open the last package in the basket."

He did so and announced, "Oh look, it's almond cake!"

They laughed at the expected dessert.

When the very last morsel of cake had disappeared, Seth said, "Are you ready for more surprises?"

"I'm *always* ready!"

He got up. "I'll go get it." He went to his bedside table and took out an envelope, then walked back to the kitchen and handed it to Julia.

"Ooh, this looks interesting." Julia screamed with delight when she opened the envelope and found tickets for a European honeymoon trip.

She kissed Seth on both cheeks—in the European way. "This is wonderful and the dates coincide with leaving your job!"

"Yes, Jules, we'll have the time of our lives. Happy anniversary!"

He continued, "However, I have one more surprise for you. Come and sit down."

"*Another* surprise? Then I'd *better* sit down!"

Seth opened the pantry and reached to the back of the highest shelf. He withdrew the architectural drawings he'd stashed there the previous day.

She said, "You sly dog. When did you hide them there?"

He smiled and placed the rolled-up drawings on the table in front of her. He said, "Go ahead and unroll the drawings, Jules."

She held the center of the roll and slid it to the left to reveal the drawings. "This looks like a chalet, it's beautiful! Is this your first independent project, Seth?"

"Yes, in a manner of speaking. What you have in front of you are drawings of our vacation home to be built in the Catskills."

She jumped up and practically knocked him over with her exuberance. "Seth! You're amazing and our vacation home will be so much fun!"

He hugged her and said, "That's my plan, Jules! *Now*, it's time to pop open the bubbly!"

They sipped their champagne while Seth described the chalet in detail.

When they went to bed, they talked about their honeymoon and the places they would visit.

They drifted off to sleep with thoughts of far-off lands in their heads.

Thor had been asked by the Swedish authorities to assist in the numerous reopened investigations of kidnappings dating back as far as 1930.

He, of course, was thrilled and gladly accepted. He planned to move his headquarters to Stockholm so he would be in the heart of the police activities.

Before Thor left for Sweden, Julia asked him to meet her for coffee at Sven's deli.

He rushed in, kissed Julia on the cheek and said, "I'm sorry I can't stay long, Julia. I'm meeting Thora and I plan to ask her to marry me!"

"That's wonderful, Thor! Then you'll need this." She reached into her purse and touched the velvet box. Her heart jumped with the emotion she felt.

She handed the box to Thor. "Tom would want you to have the diamond ring his grandmother gave him."

Tears fell from his eyes. "Julia, I had forgotten about this ring. Are you sure you want to give it up, sweetie?"

"Yes, Thor. It's yours to give to your beloved."

Julia was surprised that her heart still ached when she thought of Tom's death.

Thor looked at her. "I know. It still hurts me too."

He hesitated for a moment. "I accept this ring and consider it an honor to be able to give it to Thora. Tom had a big role in finding her."

Sadly, she said, "Yes, he did."

Another full circle, Julia thought.

"You'll be leaving for Sweden soon. Will you be married here before you go?"

He laughed, "Well, that's *if* she agrees to marry me!"

"Of course, she will, Thor!"

He got up and said, "Sorry, sweetie, got to go. You and Seth will be our witnesses, Julia. Bye."

She laughed as he ran out of the deli. She thought how very happy she was for her dear friend and for her cousin, Thora.

Thora and Thor were married a week later at City Hall with Seth and Julia as their witnesses.

After the ceremony, Seth suggested they all go to lunch. Thor announced they were leaving for Sweden right away. "Thora has packed enough for a two-year stay," he said as he hugged his new wife.

She pretended to be annoyed with him and said, "Thor, you exaggerate!"

Julia threw her arms around Thora and said, "I will miss you. Will you promise to visit us soon?"

Thora glanced at Seth and asked, "Do you want to tell her?"

"Tell me what?" Julia asked.

Seth replied, "Jules, after our honeymoon, we can set up shop in Sweden for a few months. But only if you want to."

Thor chimed in with, "I can use a good investigator, Julia. What do you say, are you game?"

"You *bet* I am!" She hugged Seth.

Then she hugged the newlyweds. "Congratulations, you two...I'll be seeing you!"

The memorial service for Tom took place three weeks after Thor and Thora were married. It had been arranged for them to come home from Sweden for the memorial.

Tom had no living relatives and Julia knew him better than anyone, so she planned a simple service on her own and asked Thor to talk about Tom.

Tom would not want a church service. He was a spiritual man but he was not one to attend church.

Julia decided that a luncheon would be appropriate. She called the Plaza Hotel, where Claudette and Javier lived, and reserved a small dining room.

Julia arrived early for the luncheon that would commemorate Tom's life. She wanted time to reflect; time to prepare for closure. After all, she had come close to being Tom's life partner, his wife. While she was very happy with Seth, there was a part of her that hadn't quite let go of Tom.

Julia insisted on setting the dining table herself. She stood and admired the centerpiece she designed using the bird of paradise flowers. Since the flowers were not in season locally, she'd had them flown in from Hawaii.

When she had completed the setup, she sat at the head of the table and touched a soft white linen napkin that she'd lovingly folded and placed there. That seat would remain empty for the service.

Her mind was full of thoughts of Tom. Time seemed to stand still as she watched a parade of memories of him float by in her mind's eye. She'd heard that when you die, your life passes before your eyes. However, she was visualizing memories of her life with Tom, and she wasn't dying. But of course, their relationship was dying, finally and completely.

Just as the "memory parade" was coming to an end, she heard Tom's voice loud and clear. He said, *"Julia. Beautiful Julia. Don't be sad for me. My reason for being was fulfilled when I saved your life. From my vantage point now, I see that you and Seth are perfect together. It makes me happy to see you happy.*

"Please dry your tears now. When you cry, I cry with you. Your grief holds both of us from our individual progress. I understand that the human part of you grieves. When you look backward and think of me, you discover grief anew. I offer you the true understanding of life. It's ongoing and wonderful. In what is termed the afterlife, there are no constraints, no encumbrances. The life work continues after the death of the body. The soul-mind creates whatever is thought of. You might call it imagination, but imagination has no form. Time is needed to manifest what you wish to create on earth. In spirit, time does not exist, there is only the now. Therefore, whatever is thought of in the afterlife simply manifests instantaneously.

"It is understandable that these truths are not easily comprehended. You deal with flesh and blood and gravity. The greatest challenge faced in the afterlife lies in trying to assist incarnate souls to understand the intangible. Few can hear with their heart as you are doing now, Julia. Because you see and hear beyond the tangible, life is so much more joyful for you than for many others.

"I truly appreciate that you are honoring me today. Thank you, Julia. So, celebrate my life today with your husband and your friends. Then go on with your life in all the ways that inspire you and bring you joy.

"I will say goodbye, Julia. There is someone here who wishes to speak to you."

Julia heard the chuckle. Her Uncle Per said, *"Julia, we are all with you today to honor Tom. It is also appropriate to honor you for writing the journal. Your work, with Tom's assistance, finished what I could not. Many lives were changed for the better because of your writing.*

"You also connected Mrs. Wellington to the widow of her beloved nephew, Henrique Pulaski. He is here and wishes to thank you.

"None of these connections would have been made if you had not been able to listen with your heart, Julia. There is not enough time for the others to thank you. I will speak for them.

"First, the Blue Tango Team: Hans, Karl, Wilhelm, Henrique and Will want to thank you. Of course, Raya and I are part of that group and we offer you thanks as well.

"Next, Inga wishes to be acknowledged to you. You will remember that she was my secretary and later, Nash Bjorn's mother. She is happy that Thor Jr. and Nash are in your life. More than that, when you and Thor found Thora, Inga was ecstatic, especially because Thora was taken while in her care. That had added to her anguish about the loss of Thora, and you've reconciled it by finding Thora.

"Claudette's parents, Marie and Franz, are present to thank you for finding and befriending their beloved daughter. They also are thankful that you reconnected her with Javier.

"You know Thor's friend, Sven, and his wife, Ingrid. Sven's Uncle Sven was my loyal friend with whom I lived and worked. He thanks you for accepting his nephew and family into your family.

"And now, Thor Sr. wishes to compliment your intuitive and investigative skills. He says that you've righted many wrongs. He's happy that his son precipitated the investigations and that he was smart enough to add you and Tom to the mix to get the best outcome. He notes that the three of you worked together like a well-oiled machine and were able to complete the work of the Blue Tango Team in fine style.

"Seth is to be honored today as well. He introduced you to Thor Jr. who put together the investigative triad that went to Montreal and found Thora's adoption file, and the files of other kidnap victims. That work will continue and reconnect many more families.

"Julia, lastly, Raya is eternally grateful to you, and to Thor and Tom for finding our Thora.

"Well, your friends will be arriving soon. Goodbye for now, Julia. Don't you worry, I will visit from time to time."

Julia smiled and looked at the wall clock. Barely one minute had passed while Tom and Uncle Per spoke to her. It seemed much longer. She was deeply humbled by the outpouring of gratitude and support from the people she'd come to love and admire as she wrote the journal.

Seth was the first of the guests to arrive. He took one look at Julia and said, "Sweetheart, you look as if you've seen a ghost. What's wrong?"

She smiled and said, "Nothing is wrong, Seth. Everything is perfect!"

He kissed her and said, "I know today is difficult for you. I'm right beside you."

"Thank you, Seth. I've finally come to terms with Tom's death and I have a hunch he'd appreciate this memorial and that he is at peace."

"I believe that too, Julia. And I believe that we, as humans, cannot comprehend the afterlife. After all, we have enough to keep us busy right here."

Julia threw her arms around her husband's neck and said, "Seth, *you* are a wise man!"

They were interrupted when Thor bounded into the room in his inimitable style. "Okay, you two lovebirds, let's get started!"

Thor looked at Julia. "How are you holding up, sweetie?"

"I'm doing very well, Thor. Thanks for asking. Where is Thora?"

"She's in the lobby waiting for Claudette and Javier. Everyone else should be here soon."

Thor turned as Thora came into the dining room. "And here is my beautiful wife now!"

All the guests arrived with Thora. One by one, each greeted Julia, Seth and Thor.

Thor took his place at the podium and tapped on the microphone to get the guests' attention. Julia thought of the first time she heard Thor speak at the Central Park festivities. "Welcome to all of you. Please find your seat at the beautiful table Julia has arranged. You will find a name tag at each place setting."

Claudette and Javier sat next to Mrs. Wellington. Sven and his wife, Ingrid, were seated next to Thora. Nash sat next to the place where Thor was to sit.

Julia and Seth sat next to the empty chair at the head of the table—the place saved for Tom.

When everyone was seated, Thor once again called for attention. "We are here today to honor Tom Pierson. Julia knew him better than any of us, but she asked me to do the honors.

"Seth and Javier met Tom through Julia. The rest of you did not know him personally but knew of his work with Julia and me. That work is the reason that Tom is no longer with us and why he is being honored today.

"I knew Tom to be a serious-minded man who cared deeply about helping others. He did that by using his investigative skills.

"In the course of our investigations to locate people saved during World War II by Julia's uncle, Per Lundgren, and my father, Thor Bjorn, Sr., Tom lost his life.

"However, Julia and I used Tom's notes, and we were able to find Thora Lundgren, who had been kidnapped when she was an infant. Then she was adopted by an American family who were not aware that she'd been kidnapped from Sweden.

"I'm happy to say that Thora Lundgren is now my wife." Thor winked at Thora and then continued. "Julia and I discovered Thora living in Tarrytown, New York. Tom's notes led us to her and we are forever grateful to him.

"The connections that Julia and I made, using Tom's notes, was miraculous.

"However, I would be remiss if I did not mention the journal that Julia wrote. The search for those rescued from Europe during the war began with Julia's research of her Swedish roots. She discovered that her Great Uncle Per had been a Swedish diplomat during the Second World War. He subsequently joined an underground effort, the Blue Tango Team, to rescue people from Europe.

"Through the journal, Claudette and Javier were reunited last year after being rescued in France in 1940. They were only three years old when Per Lundgren and the Blue Tango Team found them. Claudette's parents, Marie and Franz, were also rescued at the same time, as were a few friends and family members.

"Julia also wrote about a group of children kidnapped from Poland. They were being taken to work camp by the Nazis. The Blue Tango Team tried to rescue all the children with the help of my father, but only eight were saved. Those eight made it to North America. One of the boys was Henrique Pulaski, nephew to Mrs. Pulaski Wellington. Fourteen years later, Claudette met and married Henrique in Montreal, where he'd become a successful banker.

"When we met Claudette in Montreal last year, she'd been widowed for ten years. She *did* remember her childhood friend, Javier, and she wanted to see him again. As it happened, Javier worked in the Manhattan building where Julia lived, so we got them together. Now they are married and living out their golden years right here at the Plaza Hotel!

"And now, due to Tom's contributions, I am working with the Swedish authorities in Stockholm to solve kidnapping cases that had gone cold decades ago."

Thor took a long pause and a deep breath. He looked at Julia. Then he looked skyward and said, "Tom, we all thank you. It has been an honor to know you. Julia and I vow to continue the valuable work that you began."

Thor bowed his head and ignored the tears that fell on his shirt directly over his heart. He then looked up just as all eyes went to the head of the table, where the empty chair sat. The chair moved just enough that no one was sure it had actually moved. They all smiled through tears.

Thor waited a full minute before he announced, "Let's eat!" He took his seat between Thora and Nash.

As the luncheon was being served, he leaned over and whispered into Thora's ear, "Did I tell you that your engagement ring was given to Tom by his grandmother? She wanted it to be worn by a woman who was loved by a man as much as she was loved by her husband."

Thora kissed him gently on the cheek and whispered, "You never told me that, Thor, but somehow, I knew. I'm sure I am loved by you every bit as much as Tom's grandmother was loved by her husband."

After the luncheon, everyone went off in different directions to enjoy the rest of the sunny day as if it were an ordinary day. To Julia, it was anything but ordinary. It was the day she became completely happy with her present life, without reliving the past pain of loss.

She took Seth's hand and said, "You make me very happy, Seth."

He laughed and said, "That's my plan, Jules! Come on, it's a beautiful day. Let's walk home."

About the Author

Linda Lee Keenan was born and raised in upstate New York and has lived in the northeast all her life. She has a varied professional background as a Paralegal, Real Estate Appraiser, Interior Decorator and Adjunct Professor of History.

She was a non-traditional college student, beginning her studies late in life. She earned a Bachelor of Science degree with an emphasis on legal studies at Post University in Connecticut while working as a Paralegal. She minored in History and it became her passion. She went on to earn a graduate degree in International History from Western Connecticut State University.

An avid interest in the Second World War has led Linda to write this second novel on the subject. Her first historical novel, "With Love from Poland" tells a story of family and friends who join to form an underground organization to escape from Cracow, Poland, after Hitler attacked in 1939.

One of the books that influenced Linda is "Looking Backward" by Edward Bellamy, a utopian novel published in 1888 about the year 2000 from the perspective of real life in 1887. Bellamy's book, together with Thornton Wilder's play "Our Town" helped to shape her outlook on life and thus is reflected in her writing.

If you enjoyed reading "The Journal," I'd appreciate a quick review. www.amazon.com/author/lindakeenan . Thank you!